WISHING FOR LA LUNA

RITMO Y DESEO

J L LORA

Larimar

Stay Safe - Trigger Warnings

Your safety matters. Rio and Luna's story explores toxic relationship dynamics, destructive choices, and emotional conflict. They're scarred, sometimes messy, but their growth and healing are at the heart of this story.

To avoid spoiling any aspect of the story, a list of all triggers is available for your reference on my website. To access, please go to:

http://bit.ly/46A3vVh

Also, please remember this is book one of their journey. Book two will come out in 2026.

__For my Ficha Mundial Girls,__ I couldn't have chosen a better group of women to embark on this journey with. Love you, girls!

A special dedication and thanks from the bottom of my heart to __La Madrina__ of Wishing for La Luna, __K. L. Hernandez__. I couldn't have done this without you!

To my dream graphic artist, __Djilas Gomez.__ You made Rio and Luna come to life for the cover. They're perfect in every way.

JL

1

Rio

Coñazo, I already regret this.

The last place I need to be is an industry party.

I weave in and out through the two-sided hallway. It's hot, infused with the clashing smells of bodies, perfumes, colognes, and refined weed. My goal is to avoid the crowd of people who stop dancing to try to get my attention and instead head into the living room area of the penthouse, near the balcony. The tightening in my chest is intense. My breath comes in choppy intakes as I stand near the window. The air hits my face, and I can't breathe it in fast enough, so I push my hoodie back. I need a minute to center my gaze on the millions of lights in front of me in the postcard-like, breathtaking view of the Manhattan skyline with its skyscrapers, bridges, and the Hudson River on the horizon.

"Rio," a gravelly voice I would recognize anywhere calls out from behind. I turn to see Niko, owner of this view, rushing my way with a smile that splits his face and is brighter than the yellow jersey he's wearing. His arms go around me. "We've missed you, *Manito.*"

His hand claps my shoulder hard, like he's only Nikanor Romero, my friend of more than fifteen years, not Niko *El Rebelde*, the superstar who turns every musical note into gold and any venue into a street party. He's one of the few true friends I have and one of the two people in the industry who could lure me out of the house these days. I can't help but return the grin.

"It's good to be back," I say, and it's not necessarily a lie, just not the whole truth. "I'm still trying to get into the groove of things."

He bobs his head up and down. "I get it, and what better place to start than with your friends? We'll jump in the studio later. For now, you play. Hay *muchas* shorties. Have fun. I need to check that we are all set with the equipment, but I'll be back to get you. *Tu sabes que Vampiro* is mad *cabrón* about having everything just perfect."

I nod. Calling our music producer, Vampiro, temperamental is putting it mildly. The man wouldn't think twice of walking out and messing up our plans if we don't have every detail ironed out to perfection.

Niko leaves me alone to look around the room. I'm trying to keep an open mind, but industry parties are not my *vaina* right now. I want nothing but to be away from people, locked in my room, but Niko invited me to record tonight. Our song is destined to be a banger, and I'm excited for my verse. I've been tweaking and perfecting it. The music grows louder. *"Energia"* by Alexis y Fido booms from the speakers, and everyone screams. Great song, just not in the mood. I retreat to a corner near the balcony to sip my beer, avoiding eye contact. Hopefully, the message is clear: *no me jodan.*

"Excuse me," a feminine voice says from behind me.

Fuck. Do people not get the hint when others don't want to be bothered? I try to school my face to something neutral and force the annoyance from my voice as I turn and reply, "Yeah?"

And holy shit. Brown skin like *chocolate de agua,* tight curls for days, and small almond eyes in a heart-shaped face that I've never seen before but I would have definitely remembered. My gaze drifts lower, and yeah, I would have screenshotted and filed away all those curves in jeans and a deep-red, sweetheart-cut shirt that frames her generous chest in my brain.

Si, I would remember her.

"You're blocking the drink table," she says, luscious lips stretching in an almost hesitant way.

I blink a couple times and look behind me, only to flush. Heat rises up my chest to my face way too fast. *What an ass I am.* Here I'm thinking she's coming to cozy up to me, but all she wants is a drink. I move slightly and say, "Sorry."

"It's all good." She moves past me and stops, eyeing the table like she's lost.

"You can't go wrong with Brugal, Coke, and lime," I offer.

"How traditional of you," she says, and the smile she turns on me brightens her face.

I extend my hand. "Rio Castillo, and I can mix it for you, if you want."

She takes my hand in her softer and warmer one. "Luna Santos, and I would love that, if it's no bother."

"Not at all." I mix the drink quickly and hand it to her. Behind her, there's a window, and her namesake, the moon, is high in the sky. It almost glows like a halo behind her. "How lucky am I?"

"Como así?" she asks in an accent that's a nostalgic callback to my people.

De lo mío. Dominicana.

I point at the sky beyond the window. "I'm in the company of two *lunas* in one night. That's got to be a good omen. Or maybe you are *la Diosa Luna*?"

"I never heard that one before." But she laughs. It's a little loud, but her eyes glow like jewels, *gotitas de ambar*, against the light. I can't help but stare at that full mouth and throw my wish to be alone far away.

"You want to sit?" I ask.

Her eyes brighten, and she nods, leading the way to a small couch nearby.

"So, are you one of the models in Niko's video?"

She laughs again, shaking her head, making me lean closer. "Does that actually work? Are girls, like, 'Omg, Rio thinks I'm a model,' and then they lose their mind and self-control?"

She knows who I am.

It's my turn to shake my head. "I didn't mean it like that, but stop playing. You know you're gorgeous."

"I don't know about that."

I purse my lips, pointing them up toward my nose, in a very Dominican gesture meant to let her know I don't believe her. "Does that work? The whole modesty thing? Because there's no way you don't know how bad you are."

Her lashes flutter. "Thank you. You're sweet. You looked annoyed when I approached you. I thought you were going to chew me out."

"Sorry about that. I hate these things... I'm usually better. I thought you were a groupie and... Man, I'm so embarrassed."

She grimaces. "Um, I'm definitely not a groupie, but full disclosure, I'm a fan. '*Dime Mami*' is my favorite song. I actually came to tell you that."

I'm caught off guard by her admission, but I can't stop staring into her eyes. Her embarrassment is cute too. *Definitely not turned off.*

I open my mouth to tell her it's okay, but her hand shoots out to touch mine. "I'm not here to bother you. I can go do something else. I just wanted to say how much I love your song."

Her hand is so warm. Her gaze holds mine, and the tightening in my chest is sudden.

"You're not bothering me," I tell her. "It's actually good to hear. I've been away for so long, I wonder if anyone remembers me at all. So, what do you actually do other than listen to my music?" I tease.

She scoffs. "*¡Qué arrogancia!* I said *one* song. You assume I meant your whole discography."

I shrug, enjoying the feistiness in her voice. "Maybe it's wishful thinking."

She holds a hand up to her heart. "I'm not confirming nor denying that I listen to all three albums regularly and the mixtape."

Jesus, she's gorgeous.

"Favorite?" I ask.

Luna taps her chin, but the twitch in her lips gives her away. "The mixtape, *After the Rain*. You were raw in it." She presses her hand against mine, sending a wave of heat over that area of my skin. "Don't get me wrong, all three albums are awesome with great bangers, but they're more commercial. The mixtape feels intimate, like we're sitting in a living room and you're telling me the story of how she broke you."

They. All of them broke me. Some with a breakup, others with silence, but nothing compared to the last…way after I released the mixtape. She couldn't deal with my mess.

But I don't get caught up in that, because the intimate moment she described feels like this moment. I can't remember the last time someone touched me while talking, other than fucking, and I…don't hate it—quite the opposite.

"I was younger then, and I had plenty of heartbreaks to talk about."

She lifts her hands. "No judgments. Just grateful because it got me through a breakup."

I blurt out the first thing that comes to mind. "Now, what *pariguayo* would break up with you?"

Her gaze narrows on me. "*Vas a seguir?*"

I can't help but laugh. "I mean it."

"Every single time with every single girl, I'm sure." Her tone is drier than the air outside.

I laugh again. This time, Luna's mouth curls into a small grin.

"Seriously, though, what do you do, *Diosa Luna*?"

"Hahaha, cute. I'm a social media and marketing manager."

"That sounds like a fun job," I say, because I'm 100% sure I could not do that. I do the bare minimum on my own social media. It grates my team to no end.

"I love it." Her eyes gleam, lighting up her face. "It's finding ways to resonate with people and audiences. We do it for restaurants, stores, and brands."

"That makes sense. It's like testing songs to see which one makes people feel the music and dance. But those are all different. What does your heart call out to most?"

I want to know what she's into. It's been a while since I had a conversation like this with someone. I haven't wanted to. With her, I want to keep talking.

"There's an up-and-coming fashion-and-lifestyle brand called *Morena & Miel*, which I happen to love. Creating social media for it is my favorite thing in the world."

"Why?"

"The products are original, and everything is carefully chosen. The pieces are well thought out and one of a kind. I love unique things—like that charm." She points to my Cuban link chain.

I touch the center where the special skeleton key hangs, and I'm flooded with all the feelings and the call of something deep inside me. I'm searching for words to say but can't come up with anything. I close my fist around it.

Her face goes from curious to soft as she watches the gesture. "It's absolutely gorgeous."

There's warmth in her voice, so I find myself telling her more than I usually share. "It's a key, actually."

She blinks. "Really? What does it open?"

My *casita, mi museo de recuerdos, and my whole soul.*

"The most valuable thing I own." I scoot closer to her, press the side tab on the shank, and it triggers the barrel, and then I twist it until the key bit pops out.

"That did not just happen." The light dances in her eyes, and her lips part.

And it hits me that I've told her too much. I don't want anyone to know about the charm being a key or for anyone to know about the *casita* back home. "Hey, do you mind not sharing that?"

Her fingers drag across her mouth, and she makes a twisting motion with her finger. "My lips are sealed."

Her face is so close I can't help but stare into it. "*Diablo, qué carita tan bella tienes.*"

"Stop," she says but doesn't pull away.

"No, I'm serious." I brush the backs of my fingers over her velvety soft cheek.

She sucks in a breath, and her lips press together, like preparing for mine. I lean over.

"Rio, let's go," Niko calls out. "Vampiro is ready."

But I am lost in the gloss of her eyes, the lingering sigh she releases, and the warmth that radiates from her skin. It's entrancing. I reach for her face.

"Rio, come on. Where are you?"

I drop my hands, and I clear my throat. "I'm sorry, I have to go record."

She blinks fast a few times, slowly shaking her head and looking away. When our gazes meet again, she shoots me a tentative smile and pushes to her feet. "Thanks for the chat. It was nice to meet you."

She walks away, and I start following Niko.

No, I can't let it end like this. It's been a while since I felt connected to anyone, and I don't want this moment to end. I rush back after her, and I grab her hand. "Luna."

She turns, and we're facing each other. The question is etched in her expressive eyes.

Yeah, I need to see her again. "Can I get your number?"

Luna

ME

OMG, Sel. I have so much to tell you. Where are you? I'm coming to you.

I cannot wait to tell my cousin about meeting Rio Castillo. I didn't know he would be here. He's hotter in person—as if that were possible. That full mouth, that pretty boy face, lashes for days, brown-almost-black eyes, and those lips—the videos do not lie. He's got me so giddy.

That part is probably not okay. I've been around enough celebrities to know that some are complete assholes. Not him, though. I'm still smiling as I run downstairs. Adina's waiting for me outside the building, and I'm ready to go.

I can't believe that just happened. I just wanted to tell Rio how much I loved his music, but when he turned around and looked at me so mean, I made the excuse of trying to get a drink. But he turned out to be so sweet. He even flirted with me! His eyes seemed so sad, a little dull, and he was awkward, but that went away as we spoke. *And he almost kissed me.* My chest still burns, thinking about him.

I even got his number. And he's already texting me!

I open the door to the street, and my friend Adina Belmont, also known as *Adi in the City*, stands there in all her glory—tall, beautiful, 10/10 body, glorious black hair, and a scowl so mean it could bring a star down from the sky.

"Where the hell have you been?" Her tone is harsh, as it usually is when she's ticked off.

"I was upstairs. Where were you? You disappeared on me. I was looking for you for a while," I say.

But that's how I ran into my favorite artist and then figured she would find me. *No regrets.*

"Working on setting up a collab. I'm here to network, too." Now she's got her back up and won't look me in the eye.

"Okay, you were doing your thing. Why are you mad?"

She rolls her eyes. "Who says I'm mad? I just couldn't find you."

"Well, here I am." There's no way I'm going to engage in whatever mood she is in now. I'm not letting her bring me down this time. I'm flying too high. I need my hype woman right now, my cousin Sel, because she's going to die when I tell her I met Rio Castillo. I just need to make sure Adina gets home first. "Are you ready to go?"

"No. Rio's here. I want to meet him."

His name stirs a fluttering in my belly, and words rush out of my mouth. "He's in the studio. But don't worry, you'll get to meet him soon."

She frowns. "What? How do you know?"

Her eyes bulge, her words suddenly overpronounced. It's what kills the fluttering and puts out the excitement. I know her well enough to know something went wrong—someone stepped on her toe, or had the same shirt, or maybe a guy she liked said hello to someone else—and now she is in a bad mood. It's a signal that I need to get away from her. Growing up together, I've learned that I love this chick with all my heart — she's my sister in my heart — but sometimes I need to love her from another borough.

"It's no biggie. I was talking to him upstairs. He has my number. We're probably going to hang out, and I'm definitely going to make sure my bestie gets to meet him."

Her gaze narrows, and her face goes red. She takes a step toward me. "Lulu, what the fuck are you doing?"

I blink a few times, my mouth drifting open. *Huh?* "I...what?"

"I'm talking to him. I was supposed to meet him inside but got caught up in business."

I'm stunned. *Is this a joke?* She never mentioned this.

"You told me earlier that we came to see Niko and Chico Spark. You never mentioned him."

"It was between him and me. Do I have to tell you everything? Like, Jesus, you're my friend. You heard me talk about him. I thought I could trust you around my dude."

Has she been snorting again?

I touch her arm, pulling her a few steps away from the entrance. "Adi, I didn't know he was your dude. We talked about his music. How can I know if you didn't tell me?"

She shakes my hand off.

"Anyway, you can't talk to him. You will not do this to me. I can't be friends with someone I can't trust," her voice rises, drawing stares from people. How long will it be until someone pulls out their phone, and we end up in one of the gossip rags?

"Calm down. We can talk this out."

"What is there to talk about, Lulu? Stay the fuck away from him. He knows you're my friend, because I talk about you. He can't help it. He's a flirt. But me and you know better."

She's not making any fucking sense, but I don't care anymore. I'm over it. I want this night to end.

"Fine. I will stay away. Can we go now?" I already regret not going out with Sel to come here. I should've known better when she invited me and I got that uneasy feeling in the pit of my stomach.

"No, I don't want to leave. Let's go inside so you can tell Rio not to talk to you anymore."

Hell no. This bitch has lost it. I'm not making an ass out of myself. "Adina, it's not that serious. It was innocent flirting. I'm not ruining a friendship over a dude, but I'm also not going in there to cause a scene. You're an influencer, and I'm in PR. Those people inside could end our careers."

"You don't even have a PR job yet. No one knows you like that. I said we're going inside!" She grabs my arm.

I inch forward and point at her. "Get your hand off me. I said I'm not going back in there. In fact, you can go inside by your damn self!"

She releases me, stepping back with bulging eyes.

I walk away from her.

"Lulu," she calls out, but I keep walking until I turn the corner. I'm seething and pull out my phone to order an Uber. My face is so hot, and I'm so angry that I could chew glass and not bleed. This all could have been prevented. She could've just said she was talking to that man.

Then the phone starts to ring. It's Adina. I hit the side button. But she calls again and again. I ignore every call.

A message from my cousin comes through.

SEL

I'm in The Heights. Dropping a pin. Get your ass here.

ADINA

I'm sorry. Come back. Please.

You're my best friend. I love you.

I would hate it if this got between us.

The Uber is right around the corner, and I walk down the block to the light to meet the driver. Five minutes later, we're headed uptown. I lay my head back against the leather seat of the sedan and breathe, letting everything settle inside me. I'm so mad, and I don't know if it's all Adina's fault. Rio is obviously a player who was trying to mess with me while talking to my friend. There are plenty of guys in the world she moves in who think talking to or messing with an influencer gives them free access to her friends.

He got you with those sad eyes and the 'key to the most valuable thing I own' story. You forgot what Perla, his ex, said about him. *He's emotionally unavailable and a cheater.*

I just know Sel is going to tell me that my first mistake is to trust any man. You would think I would know that after my last two pathological liars I dated.

Adina keeps calling, but I put my phone in do-not-disturb mode. I keep an eye on the messages in case Sel says anything else, but when it pings, it's a message from him.

RIO

I may be done sooner than expected. Where do I find you?

I close my eyes and see a crimson tide behind my lids.

ME

You don't. Do not message me again.

RIO

Huh?

ME

Adina is my best friend.

And then I block him.

I open the window, and even the October air doesn't cool me off. When I arrive at the club where Sel is hanging out, I find her chatting with a group of guys, oblivious to how some of them are staring at her. Her jeans are tight, but she's wearing an off-the-shoulder shirt and flats. Her makeup is natural over her golden, amber-toned skin. She takes one look at me and walks away from them. Her hand hooks around the same arm Adina snatched earlier, but my cousin secures it against her side.

Ten minutes later, her jaw is working, and her hands are flexing into fists. "You see? That's why she doesn't want me to come when you two hang out. She can't pull that shit on you with me around. Is that bitch snorting again?"

"I don't know, but I'm ignoring her and have already blocked him. I'm not losing a friend over him."

"You know what I always say: men are good-for-nothing dogs. And no, you don't turn your back on your homegirl over dick. But your girl is *trippin'* big time, as always. To yell at you like that when she never told you, like fuck, it's definitely giving coke."

Her tone yanks a laugh out of me despite the headache brewing in the back of my head. "I think I need to eat something."

She tilts her head to the door. "Let's hit the *Yaroa* food truck."

We head to the food truck spot, and the smell of seasoned meat and fried plantains layered with cheese is so comforting it dulls the throbbing at my temples. But I'm still...annoyed? Disappointed? "He seemed so sincere."

"Maybe he was. Maybe your girl was bugging like she always does when guys pay you attention. It's also possible that he's used to selling that *carita de niño lindo* to everyone. You know he's always knee deep in panties. And he probably saw you and wondered what you were doing with that *huevo sin sal*. Let's forget him and her tonight. After we eat, we'll go back and dance our asses off. They have 90s reggaeton followed by Anthony Santos' hour."

Jesus. How am I going to survive an hour of dancing to Anthony Santos—no relation to me—with this headache? Every single one of his songs is pure cardio, and they last more than five minutes. But I need a distraction, or I'll get in a funk. "Yeah, let's do that."

He didn't seem like a conceited jackass or entitled, like some of the people in Adina's circle can be. That's what is so freaking annoying. I wish I had walked away faster. It would've stayed a cute fantasy. The big star pays attention to me, and the connection is instant enough for me to still feel his breath on my lips. I could kick myself. I don't want to talk to him or see him. I don't even want to hear his music. *Rio Castillo can go straight to hell.*

2

Rio – Six months later

I'm in fucking hell.

And about to get doused in gasoline.

The fast clicking of stilettos echoes closer, reaching me along with the feminine scent—musk, cashmeran, jasmine—of the expensive perfume I had specially made for her birthday.

Hurricane Maeven is here.

I don't lift my gaze from the spotted dirty tile and the nine hundred and ninety-two spots I've been counting, not even when the long sigh, charged with what I can only assume are large doses of fed-the-fuck-up, fills the room.

"When I accepted this job, I made it abundantly clear, Riomar Castillo, that I'm not here for this kind of fuckery." Maeven's voice is sharp and tight, and she doesn't stop there. "You had a wonderful day today. Your new album is trending on social media with people calling it an instant classic. We announced your tour, but instead of shaking our asses to your songs in a club flowing with champagne, I'm here bailing you out of jail."

I still don't look at her beyond the five-inch heels with bows on the backs. "Did you know there are 992 stains on these tiles?"

She pushes closer. "No, but when you look for a new publicist, for the right amount of money, you may be able to find 992 candidates that will be willing to put up with this shit."

She pivots back to the way she came. I push to my feet, raising my gaze from the floor.

"Don't leave, Maeven," I say, finally looking up at her.

Her hair is pulled into a high ponytail that dangles even as she pauses. Her jeans and red top with what looks like a keyhole in the front make her look relaxed and laid back, but her face gives more of an on-my-last-nerve vibe. It's accentuated by the reddish hue on her brown skin, most likely from annoyance. *That's my fault.*

"Why shouldn't I?" she asks while glaring at me as if she could disintegrate me with her gaze.

Yeah, she's pissed at me, and I can't blame her.

"It wasn't my fault. Noryel came in looking for trouble. I was having a good time, chillin' with my people, until that asshole started throwing shots until he threw a glass at us. I went over there and showed him I didn't need a glass to make a point." I flex my fingers against the raw pain in my knuckles.

"Rio, you broke his nose and dislocated his shoulder. He won't be able to make his next gigs."

I shrug. "He had it coming."

"Yeah, I won't argue with you there because everyone knows Noryel DD was in real need of an ass whooping. But it didn't need to come from you. It was reckless. You keep acting like a hot trigger and falling for traps constantly. This shit is getting old." She turns her finger in a circle as if to say *look around us.* "Do you know the kind of favor I had to pull so charges weren't pressed against you?"

Anger storms up my spine. She doesn't have to do me any fucking favors.

"No, you don't. Because I, Esme, and Kresh are constantly bailing you out. I should cut my losses with you, Rio. I could be making this money with someone easier to manage."

And now she throws the whole team in my face. Esmeralda "Esme"

Fernandez is my lawyer, and Lucrecia "Kresh" Bravo is my agent. Both work in tandem with Maeven to manage my career. But at this point, I don't care. "Do it, then. I don't need you. I don't need anyone who doesn't want to be here."

I sit back down on the chair.

"Get up. I'm not doing this here."

She turns on her heel, walking in quick, New York strides. I follow because I'm not dumb enough to stay in jail if I shouldn't even be here. Outside the room, the cops are waiting for us. Esme, with her asymmetrical bob, is talking to them. Her no-nonsense lawyer expression is on full display as she nods.

The officer who arrested me hands me my jewelry and phone. "Stay out of trouble."

"Fuck you," I say back.

Maeven stops walking to pin me with what I recognize as her *shut-the-fuck-up* look—flat lips and a scowl that could scare the hair off a Maine Coon. I smile and follow her out.

Outside, a large Suburban is waiting for us. We hop in, and Esme leans close, her eyes sharp on mine. "Stop fucking up. You're lucky we were able to secure witnesses who saw him throw the glass your way before they got paid off. But you can only get lucky so many times, Rio. It's getting old. We don't want you to ruin everything you've got going on."

I nod. "Thank you."

We drive up the West Side Highway to Riverdale to drop off Esme. I'm always struck at how different from the other parts of the city it is. If you went by the all the lush trees and the mixture of private homes and exclusive buildings, you wouldn't think there are subway stations and poor neighborhoods just miles away. The suburban feel is like a mirage. I don't get to contemplate that much as we are soon headed to my place in the Upper West Side. Maeven stares out to the night river view as we maneuver back on the highway. The silence in the car is heavy, other than the driver's loud gum smacking. Maeven's not on her phone like she always is. This time, she's pensive, her leg tapping on the floor of the car like a ticking time bomb.

She's going to quit. *And she should.* No one signed up for this shit, but she's getting paid well, so fuck her. If she wants to walk away, good-bye. I'm not begging anyone to stay, even if I lose opportunities. So what? I can make more songs, and I can hire another publicist. One that doesn't nag so much.

Except, she's like family, with a fierce and protective presence, taking care of me during my worst times.

I'm not forcing anyone to stay, though.

When we get to my place, she jumps out of the car, and we head into the building. Tito, my cousin and bodyguard, is waiting for us at the door, wearing fresh clothes and a baseball cap. He's built like a linebacker, pure muscle on every inch of his body. His imposing body is at odds with the worried expression on his face. His brown skin looks a little ashen too. We got separated when I got arrested, and he was probably the one who called Maeven and Esme.

He claps my shoulder and ushers us into the building. "How was it?"

"It was fine. Almost had to fight someone there too." I look at Maeven as I say it, but her face remains blank. I want to piss her off so she can quit and walk away without dragging this shit out. I hate when people make up their mind and then keep pushing shit off.

Tito looks at me, his eyes panicky, his mouth pale. He knows she'll dump me too.

"Maeven, what were you getting into?"

She doesn't bother to look at us. "Esme and I were having dinner with Vale and Alondra. We were working on their wedding plans."

Shit. Alondra is Esme's best friend and Maeven's cousin—they're all like sisters. She lives in North Carolina with her fiancé Valentin. They're in town to discuss wedding planning and were supposed to meet us after to celebrate my album release.

Yeah, I'm getting my ass dropped today.

The music blares before the door opens to my penthouse. It's not any music. It's my music, my art, my pain, *mi alma.* The people who were partying with me at the club are all here. When everyone sees me, they scream my name.

A few girls surround me, and someone hands me a *Presidente* beer.

Maeven intercepts it instead, her eyes pelting me with that look I can't decipher. "Tell them all to get the fuck out."

"They came to party with me."

"Tell. Them. To. Get. The. Fuck. Out." Her voice booms through an open mic. Conversations diminish. The DJ stops playing. All eyes are on her as she blinks a couple of times but doesn't miss a beat. "You all heard me. Get out. You're not Rio's friends. I didn't see any of you trying to get him out. All you're doing is mooching off his alcohol and food."

"*Y quien es esta cabrona?*" one of the women says.

Maeven points to the door. "I said, get the fuck out!"

In a matter of a few minutes, the penthouse empties, except for me, her, and Tito. "Go wait outside," she tells him

The minute the door closes, she stares me down. "What the fuck is your problem? Do you think this is a game? You're fucking up your life and damaging your career. You're either drinking, getting high off your ass, or fighting."

"I thought you were quitting," I say with as much sarcasm as I can muster.

"I should. I should walk away and leave you to your mess."

"Why don't you? I don't need you. I don't need anyone."

She jabs a finger into my chest. "You don't want to need me, but you do. Your tour is not selling very well. Your name is more associated with fuck-shit behavior than music these days. That album is a masterpiece, but people won't know it because of your antics. But that ends right now. You're going to get your shit together if it kills me. I booked you an appointment with Dr. Jacinda Smith. She's a psychologist, very discreet, who can help you work out some of your issues."

"I don't need to see a counselor. I'm just wild."

She holds my gaze, unmoved. "You're not wild. You're letting your hurt get to you. You're acting dumb. If you keep going down this path, you're going to do something that's going to fuck up your career for good. How long until someone you're hanging with plants something on you? How long until one of these little thots you keep hanging around with accuses you of something or gets knocked up because you're too drunk or high to realize it?"

"I'm not—" I stop. "Tito is always there."

He's my best friend. I trust Tito with my life.

"Yeah, but you put yourself in situations he may not be able to get you out of. You're destroying yourself and will probably take him down in the process because he's trying to save your ass. You know why he wasn't at the jail with you?"

I shake my head.

"Have you seen him wear a hat before?" She doesn't wait for my answer. "Neither have I, but he's wearing one tonight. Why do you think that is, Rio?"

"I don't know."

She pushes close and points to her head. "Because he had to be taken to the ER. Someone hit him with a glass bottle, and he was bleeding. Of course, he's covering it up so you don't see it. He will go down protecting you."

Oh shit.

I open my mouth, but she stops me with her hand in the air.

"Do you think this is what Fer would want for you? Do you think seeing you like this lets her rest in peace?" Maeven's gaze drifts to the glass butterfly hanging in front of the window. Maeven herself gave it to me as a gift on the worst day of my life.

Pain breaks out in my chest like she sucker punched me. I flinch. My body fights the urge to sink to my knees. "*No hables de ella.*"

Maeven shakes her head. "I don't want to talk about her. It breaks my heart to see the pain in your eyes when I do, but maybe it's time you did."

I shake my head and move to the window to stare out at the Hudson River. "*No lo voy a hacer.*"

"You have to, Rio. Have you noticed you immediately switch to Spanish when you talk about your mom?"

The pressure in my chest intensifies, and the thirst dries my throat. It's been over a year, and my fingers flex, still feeling the softness of her hand in mine as her breath faded away. I still see the peace descend over her features on her last exhale when she slipped into what seemed to be a dream with a hint of a smile on her face. I swallow, not wanting to scream her name like I did in that moment.

Maeven's hand settles on my shoulder. "It's time. I don't want to leave you. It would break my heart and Fer's. In her last days, I promised her I would take care of you. That's sacred to me because she gave us a chance when we were newbies to manage your career, and she was like a mom to me. Everyone else is a client, but you're like a little brother to me and Esme. You've got to meet me halfway."

I want to tell her to fuck off. Hearing *her* name hurts more than the punches from the fights or the mornings when I wake up with a pounding headache and throwing up into a toilet.

And then I hear that raspy voice that time can't fade in my head. *Her voice. Eres mi orgullo.*

Except, the person in the reflection is no one's pride. I know I have to change. I need to do something different. I just don't know how.

"I don't want to go to rehab. It's not that bad."

Maeven nods. "Okay, then. Show me. Let's start with therapy and get ready for the tour. In the meantime, I'll work my magic to fix your image." She points at me. "I need you to promise... No more fighting. No more drugs. And no more than two drinks a night."

"Deal."

She looks down at her phone and back at my face. "And here's where we start. Next week, Chico Sparx is playing at the Coliseum. You're going to perform the new song you recorded with him and Niko. It's releasing the day before. Niko won't be there, but you and Chico will do well together. He will also let you sing one of your album's songs. The girls will love it."

I start to shake my head because there's no way I feel ready for that. But she's got that not-budging look in her eyes.

Maybe it's time I get out on the stage again. I'll have to do it for the tour anyway.

"Okay."

After Maeven leaves, I sit on the couch, with my phone in my hand, scrolling through my social media feeds. The fight with Noryel is being discussed everywhere, with people commenting.

Noryel had it coming. He's been a real POS lately.

Yeah, about time someone gave him a good salsa.

But mostly, people are talking about me.

Man, it's time someone says it. Rio is a fucking mess.

ATP we know Rio for the fuck-shit, not his music.

Another guy agrees. *Yeah, like bruh, get some therapy.*

Someone else posts *Does Rio not have friends?*

The answer from another person has me almost throwing my phone against the wall. *Yeah, but Niko is too big to be associated with that shit. That's why he stays far away.*

I keep scrolling down my feed, trying to outrun the posts about me. My friend Zao posted to his IG page about his return to his *Barrio*. All the kids are smiling in photos with him, and a party broke out in the main street.

El Dominante back in his kingdom. Nada como #BuenosAires #RD

God, I want to go home so bad. I wouldn't get into problems there. I just can't go.

Farther down, a photo calls my attention. It's from Adi in the City's blog. Adina is standing in front of a building, making the peace sign, but the one that really catches my eye is the woman in the back, leaning casually against the wall in a jean jacket and joggers while smiling at someone off camera.

Luna.

My lip curls like hers did the last time we saw each other at a club in The Heights. I still don't know what I supposedly did to her other than flirt a little at Niko's. Ever since, she's been giving me the cold shoulder and not even saying hello when we run into each other. But it's all good. I dodged a bullet the day we met. And now I don't have time for this shit.

Because my life is in shambles.

My phone pings. It's a text.

NIKO

Bro. What's going on? This is not you. Why
you being so reckless?

ME

It's nothing, man.

NIKO

Not nothing. You got arrested. Let's talk. I
got your back.

And the sinking feeling is instant. *I'm a mess, and everyone knows.*
Niko always has it together. He doesn't need to be told what to do. He
doesn't need a Maeven to fix shit for him.

Me

No biggie. I let anger get the best of me. I
got it tho.

A call from him comes through, and I hit the ignore button.
Then another text. It's from my friend Xavier "El Flaco" Delgado.

XAVIER

I know you're hurting. You're not alone.
Call me.

I can't talk to him either. I need to do this on my own.

I leave him *on read*, close my phone screen, and flip the device away.
Doom-scrolling does nothing but remind me of what a fuck-up I am
and exposes me to people who already know that.

I grab my pen and notepad. This is how I write songs—alone in the
silence—and I have words to get off my chest tonight.

I can't believe you did this...to me.
No lo puedo creer
Everything in me arde
Y no me puedo contener

Walking around life like a powdered keg

Any friction becomes an ignition
Rapid combustion es mi mecanismo
Y todos los días vivo lo mismo

Algo tiene que cambiar
Something's got to give
Because carrying this weight
Is almost breaking me

You did this
No se por que lo hiciste
La paz no me encuentra
En ningun sitio que busque

Me quitaste el sol
You left me in the darkness
La paz no me encuentra
You're supposed to love me
How could you be so heartless?

Send me a sliver of light
A tiny star for my sky
La oscuridad no es mi amiga
It's my prison of anger, mi peor enemiga

Algo tiene que cambiar
I need you to break this chain
Porque no puedo respirar
Drowning in all this pain

3

Luna

The beat drops as I finish applying lipliner while my hips roll to the music. The song is sexy and flavorful, making your body move almost involuntarily in a way only reggaeton music can. I don't stop dancing, even as I apply my eyeshadow. Then the beat transitions to a soft, sensual vibe.

"*Es Rio*," a soulful voice croons, and my back stiffens. Though his voice complements the beat to perfection, my lips curl.

> *Mami, se que me extrañabas*
> *But no sweat cause Daddy's here*
> *Pa calentarte la cama.*

The music keeps playing, but my hips still, like my grandma's old ones, Fernandito Villalona scratched records.

"You didn't know he dropped this song with Niko and Chico?" Adina asks from my bed.

I shake my head. "Why would you play one of his songs?"

She shrugs. "Because it's good, and you should have seen the way your hips shook. You were about to twerk."

I roll my eyes at her in the mirror. "I was not. And you don't twerk for *reggaeton. Perreas.*"

"Whatever. The song is hot, and he's perfect on it." She sighs. "You don't have to hate him anymore, Lu. I'm over him."

She's not. Her gigantic crush on Rio is still going strong despite what happened six months ago. She practically drools at parties when he's there. I don't know what she sees in that sleazy shithead who gets into one mess after another.

"Nope," I say, as snappish as I can. "No one tries to play with my best friend. This beef with Rio is forever," I say in my best Cardi B voice.

Her fingers form a heart. "We can still enjoy the song, right?"

Her gaze is on me through the mirror, and knowing her like I do, I shrug. It's better not to elaborate, or she will get in her own head, and I have no desire to rehash the night when fuckboy almost destroyed our friendship. "You can enjoy it."

I apply eyeliner and grab the black sheer-swirl bodysuit from the bed, shimmying into it. Then I put on my faded jeans. She watches my every move as I slip my earrings on and finally take off my doobie wrap, carefully combing down my hair. I'm wearing it straight tonight.

"You look so good, Lu," she says softly with a tiny smile on her lips. "You always find creative ways to style all that body."

There's a catch in my belly, but I dismiss it and smile at her. *Because this ass is a weapon I proudly wield.* "Thanks, this thing is a legend." I wiggle my butt, adding, "You look gorgeous too."

She hops off my bed and comes to stand in the mirror with her phone in hand. We pose and snap photos of ourselves. She's three sizes smaller than me and has a killer body. My wide hips and big ass are a bombastic contrast to her sleek curves encased in the body-fitted jumpsuit.

"We look like a sexy yin and yang." I wink at her in the mirror.

She smirks, switching her pose. We shoot from different angles until her phone rings.

"Thierry is downstairs," she says, grabbing her jacket. Her new boyfriend, Thierry Banks, is a tight end for the Giants, and a professional douche, if you ask me. But Adina is in love, so here we go.

I grab my jacket as well, throw on my mesh stilettos, and follow her out the door. My mom is standing in the living room in her blue fuzzy robe. Her brown eyes do a double-take, her gaze bouncing from Adina to me, but she strings a small smile.

"Bellas las dos."

"Thank you, Raquel," Adina says and then heads for the door. "Lu, hurry up. You know Thierry hates waiting."

The minute she is out the door, my mom's eyes narrow on me. "Why is she wearing your jumpsuit? You spent days making it."

I shrug. "She asked for it."

"Luna, you know I love her. I helped raise her, but how many times—"

"Mami, it's just a jumpsuit, and I don't have time right now." I throw my arms around her. *"Bendición?"*

She hugs me tight. *"Dios te bendiga,"* she says, then whispers in my ear, "You still look better than her."

I chuckle. "Love you."

"Love you too, *Mariposita.* Remember, I'm going out with Darren tonight."

I smile. I love that Darren, Mami's boyfriend, is taking her to dinner and a lounge. "That's right. Show me your outfit."

She opens her robe to reveal the slacks and cross-wrapped halter top that go together beautifully. The large, scalloped earrings are a great accessory, and her hair pulled back into a bun completes the look.

"I'll drape the sweater over my shoulders like you told me." She makes the motion with her hands to illustrate.

I kiss my fingers like a chef with a signature dish. "Perfection. Meghan Markle would be proud. Wear the black-and-gold mules with it."

I rush down the stairs as fast as my heels allow me and step out into the cool night air, still smiling. I'm so happy when Darren takes Mami out, and she gets to do more than work. Thierry's Maybach is parked right in front of my building door. All the guys on the block stare at it.

"Damn, Luna, let me come with you," one shouts.

"Luna, tell your friend to let me borrow his car real quick," yells my neighbor out of the window.

I laugh and wave, then climb into the front seat of the vehicle and say hello to the driver.

"Hey, Luna, looking good," Thierry Banks chimes from the back.

"Thanks," I say, only slightly turning to look at him.

"What about me?" Adina asks.

"Baby, this little catsuit thing you got on is going to get you in trouble tonight. It's so fucking sexy." He whispers something in her ear that I can hear as if he had yelled it. "Maybe I'll fuck you in it."

I try not to wince and keep my eyes on the road as the driver maneuvers us out onto the Major Deegan Expressway. Adina's giggle from the backseat fills the car, along with the kissing noises, rustling of his hands over the fabric of her clothing, and—dear God—the slurping.

She can definitely keep the jumpsuit.

Emails for Enlace, the small PR company my cousin Sel and I run together, become my saving grace, as I dive into them. I respond to a couple messages and then review the social media comments for Amber Bijoux, one of the companies we work with, mining the data to create and curate content. People are loving their new bracelets. A couple of celebs have tagged us in their posts. I copy some quotes and add them to my OneNote app, along with the dates. Next month's calendar is mainly done. I just love how organic it will all feel. Having quotes is automatic content you don't need to edit.

Soon, I'll be working for my dream company, Elevate, as a public relations specialist. Elevate has high-profile clients, and I'll get to help them manage those portfolios and PR management for their clients. I've never wanted to be in front of the camera, but helping people manage their image has always been a dream. It's also where the money is. Sel and I will need to hire someone to help us with Enlace until I settle into my new job and can handle both workloads, because I do not want to stop doing this.

"Luna." Adina's voice penetrates the work fog.

"What?" I ask, looking up to find we're already close to the venue.

"What the hell are you doing? I'm talking to you." Her tone is tight, tinged with annoyance.

"Oh." I look down at the screen and hit save. "Gathering some data for work."

She groans. "Do you ever turn it off? We're going to a Chico Sparx concert, and you're here working."

I don't miss the way the driver's eyes slide to the side of his head to meet mine. I can almost hear the comment "some of us have to work for a living" hanging in the air. But Adina doesn't know better.

"Girl, I am riding in a car, doing nothing. I might as well put my brain to good use."

"We're here, and you're hanging out with us. We need your attention too," she whines.

"I'm letting you and Thierry have your time alone," I insist. Because there's no way I'm going to be sitting around watching them make out, even if their tongues didn't slip out of their mouths so often.

Yuck.

"I'm obviously not doing it right because she's more worried about you than me." Thierry's tone is testy.

"It's not that, babe. You know you're my number one, but I want my number two to chat it up with us."

More slurping sounds, and I'm ready to jump out of the still-moving vehicle. Thankfully, we arrive, and in the next two minutes, we are ushered inside the Coliseum. The interior is designed like a Roman amphitheater, with the stage situated in the center.

Thierry takes us backstage, where we get to say hello to Chico Sparx. He's short but muscular, with a sharp sense of style. His baby face does justice to his name. He hugs Thierry and Adina, who turn away to greet someone else. Chico turns to me and despite meeting him at a few parties, I'm not famous, so I always feel like I have to introduce myself. "I'm Luna Santos."

His eyes light up. "I remember you, gorgeous Luna. We definitely need to have you in one of our videos." His gaze drifts behind me. "Rio, let me introduce you to some friends."

My back stiffens, but he's in my line of vision before I can even fix my face. Our gazes meet, and his eyes do a quick scan over me. Then, he makes that face like he just had a shot of vinegar. *No, he's not happy to see me either.*

Thankfully, it's been a while since our paths have crossed. I let my gaze slide over him, too. Is it me or does he seem a little more jacked? The black t-shirt clings to his body like honey to a jar. Yeah, those shoulders and arms have definitely filled up since the day we chatted at Niko's party.

"Hi, Luna." The face that makes thousands of girls scream and panties rain on the stage dissolves into a half-smile. It's tight, polite, and dry.

"Rio," I say, matching his energy.

"You know each other?" Chico asks.

"Yeah," we both say but don't elaborate.

Chico opens his mouth, but Thierry hands me a drink. I thank him and take a sip while all three men stare at me.

Chico looks at Rio. "I was telling Luna she should be in one of our videos. People would love her face and her body—no offense."

"Hi, Rio."

He turns to Adina and smiles from ear to ear, and it's genuine, unlike his strained expression for me. "So good to see you."

I fight the urge to roll my eyes. *What a perro.*

They exchange pleasantries while I chat with Chico and Thierry. I take a big sip of my drink, suddenly thirsty. It's only when Rio walks away that I can easily breathe. I hate that man so much that I'll never be comfortable around him. I just wish he wasn't so fine.

I need to vet the places I go with Adina more carefully from now on to avoid running into him.

When we get to our seats, she leans to whisper in my ear, "Rio is such a dog. He was coming on to me with Thierry only a few feet away."

Funny, I didn't hear any of that. He talked to her about the weather, her new energy drink campaign, and his upcoming tour. At no point did he seem to get close to her. But I wasn't paying close attention.

All I can say is, "Oh, wow."

"What did you and Chico talk about?"

My mind goes blank. *Fuck, I can't remember. Wait, he kept asking if*

I would be in one of his videos. I know better than to say that to Adina. "Just chit chat. Nothing big."

"You sure?" She stares me down, but the DJ starts the warmup. She leans over. "This concert is going to be so good. I can't wait to see him perform his song with Rio."

I frown at her. "How are you not disgusted?"

She shrugs. "The song is fire. It also feels kinda good to know he still wants me. He's been hitting the gym hard. He looks yummy right now."

"I guess, if you're into that."

She laughs, her eyes peeled on me. "Come on. You thought he was hot."

"Until I found out he was a dog trying to play us both."

"I think he was just drunk the night he made a pass at you. It happens. I can forgive him. Let it go, Lulu."

"You can," I say, because I still hear the anger in her voice when I told her he asked me out. The whole thing changed our friendship. I no longer feel like I can fully be honest with her, even about the little things. Something always stops me. Maybe it's that I finally began to see all the things Sel has been saying for years about Adina being an *envidiosa.* "Let's forget him."

"You need another drink," she says to me then turns to whisper in Thierry's ear.

There's a slight numbness in my cheek. I need to slow down. "No, I still have some of this one left. Maybe later."

She thrusts a new full glass into my hand, and when I sip, I can taste the intensity of the alcohol and something sweeter that sticks to my tongue. The buzz begins, and I place the glass next to me on the floor as the music starts with the classics.

"Let's take it back with some classics before we get to Chico," the DJ practically screams into the mic.

"*Noche de Sexo*" comes on, and everyone starts screaming when it transitions to "*Dime Mami.*" I'm on my feet, so buzzed that I forget how much I hate Rio, and dance with my hands in the air like the first two hundred times I've heard it. The music feels more intense. I match it with my movements. When Chico brings out Rio, everyone screams.

I'm in a zone, watching him move to the music and dance for the audience. I follow along with my hips.

A rush courses through my body, and I could dance all night like this. I close my eyes and sway, letting the feeling drive me. When I open them again, Rio is practically right in front of me. I blink a couple of times, and he's back on the stage. *Jesus, I'm twisted as fuck.*

I'm only on my second drink. *Why am I flying like this?*

4

Rio

"You killed that!" Chico screams as he makes his way to me backstage, bumping my shoulder. "They sang your verse at the tops of their lungs. The crowd missed you."

I smile because it really feels good. I worried what that would be like after being gone for more than a year and a half. But being onstage felt like coming into my second skin. Yeah, they're here for Chico tonight, but they remembered me. That's good enough for me right now. I still have a long road to my tour-kickoff concert and only a few months to prepare.

I change my sweaty shirt while Chico goes to change for his next set.

When I exit the dressing room, I see her alone, standing by the wall. *Luna.* She's staring right at me, but her expression blank, unlike the way she was dancing in the audience. She was really working those hips, shaking them to my music, but now it's like she doesn't even know me.

Why does she hate me so much? I want to close the distance between us and ask her what her problem is. All I did was ask her out, and one minute she was into it, but the next, she texted back as if I had done

31

something to her. Now, every time I see her, she acts like a pure *loca*. *Why are the hottest ones always unhinged?*

Thierry comes out of nowhere to stand by her. He hands her a glass of water, and then his hand goes to her waist and drifts to her ass. He pulls her to him, and her head lolls to his shoulder. Then, like he's done it a million times, his head comes down, and he tilts her neck up to kiss her.

I'm stunned. *That's her friend's boyfriend.*

But her hand is shoving at his side.

And the alarm bells go off in my head.

"Something's wrong with her," Tito says.

I take my gaze off them and look at him. "You see that too?"

"She looks like you when you were on the Vibe."

Vibe is something someone gave me months ago to take the edge off. The flashback is quick and strong. I couldn't feel a thing with my skin being so numb. People kept pulling me. I didn't want to go but couldn't say no. Looking at Luna brings it all back.

Then I hear her voice clearly. "I don't feel good. Leave me alone."

She is pushing at him, but Thierry brings her closer.

I take a step forward, and Chico's hand is on my shoulder to stop me. "Stay away, man. It's none of your business. That's how that crowd parties."

I look at him, but I hear her say, "No, I don't want to."

As much as I don't like this chick, I need to make sure she is okay.

I shake Chico's hand off my shoulder and cross the distance. "What's going on?"

Thierry smirks at me. "What does it look like?"

Luna's eyes are glassy. Her body is unstable, like she can't stand on her own.

"She's not okay. Are you trying to take advantage of her?"

Thierry laughs. "Yeah, right."

I ignore him. "Luna, you want to come with me?"

She doesn't move, but whispers, "Yes."

I step forward.

Thierry holds up a hand. "Back off."

His bodyguard remains by his side but doesn't move. He's staring at Tito. My cousin is big enough for him to think twice.

I extend a hand, and Luna latches onto it. I pull her, but Thierry holds her back.

"Let her go, man. She said no. That means you fuck off." If I have to tell him again, it won't be with words. My hand flexes to a fist, ready to do the talking for me.

"Mind your fucking business, man," Thierry shoots back.

"What's going on?" Adina rushes to his side, but her gaze is on me.

Thierry points at me. "Luna is not feeling good, and this asshole wants her to go with him."

She looks from Luna to me, pressing her lips. "No, she hates him." Her phone pings, and she looks at it. Then her face goes pale, and she turns to Thierry. "What the fuck?"

On her phone screen is the image of Thierry kissing Luna. In the next second, she turns to Luna and tries to slap her. "You bitch."

Both bodyguards step in the way. I move Luna back, but in that moment, she tugs at my hand.

"I want to go home." Her voice is soft, almost fading, provoking a heaviness in my stomach.

I'm going to make sure she gets there.

I move her away as Adina is screaming in the background. "That fucking slut. She always wants what I have. I can't believe you, Thierry. Why her?"

I take Luna out of the place.

"Get me an Uber."

I shake my head at her. "You can't go home alone. Tell me where you live, and I'll take you."

"But I hate you. You're a dog." Her eyes are darting from side to side.

"I know, but we have to get you home."

"Call Sel..." She sways against me with her full weight.

I manage to catch her, but her eyes roll back. My heart drops as I hold her with one hand and pat her face. "Luna."

She doesn't open her eyes or look at me again. My heart is pounding so fast I'm barely aware of the yelling around me and the gathering crowd.

A hand presses on my shoulder. Thankfully, it's Tito. "We have to get her to a hospital."

I pick her up, her limp body heavy against my chest, and we load her into the backseat of my waiting SUV. I place her head on my lap as we drive away. I keep patting her cheek, but she's out cold.

"Let's go to St. Anthony's. It's the closest one. Rio, you need to call Maeven," Marco, my driver, says.

I look away from Luna to the front of the car. His usually jovial face is now marked by a deep frown. "What? Why?"

"You didn't see people snapping photos and videos? This girl's face is already all over the place after she kissed Thierry."

"*He* kissed *her*. Forcibly. She was practically a zombie."

"It won't matter. The internet is already on it," Marco insists.

I clench my teeth. There's never a moment where there's not a fucking camera around. "This just happened."

"No kidding. People are going live on TikTok. This shit is going viral. Maeven won't be happy," says Tito, holding up his phone.

"What else is new?"

Five minutes later, we pull up to the emergency room. When they take Luna away, I pull out my phone and call Maeven.

"Rio? What's wrong? Why are you calling me at this hour?" She's out of breath.

"We have a problem. There's this girl, Luna, who seems to have been drugged—"

"Get off me. I gotta go," she tells someone. "Rio, did you have sex with that impaired girl?"

"What? No. I took her away from Thierry Banks. He was kissing her against her will, and then his girlfriend, Adina, wanted to beat her. We brought her to St. Anthony's. She's in the ER. Marco said I should call you—"

Her audible breath fills the line. "Hold up. Are you talking about Luna Santos?"

"Yeah, she's out cold. You know her?"

"Yeah," she says, and there's all kinds of rustling on the other line. "Help me find my pants. Luna's my old intern. I'm on my way, Rio."

5

Luna

"Luna," my dad calls out.

Papi?

I turn around and run looking for him, but it's dark. I can't see clearly. Then, my grandma is there, sitting in her kitchen, rolling pasteles. She grabs my hand, the masa sticking her fingers to my skin. Her touch is comforting, and I miss the warmth of her leathery skin so much. "Go back."

"Luna!" My name is a scream that jolts me awake, followed by beeps and arguing voices.

"You all need to leave, Mrs. Belmont. My daughter doesn't need this mess right now. Please go home."

Mami?

"That's all you have to say, Raquel? Adina is devastated. You're supposed to love her too."

Bethany Belmont's tone is angry and loud. *What the hell is happening?*

"Lulu, wake up and talk to us. I can't fucking believe you did that to me." Adina's voice cracks, and I fight to open my eyes, but I can't.

35

"Stop yelling at her, or I'm going to whoop your ass like I should have done a long time ago."

It's Sel's piercing voice and take-no-shit tone. *Why is she so angry?*

Another voice, one I don't recognize, rises above the loud chatter. "You need to go. This is a hospital, and there are other patients. Only her mother and cousin can stay."

"*Mami*," I force out, prying my eyes open.

"*Mariposita*, thank God." My mom is at my side, but I can only see her outline. It's blurry, but I don't need to see her. I feel her hand on my face. "How are you feeling?"

The love in her tone and the warmth in her touch make my eyes fill with tears. "I feel sick."

"I'm sure you do. And you're going to blame it on the alcohol, aren't you?" Mrs. Belmont says from my mother's side.

"What are you talking about? What happened?" I ask.

"Oh, don't bullshit us. We all know. The whole world knows what you did. It's everywhere. Just make sure you don't try to throw the blame on someone else."

My head pounds against my skull so hard my stomach turns. "What the hell are you talking about?"

"You know very well what you did. Stop playing games. The drinks were not even that strong. Too many people saw!" Adina yells.

"Titi Raquel, say the word, and I'll dog walk this little bitch and her mom," Sel's voice rises.

My gut twists violently, and my stomach feels like it's tearing itself from my body. The nausea rises fast—so fast I almost have no time to turn my head. Someone shoves a bedpan in front of me, and I vomit into it. The bile surges, and there is so much I think I'm about to choke. My stomach heaves. At times, the panic rises because I can't breathe, and I feel like I'm going to drown in it. Tears flow just as fast. I can't stop. Then I have nothing else in my stomach, and all that's left is pain as I fall back into the hospital pillow.

There's no noise in the room except for *Mami's* humming. Through my half-closed eyes, she wipes my mouth and face with a moist towel.

"It's okay. I got it," my mom says when a nurse comes close and presses a cold rag to my forehead.

"They're gone," Sel says.

"Thank you. Can you please let the nurse's station know that they're not to come in this room without me?" *Mami* tells the nurse.

"Yes, Mrs. Santos."

"Thank you. My daughter doesn't need to talk to them right now. She's gone through a lot. We need to find out what happened first."

"I'm pretty sure she was drugged," Sel says. "Luna doesn't get drunk with them because they're weird as shit. We all know that's how these dummies party. I wish I could have gone with her."

"Me too. I always feel better when Luna is with you. I hate when she hangs with Adina,"

Everyone must think I'm asleep.

"Honestly, and you didn't hear this from me..." The nurse leans closer, their backs turned to me. "We think she was drugged as well. But we have to wait for the tests."

"She's going to be okay, right?" The crack in Mami's voice is as painful as the cramps curling in my stomach.

What the hell is going on? Why were Adina and her mom screaming like that?

"Luna, can you hear me?"

I barely have any strength left, but I nod.

"Go to sleep. It's going to be okay." Mami begins to rub my forehead to the middle of my head, but I'm in so much physical pain. Worst of all, something happened, and I'm in the hospital. Adina was accusing me of something, but what was it? I've never heard her or her mom sound like that. I just don't get it.

Exhaustion wins over my body, and I can't keep my eyes open, so I drift off. Tomorrow. I'll remember and clear the air with them tomorrow.

6

Luna

My gaze doesn't move from the beige walls. In the time since I've been awake—ten minutes, according to the clock on the wall—I've been trying to make sense of what's happening. I'm alone, confused, and my head hurts.

Acidic sand coats my tongue—not that I've ever tasted something like that—and I can barely swallow. When I manage it, the nausea rises in waves.

"I can't let you in there. Only family can come in." Someone's voice rises outside the room, rattling my head and blurring my vision.

"We are like family," Mrs. Belmont bellows.

I open my mouth to call out her name, but the wave of nausea has me pressing my fist against my mouth and doubling over. Their panicked voices seem urgent, but I don't have the strength to move or call out. I feel too shitty to deal with whatever emergency Adina has concocted. As much as I love her, I don't have the energy for her.

"Mom, calm down. They won't let us in this way. We grew up together. I need to see her." Adina's voice rises as well.

"Yeah, you're right. I'm sorry, Nurse Krista. Can I show you something?"

After a couple minutes of silence, the nurse says, "You have two minutes. Hurry up before the head nurse comes."

My heart quickens. *They're coming in.* I pull the blanket up to my neck to cover myself. In the next second, they open the door and walk in.

Mrs. Belmont is by my side in my next breath. "You're going to keep your mouth shut and go away."

"Keep my mouth shut about what?"

Her face moves closer to mine. "Don't fuck with me, Luna. I'll make sure you and your mom have to sell your asses to live."

I'm shocked into silence. I've known this woman since I was seven. She's never spoken to me like this before.

"I can't believe I thought we were friends. How could you?" There's so much venom in Adina's voice my stomach turns.

"How could I what? Are you high?"

"Shut the fuck up," her mother says. "Don't ever let that come out of your mouth again."

"What the hell are you doing here?" A tall woman in scrubs is standing at the door. "Only her family is allowed to see her. Please leave." The nurse's voice is final.

"She owes me an explanation," Adina insists.

"You'll have to wait for that."

"Do you know who I am?" Mrs. Belmont says, in a tight, between-the-teeth kind of tone.

A snort follows amusement as the tall woman openly stares at her. "We do know who you are. You are the queen of the East Side. But here, I am the head nurse, and outside, there is a police officer. Either you leave, or I will have him escort you out. If I were you, I would leave before Mrs. Santos or her niece comes in, because I'm sure they won't take kindly to you being in here."

Mrs. Belmont curls her lip like she's about to spit on me. "Remember what I said."

Adina's look is pure hatred as she follows her mom out. Angry steps fade away, and the door swings open. The nurse comes closer, checks on the machines, and then meets my eyes.

"Sorry about that. They shouldn't have been here. How are you feeling?"

I shake my head.

"You don't have to worry about them coming back. Neither the police officer nor the staff will allow it. We'll deal with the nurse that let them in."

Except, they just got in to see me.

"Why is there a police officer outside my room?"

Her gaze darts to the floor for a second. "Because people have been trying to get in to see you."

"Who?" I ask.

"Vultures. Gossip bloggers. Paparazzi."

"That doesn't make any sense. I'm not famous."

The nurse shakes her head. "You weren't famous yesterday, sweetie. Today, you're the most famous person in New York City. You're trending on social media, along with that girl that just left and her football boyfriend."

My stomach roils as the same anxiety of earlier that morning comes back with a vengeance—my mother's worried face, Adina's look, her mother's words, all a bunch of foggy memories that don't connect.

"What the hell happened? I can't remember anything except for this morning."

The nurse's eyebrows shoot up. "Your mom is on the way back. She will talk to you and tell you everything."

I stare at her. "Why can't you tell me? You obviously know."

"I'm not at liberty to say, Luna."

"But why?"

A rap on the door pulls our gazes in its direction.

A male attendant is staring right at me. His eyes search for something on my face. Then he abruptly looks away at the nurse. "The detectives are waiting outside."

"Tell them the doctor has to see her first. Then go get Doctor Mendez."

He walks away, closing the door softly behind him. Within seconds, fast steps grow closer, and the doctor walks through the door and beelines for my bed. "Hi, Luna. I'm Doctor Mendez. How are you feeling?"

"Confused," I whisper.

"It's normal. We did a blood test on you, and it came back positive for dangerously high levels of Vibenzine."

I shake my head. What? I don't know what that is. "I'm not on meds."

She nods. "We know. The agent we found in your system is not a prescribed medication. It's a cross between a Benzodiazepine and a hypnotic agent. The street name is Vibes."

My heart drops, and my hand settles at my throat. Vibes is a party drug people take to have an extra good time. I've never needed something like that, but I've been around it. I'm both shaking my head and trying not to heave. "No, I wouldn't take that. I don't do drugs..."

I trail off because Adina and her mom's visit come to mind. *Keep your mouth shut.*

"Just breathe and try to remain calm. The drug is still in your system, and your body did not react well to it. You had a big allergic reaction and are lucky you were brought in right away."

Calm? How can I be calm? "But the cops are here."

"They can't talk to you if I don't say it's okay," she whispers.

"My head hurts. I can't remember anything but the screaming this morning."

The nurse nods, her gaze on the doctor. "Mrs. Belmont and her daughter had to be removed. I thought your mom and cousin were going to beat them."

"My...my mom? My mom doesn't fight. She is very respectful of Mrs. Belmont. She works for her and would never."

The nurse chuckles. "The mama lion came out of her. I would've beaten her ass too. No one knew what was happening with you. You were convulsing, and she kept screeching."

"But why was she worked up?" My breath hitches, my heart beating out of control.

The nurse's hand latches onto my forearm. "You really don't remember, do you?"

I can only manage a shake of my head. "Tell me."

"I'll be back to answer your questions. Let me go speak to the detectives and ask them to come back." Dr. Mendez steps out of the room as the door swings open. My mom appears shortly after.

"*Mami*, what's happening?"

Her face is so serious, with dark circles around her eyes that I haven't seen in so long. I don't think my stomach can sink any lower, but it does. "It's okay, *Mariposita*. I have a lawyer and a publicist coming. Bethany is already up to her games with you. I'm not letting her."

Bethany. Not Mrs. Belmont.

"What are you talking about? They wouldn't do that."

Except, they were just here talking so roughly and threatening me.

My mother's gaze hardens. "What did you do yesterday?"

Taken aback by her tone, I blink a few times, trying to find the answer to the question, yet nothing comes to me. "I don't know."

"You left the house around eight last night. You and Adina went to a concert."

I shake my head, but the memory flashes before my eyes. Adina was wearing my jumpsuit, and I got into the Maybach. "Yeah, we went to The Coliseum for the Chico Sparx concert, and then...I don't know."

"Luna, there are photos of you kissing Adina's boyfriend, and then you passed out. The young man and his bodyguard couldn't wake you up. They brought you to the hospital. The doctors had to pump your stomach. There was a drug in your system."

A dark, bitter taste coats my mouth, and I press the back of my hand to it. No, I would never betray Adina. Thierry is gross. He cheats all the time. Every week, some new chick goes to social media with an I-hooked-up-with-Thierry story.

"I don't do drugs. I had a couple of drinks. Adina did too."

Was this one of Adina's sick jokes?

My mother's worried eyes and flattened mouth are all the responses I need.

"*Mami*, you have to believe me. I didn't take anything. You know I wouldn't."

My mom sighs. "I know. But you have to remember, because the police want to talk to you."

"I don't know anything. I don't remember even being...who's the man and the bodyguard?"

"He's coming over with his publicist and lawyer. She's the one that told me to wait for them and to hold off on talking to the police. I need to talk to a lawyer too."

I start to shake my head, but then I hear the voice in my head. *I wanna go home.*

What the hell? Who was that? I try to jog my mind, reaching for the memory, but it won't come to me. The door opens again, and the doctor walks in, followed by a man and a woman, both wearing blazers.

"Hi, Luna. We were waiting for you to wake up. These detectives need to talk to you."

The woman steps up closer, her gaze firmly on mine. The man watches me.

"Luna, I am Detective Martinez, and that's Detective Bryant. We need to ask you a few questions about your evening last night."

I look at Mami, then at the doctor, before finally looking at Detective Martinez again. "I don't remember anything. I am trying, but my brain is...like, foggy."

"That makes sense. There were high levels of Vibenzine in your blood."

"I was having mixed drinks only," I say louder than I mean to. I'm tired of not knowing everything.

The detectives look at one another.

"Luna?" Detective Martinez calls out.

"I don't understand any of this."

"That's normal," Doctor Mendez says. "The levels of Vibenzine in your blood were high enough to kill you. It's bound to cause a blank spot in your memories--"

Detective Bryant cuts off the doctor with a look.

"Let's go over what you do remember."

I nod. "Last night, I went to a concert with Adina and her boyfriend. She's my--"

"This is Adina Belmont and Thierry Banks you're referring to?" Detective Bryant asked, while Detective Martinez jots it in her notebook.

"Yes. We got ready at my house, and then her boyfriend picked us up."

"Recount the night for me."

But I don't get to because I start heaving, and in the next minute, three people walk into the room. One of them is Maeven Tatis. I interned for her a year ago. I can't see the other, but the third is the one that speaks.

"Hello," says a pretty brunette in a suit, her hair in a sleek bob, and perfect cheekbone lines. "I'm Esmeralda Fernandez, Luna's lawyer. I need a moment with my client."

"She's not under arrest," Detective Martinez informs her.

Esmeralda shrugs. "She's also in no condition to talk to you."

I gag, and the nurse shoves a plastic basin in front of me.

"We'll be back, Luna. But here's my card if you feel better before we return." Detective Martinez leaves the card on the rolling table and turns to leave.

When she moves, I realize a tall man is standing by the door with a shocked expression. No, not just any man. Rio Castillo.

Then my stomach jumps, and I manage to turn my head right in time as the water I've been drinking flies back out of my mouth and into the basin my mom is now holding.

I just want to die.

When my stomach settles, I lie back on the bed, avoiding all their gazes, praying for death to just take me now.

Out of all the people in the world to see me like this, it's him.

My mom goes to the sink and washes her hands. "Thank you so much, Rio. I'm Raquel, Luna's mom. I can't thank you enough for what you did. You saved my *Mariposita's* life."

She offers her hand, and he takes it. Then she throws her arms around him anyway.

The man and his bodyguard brought you here.

And I hear his voice in my head: *"Luna, you want to come with me?"*

Oh God, please. Just take me.

"*Mariposita*, they're here with a proposal to help you," Mami says.

I turn to the side with my back to them. "Help me how?"

Maeven steps up. "Hi, Luna. I'm sorry this happened to you, but there's no time to waste, and we need to act quickly. Everyone is out for you, and the Belmonts have already begun to line up their chips for the game, even though we don't know how you got the Vibes in your drink."

"Thierry gave her a drink when we were talking," Rio says.

The sound of his voice grates my insides. *Can he stop talking?*

"Do you remember that, Luna?" Esme asks.

"Not really. I don't take drugs...ever. I don't commit crimes. But I woke up to screaming, and the Belmonts were here threatening me. The funny part is, I don't know why the police are here. And I really don't understand why you're here either."

7

Rio

She looks so helpless, but the disdain in her voice is still there. Her eyes cut right through me as they always do when they land on me. I hate that Maeven and Esme brought me here. I happened to be in the right place at the right time to help her, but she's not even grateful for that. Her mom is so warm and appreciative, but Luna looks at us like bugs that she wants to spray away.

"The Tatis Media Group is here to represent you, Luna" Maeven says, pointing between her and Esme. "You see," Maeven continues, "with the Belmonts lining up their game pieces, you need to be ready to play. They all know how to cover for themselves, and from what your mom told us, they're setting you up like the fall guy. They're feeding into the rumor that you came on to Thierry. You are taking a massive beating on social media. And I think we can use what happened to make sure you come out on top."

"How?" her mom asks.

"Well, Rio happened to be there to help her in her time of need. And, unfortunately, no good deed goes unpunished, which is feeding into his own reputation. Rio and Luna can help each other—with my guidance, of course."

"I can't afford you." Luna's voice is tight, the strongest it's been since I came into the room. At least she is engaging. She looked so despondent just minutes ago.

"Darren said he will help," her mother assures her, but Maeven steps up.

"We will work pro bono for you." She hooks a thumb toward me. "This one is already paying us."

I don't really care about the money. I can afford to pay her. I know she can do it, because *Capicú*, my record label, is losing patience with everything that's going on. The last thing I need is for our parent company, *Ficha Mundial Latin Entertainment*, to step in. "What would we need to do?"

Maeven's lips quirk a little. "Fall in love."

I whip my head around so fast my brain rattles like she hit me with something. My gaze lands on Luna's, whose eyes are as round as *cafecito* saucers.

She pushes herself into an upright position. "I'm sorry, but what did you just say?"

Maeven looks between us, her shoulders up like a boxer expecting the punches, and sighs. "Look, saying the two of you have big problems is like saying water is pouring from Niagara Falls. Your reputations are in shambles." She looks at me. "In the eyes of the public, you're a fuckboy with anger issues and low sales who's trying to fill seats for a concert tour." Then she turns to Luna. "And they think you're a thot messing with her best friend's boyfriend and whoever else lands in your path."

Luna's legs swing off the bed and she shoves the covers back, exposing the hospital gown riding over her thick thighs. "Wait a fucking minute. I do not—"

Maeven cuts her off by raising her hand. "You were drugged, and I know the kinds of games the Belmonts and the people in their high-society circles tend to play. The problem is that if you go to the police now, it will create bigger problems for you. These people don't play clean. They will hang you out to dry regardless of what you say. The camera's footage from the concert conveniently disappeared. They claim they got the drinks from the bar, but no one knows how the drugs got in them. My sources tell me the Belmont money is already doing its thing."

"Show her the texts," Esme tells Raquel.

She shoots a worried glance toward Luna but grabs her phone and unlocks it. Luna turns green, like she's going to vomit again.

Must be the text messages from the Belmonts to Luna's mom that Maeven mentioned in the car on the way over.

"This is not real." Luna presses her hand to her temple. "They're threatening you. How can they say it was me?"

"Because of where you live, the fact that you don't have money. They play on perception and whatever they can feed to the public," Esme says.

"I believe you, Luna," Maeven says. "My beliefs don't change perceptions, though. But you know what does? My methods. I know what I'm doing. I'm the best in the business. I think we all know that. And I know I can turn this ship around, change both your reputations, and boost your careers...if you can set aside your egos and work with me."

Luna stares her down but says nothing.

"Please excuse my daughter. Luna is always difficult when she is sick. What are you offering?" her mom asks. "We are open to hearing what you suggest. I don't want Luna's future to be destroyed." Her gaze is on her daughter, who looks ready to leap off the bed and smack Maeven.

"Thank you," Maeven says. "All I need is six months. I will represent both of you so that we can guarantee you both receive the same treatment. The two of you just need to give me a chance to work my magic."

"How can a relationship with him fix my reputation when he used to go out with Adina?" Luna shoves a finger in the air in my direction. "It will make me look like what they say I am."

She is still as crazy as ever.

I point at Luna. "What are you talking about? I never went out with Adina."

She scoffs. "Oh, please. You slipped into her DMs and tried to hit on me while she was doing a collab. Do you know how gross that is?"

"You're out of your mind, you know that? One minute, you were eye-fucking—" I stop because her mom is in the room "—flirting with me, and the next, you told me to lose your number. Then you sneered at me at every damned event. You were not interested, and that's okay, but you don't need to throw insane excuses."

"They're not insane excuses. You—"

"Stop," Maeven snaps. "Save this fire for the cameras."

Luna scoffs. "There's not going to be any of that going on."

Her tone jabs my skin, irritating every nerve in my body. It grinds me up how she says it. Like she's better than me or something. "You know what? You're right. There's not going to be any of that shit going on. Save your own reputation. Explain to people you weren't tonguing down Thierry. You need me more than I need you."

The fire in her eyes is so potent it should incinerate me on the spot.

"Asshole," she practically spits at me.

"*Loca de remate*," I shoot right back.

"Luna Zaira. Rio. Stop." Her mom's tone is snappy, and though she doesn't stop looking at me with hatred, Luna lies back against the pillows. "Both of you listen and listen well. Maeven here is offering a great opportunity. You interned for her. You know what she charges. The fact that she's willing to do it for free speaks volumes."

"Because she needs me to fix that mess." She points at me.

Before I can push forward and tell her again what a nutjob she is, Maeven's hand slams on my chest, stopping me cold.

She doesn't look at me as she addresses Luna. "You're not wrong. I do need someone, but we both know I can get anyone I want to play this role. He is a mess, but thousands of women would jump at the chance of doing this. But you need him as much, if not more, than he needs you." She pauses, and I can't see her face, but Luna shakes her head.

Maeven nods. "You do. And you need me just as well. Your name is trending for all the wrong reasons. Elevate PR will rescind their employment offer to you the minute you're out of the hospital. You'll have no job or prospects, and the small businesses will pull away from Enlace, because the Belmonts will see to it. You don't just need a publicist; you need a master. That's me. No one else is going to do this for you for free. You can't even represent yourself because your credibility is in the same hole as your reputation. I don't say that to embarrass you. I just need you both to get off your high horses and play nice for your futures."

Luna goes a little pale and crosses her arms around her middle.

Fuck her for being so judgmental.

"Do we have a deal?"

"Yes," her mother says, staring at her daughter until she nods.

Maeven stares at me, and I nod. "Is that a yes?" she asks.

"Yes."

In the blink of an eye, Mrs. Raquel hands her daughter a basin, and Luna bends and throws up in it.

It stings that the thought of pretending to be with me makes her vomit. She called me a mess, but she's a psycho. *Yeah, this is going to be fucking great.*

And to top it all off, now I'm queasy too.

8

Luna

Four weeks later

It's a little chilly and downcast today, like my mood. I pull up the zipper on my Thiccletics jacket and proceed to stretch. People walk around me, some alone and others in groups, but no one interacts with me. There's something comforting about a NYC park and New Yorkers' ability to mind their business that suits me just fine. Through the corner of my eye, I spot a guy in a brown shirt heading my way. Last minute decision, but I pivot and walk to the entrance of the trail. I can wait for Rio there. Maeven is getting us started today.

Joy. Her message was succinct and clear.

Let's kick off this romance. The mission is simple. You're going to go to the park and walk together. Make light conversation and put some distance between the two of you. Just let people see you and take your photo. The internet and I will take care of the rest.

Simple and to the point, except...where the hell is Rio? He kept making a big deal about not having much time because he's so booked, and now he's late. Does it surprise me?

Of course not.

"Luna," someone yells my name, making me turn around. It's brown-shirt guy. He's gotten closer. "Can I talk to you for a minute?"

I don't recognize his sallow face or the crooked smile, no matter how much my mind races. So I shake my head. "I'm sorry. I have somewhere to be."

"Just five minutes. I recognized you from TV, and you're more beautiful in person. I don't blame Thierry one bit. I would've stolen a kiss and a lot more if I could."

Heat rises up my neck until my entire face is on fire, and I take an instinctive step back. I look around, immediately searching for anyone who may have heard. "Fuck off."

He takes a step toward me, his hand extended, but his gaze veers beyond me and back to my face. His smirk widens.

"Is everything okay?" a deep voice asks from behind me.

I turn around to find Rio only steps away from me with his bodyguard, Tito, looming like a menacing tower.

My stomach is knotting so bad, but relief trickles in, and I nod.

"Rio, man. It's good to meet you. My bad, I didn't realize you were here. I thought Luna was alone." He extends a hand, blinks a couple times, then drops it when Rio doesn't take it. "I mean, not like that. I wasn't going to do anything to her. I was just saying hi."

Rio frowns, stepping closer to me and searching my face. "Is this man bothering you?"

"He was leaving." I'm barely finished when brown-shirt guy takes off the opposite way.

"Friend of yours?" Rio asks, still watching the creep.

Relief segues into annoyance. If he'd been here when he said he would be, I wouldn't have had to deal with this. And now he has the nerve to ask me that?

"Is that what it looked like?"

He shrugs. "He was awfully close."

I flinch like he slapped me. "He only got that close because you were not here like we agreed."

His mouth goes slack, and he shakes his head, but I don't wait for him to say anything else and get walking down the trail.

He catches up to me in a few steps. "Look, I had a call with my agent."

"Tell someone who cares."

"I was trying to apologize. Why are you like this?" his voice rises.

"Because I don't like creeps. I hate being around them or for them to think they can just talk to me."

His face goes dark. "*Que es lo que te pasa a ti?* You don't have to call me a creep."

"I wasn't talking about you, but I guess the shoe fits."

His hand on my arm stops me. "Whatever got you *encabroná* is not my fault. It's not because of me you got cancelled and people think that you're a—"

Tito steps into my line of vision, shielding us from something. But I see them. Three women standing beyond us have their phones pointed at us.

Shit. They're either recording us or taking photos.

I quickly avert my eyes, tilt my head down, and cover my face with my hands, shaking my shoulders as if crying.

"What the fuck are you doing?" he asks.

"I think those women are recording us," I whisper so only he can hear me.

"What?" he asks.

"People are recording." I point a finger in the direction.

His gaze drifts to the side. "Fuck, I see them. We should leave. Let's abort this and try it another time."

I shake my head. "We can't. It will be all over social media. You're too popular, and unfortunately, people are checking for me these days."

"What do I do?"

"Console me. Not overly, but put your hand on my arm, and then let's keep walking." He reaches for me, and I step aside a little. "Not your whole arm." I push out between clenched teeth. "Just your hands. We're friends."

"Yeah, right." The dryness in his tone sets me off.

"Stop testing me. We already failed, and we need to fix it before—" My phone goes off. "Ugh. It's Maeven."

He stops walking. I take out my Airpods case and hand him one like we were instructed in our briefing meeting with Maeven. I put in the other and tap it to answer.

"We're both on," I say on the line.

"Are you kidding me? I tell you to go out. You don't even have to talk much. Just walk on a trail and look cute. Instead, you end up on an Instagram live, arguing. What part of the plan didn't you understand?"

"I'm sorry," I say. "This guy was bugging me and got me mad—"

"Why was a guy bothering you? Where was Rio?" Her tone is sharp, though her voice level stays even.

"I was late. I had a call with Kresh."

Maeven's sigh fills the line. "I'm going to stop being angry. It won't help anyone. Keep walking for God's sake."

"You can see us?" Rio asks.

"Yes, those girls are live. They're your fans, Rio, and the other *Sirenas* are jumping in quickly. We need to get a handle on this. Just keep walking. Get to the bridge, and once you get there, sit on the bench and talk. Don't pretend, cause the two of you obviously can't even do the small things. Discuss the last new fire song you heard. Can you do that?"

I wince, and he grimaces.

"Yeah, I think we can do that," I say.

Maeven cuts off. We keep walking.

"We pissed her off, and I don't blame her. I would be mad too if my clients didn't execute a plan correctly." I definitely need to do better. No matter how much this guy annoys me, I need to stop reacting to everything.

He shrugs. "I've pissed her off a lot lately. I think I'm a challenge she wasn't ready for." There's a slight smile on his face, and it triggers my own.

"Don't flatter yourself. I think you're a piece of cake compared to Mateo de la Cruz."

He sputters. "Shiiiiit. That guy's a fuck-up. Piece of cake, huh? Does that mean you think I'm sweet?"

I side-eye him. "I don't think there's anything sweet about you."

He says nothing. My tone even echoes in my own ears. *Damn, I sounded like a bitch.*

The flush flares over my face, making me regret my comment. "I didn't mean that in a bad way."

"No?" he asks, his eyebrow arched.

"I just meant everyone knows you're tough. You don't think twice about fighting with anyone."

We get to the bench, and as I turn to take one of the seats, I spot the three women still following in the distance.

"They must be zooming in," I whisper under my breath, turning my face down so they can't read my lips.

"Let's ignore them and stick to the script. The last fly song I heard was '*Daselo donde lo quiera*' by Mando."

I roll my eyes at him. "You *would* like that song."

"What is that supposed to mean?" he asks, frowning.

I scoff. "It's a '*Dime Mami*' rip-off."

His frown deepens. "You think so?"

"How can't you tell? Even the chorus. You should've sued them. '*Dime Mami*' is better, though."

His eyes widen a little, his lips curving. It exposes his perfect white teeth. That's the smile that sends girls into a frenzy. And it causes a weird rush in my chest. I fight through the heat in my face, trying not to break eye contact.

And then he licks his bottom lip, and my throat goes dry. "Tell me what the last fly song you've heard was."

I have to swallow a little, but I admit it's his song with Chico and Niko, "'*My Beat la Controla*.'"

And that smile widens.

It reminds me how dangerous this is—correction, how dangerous he is. *Don't forget that, Luna.*

There's a script and a six-month end date I'm planning to stick to. That's it.

Rio

Every time I sit in Dr. Jacinda Smith's waiting room, I'm as tight as the string on a brand-new guitar. My gaze bounces from wall to wall, studying the built-in bookcases and the glass digital panels, which display images of a green bamboo meadow today. It's a choose-your-own-adventure every week, as Dr. Jacinda calls it, with different photos displayed on the screens.

The thought that someone can walk in and recognize me and tag me as soft is almost as terrifying as coming in to share my thoughts with a stranger. But I promised Maeven I would do better, and I need to get mentally and physically ready for the tour.

While I wait, I deep dive into the comments on social media to see what people thought of the outing with Luna today. It was bumpy at first, but I think we managed to course correct. She even smiled and admitted she loved my last song. But social media is a different beast, where people's opinions are volatile and unpredictable. And they don't make us wait.

#Sirenas, you saw it with your own eyes. Our husband has a good friend, one poster says.

Another is a little more skeptical. *I just hope it's just friends, and Luna doesn't get her claws in him. Our husband doesn't need messy in his life.*

And there's one that triggers me. *No, Rio needs to get back with Perla.*

The tingling storms up the back of my neck and over my face. I can still hear Perla, my ex, screaming that I was shutting her out.

The message sparks a whole debate with one asking, *Is you cool? You want him to get back with the bitch who betrayed him by talking to the media?*

I continue reading the messages and shake my head. The *Sirenas*, my fans, hate Perla with a passion. She's not my favorite person either, especially after she gave an interview where she talked about the worst period of my life—and then accused me of cheating when I could barely get out of bed in the morning. More concerning is that Luna continues to take a beating online, and the *Sirenas* don't cut her any slack. Maeven says the progress will be slow, and we just need to stay on the course.

The door opens, and I'm looking up as Dr. Jacinda Smith waves me into her office. Despite being a doctor, her demeanor is inviting. Must be because her features make her look like a sweet grandma with her button nose, small mouth, and too-big-for-her-face eagle eyes that miss nothing but are also warm. Her reddish hair and almost matching ensemble of pants and top create a monochromatic look that should be all wrong, but it works.

We sit in opposing rocking chairs near the fire.

"What are we going to talk about today?" she asks.

"I went out on my first outing with Luna."

Her gaze darts around, like she's trying to place the name, until she nods. "Yes, the young woman you saved the other day. The one that is playing your girlfriend."

"Not yet," I say. "We're not there yet."

"Correct. How is she doing?"

I shrug. "She was annoyed and angry today. But that attitude toward me, coming from her, is normal."

"It doesn't seem to bother you like your last interaction."

"Wasn't too bad. She was...like the night we met before she went nuts."

"Do you want to elaborate?" she asks calmly, like she is not digging for info to bring up later.

"Maeven made us talk about music. Luna told me she likes my music."

Dr. Jacinda's lips twitch. "Is that all it takes?"

Her odd humor always takes me aback, but I find myself chuckling. "Not really. That night we met was cool. She was the first woman I had connected with in a while. She was warm but turned out to be a mirage."

Her gaze is steady on me as she says, "Well, the two of you are embarking on a joint venture. Maybe this is a good opportunity to get to know her and see why she changed her mind so quickly."

"Her friend said she had a man. I thought maybe it was guilt. But with everything that's happening, Adina seems to be the one throwing the most mud at Luna."

"I like the way you say her name."

"What?"

She shrugs, and it's delicate and soft. "Your pronunciation and cadence. *Luuunaa.* It's soft and musical. Anyhow, you have her in a place where you can find out. Maybe the two of you can reach a mutual understanding."

Hell no. "With Luna Santos? I never know what I'm going to get with her."

"I wonder if she feels the same about you."

"Huh?"

She presses her lips. "Maybe she feels like she doesn't know what she really gets with you either. Think about it." She taps her forehead. "On another note, are you continuing to journal through song?"

I'm still stuck on what she said about Luna, but I bob my head up and down. "Yeah. I kinda like it. It's easier than that first exercise about writing my feelings. That sucked."

"Some people hate journaling because they've been led to believe there's only one way to do it. But there are lots of ways. For creative minds, like yours, expressing yourself in the form of art can be therapeutic. It provides an outlet and allows you to track your emotions, much like a journey through a significant time in your life. Keep doing it."

I finish my session with her and head to rehearsals. I get home by ten, shower, and turn on YouTube. A flyover of Samaná is recommended on my home screen, and I click on it. However, as soon as the drone begins to fly over my hometown, Las Galeras, I have to exit the app. It would've flown over our property, and I already have too much on my mind. It's been a long day, and these are the times when the memories tend to catch up with me.

Instead, I choose a flyover of Puerto Rico, listening to the sounds of coquis as I work on Dr. Jacinda's homework.

Abusadora
¿Quién te dió el derecho?
To be so beautiful

Y tener por alma hierro

No quiero estar cerca de ti
Pero eres un imán
I want to ignore the way you breathe
No matter how much I try, I just can't

After spending a day of hell near you
No puedo olvidar los detalles
Your voice still whispers in my ear
Louder than el ruido de la calle

Yesterday, I touched your hand
And I swear you stared into my soul
Mi abusadora me vió tal y como soy
Yeah, you made me feel seen

Baby, mi refleccion en tus ojos fue algo que no esperaba
I wasn't ready for that.
Es Rio.
Still waters run deep.

I want to fling the notebook at the wall because this is not what I wanted to write. *Jesus. Thank God no one will ever see this shit.*

My phone pings with a text from Maeven in the group chat with Luna and me.

MAEVEN

The buzz is starting. Next step, this ship is sailing at the Knicks game.

9

Luna

I rush out of my building and beeline for the waiting SUV. Esme's husband, Ty, in his tall frame, jeans, and a jersey, is waiting outside and opens the door for me. The minute I sit and buckle up, Esme starts dropping instructions from Maeven.

"Tonight's the night. It's essential that everything goes according to plan, as the soft launch is crucial to pushing this ship from the port. You need to stick to the script and everything Maeven outlined."

Her stylish asymmetrical bob bounces along with the movement of her hands. The natural makeup strategically accentuates her chiseled features. Esme's contour game is out of this world.

"Here." She hands me a little pearl-shaped earbud.

"I have mine in my bag."

She points at the one she gave me. "You'll be using this one tonight. You have one, and Rio has the other. Maeven is going to guide you through this outing."

She doesn't trust us.

"She's low-jacking everything from our outfits to our actions." I mean, my fit is flawless. The dusty-pink, square-neck, strappy dress and blush Air Force Ones are gorgeous—super flattering to my skin. I loved this dress since I saw it in the *Autumn Lush* newsletter two weeks ago. Not to mention how loud I squealed when it arrived at my house yesterday.

"After the park incident? Do you blame her?" Ty laughs.

Esme swats him. "Maeven just wants everything to be perfect. Trust her. She truly is the best. By the end of the night, people will be talking about you and Rio for a different reason."

I nod and put the earbud in my purse. Ty turns on the radio, and they're playing a Rio artist block. I close my eyes and let his voice do what it does best: take you places. It's impressive how he switches between lover boy and *bellaqueo*.

You're always going to miss me, baby
I'm like your Fourth of July.
I know the trick to make your body whistle, crackle, and pop.
Y despues viene el boom boom boom.

His smile at the park pops into my head, and I force my eyes open. *Nope, not thinking about him while his freaky lyrics play out.* As I listen, I take the opportunity to finalize the social media calendar for Faye & Fleur, one of the companies for which I manage social media. I'm so grateful they still let me work for their business. It's a good distraction because thoughts about this outing have kept my hands shaking.

We arrive at Madison Square Garden as panic begins to set in, but the phone rings as we park, and I press my ear to answer it.

"Breathe," Maeven says in my ear. "I want you to walk with a purpose, hold on to Esme like you would with Sel. Don't make eye contact on purpose, but if it happens, give them a subway smile, fleeting without being friendly, and keep walking."

"Okay," I say.

"Don't talk back or nod, no matter what they say. Just walk, and everything will be fine. Once you're closer, I'll connect with Rio. Let's do this."

Ty steps out and hands the key to the valet, and we're walking through the main entrance. We're moving fast. An employee in the traditional Knick's blue-and-orange uniform parts the crowd for us, fast-tracking us to the court. Esme's hand on my arm is keeping me at a steady pace. Otherwise, I would run.

"You're doing great," Maeven says in my ear. "And god, you look gorgeous."

If you only knew I'm two seconds from a panic attack.

The pounding of the ball as the players warm up competes with the erratic beating in my chest. *Why did I agree to this?* I should've stayed my ass at home, under the covers, watching *telenovelas* with *Mami*. I can barely hear myself think in the cacophony of chatter, music, and practice. My throat is closing up.

"I'm connecting Rio." There's a slight pause, and then she's back. "I got you both here. Rio, touch your mustache, and Luna, touch your neck."

I do as she says. That's when I see him. He's wearing jeans and a white t-shirt that clings to those new arm muscles. When he sees me, his lips curve into a smile, causing an uptick in my pulse. I swallow and keep walking.

"Good job on the smile, Rio." Maeven sounds like she's smiling herself. "It's a great day to launch New York's *it* couple."

He's sitting next to three empty seats. We make our way to him. Ty is going to sit next to him, Esme next to Ty, and I'm sitting on the other side of Esme. It's a *let's pretend we are not on a date, but we are,* situation.

Maeven says, "When you hug, I'm counting to five, and I want you to let go to the count of three slowly."

His scent reaches me first. It's spicy and woodsy with notes of citrus and oils, and it winds its way up my nose, intoxicating my senses. I already don't like the way it hooks me and pulls me closer to him like a rope. But I give in and step into his arms, and the count-down begins.

"How are you?" he whispers in my ear.

"Dying."

When I step back, he's smiling, and his eyes do a slow perusal over me.

"Keep your eyes on her face. This is supposed to be innocent,"

Maeven warns over the phone. "Luna, take a discreet step back. You're too close to him."

"Where the fuck is she watching from?" Rio asks.

I burst out laughing.

"Go take your seat, Luna."

"See you later," I tell Rio and turn to go to my seat.

"Take your eyes off her ass," Maeven says.

A wave of heat engulfs my skin. It takes all of me not to turn around and look back at him.

The man in the seat next to mine arrives, and he calls out to Ty, who turns to me. "Can I take your seat? I haven't seen my friend in a long time."

Esme points to the seat next to Rio. "Do you mind? That's a friend from college, and I like to sit next to Ty during games so he can explain what's happening to me."

I don't get to say anything because she winks at me and then takes the seat next to her husband.

I turn back around and look at Rio, who has the same confused expression on his face.

"Fucking Maeven," he finally says.

As if she heard him, she whispers in our ears, "Don't be mad at me. If I told you, you would have overacted, trying to sell this. The element of surprise makes it look more real. Now sit next to each other and chat...about something neutral."

"Um. How was your day?" Rio asks, leaning a little into me.

A strong waft of his cologne drifts to me. "It was okay. I was a little nervous about this."

Damn, he smells good.

"Me too. Maybe it's a good thing. We're too nervous to fight."

It makes me laugh. "You're right. I don't think I've got much fight in me right now, anyway. The internet has so much smoke for me, it's unbelievable. Adina did an interview today."

His lips flatten. "I saw. I can't believe she would do that to you."

It's the same thing I have been saying to myself, but I shrug. "She thinks I betrayed her."

"She knows you didn't because she knows Thierry was the one who kissed you. You didn't consent, just like you didn't take that drug on purpose. You don't deserve this."

His gaze is so warm I have to look away.

We stick to bottled sparkling water and chit-chat about the game. The Knicks are battling, but this is not as bad as I dreaded all day.

"Were you in the studio today?"

He nods. "I recorded a remix today. It was one of the tracks that didn't make it to the album, but I'm releasing it in the deluxe extended version. It's insane."

"Oh. What song?"

He turns from the court to me. "*It's called 'Si Tu me Dejas.'*"

"If you leave me?"

"Nope. If you let me." The way his eyes glow when he says that, and the way his lips pucker the P, sends currents through my body.

I so don't like that...

"You want to hear it?" he asks.

I frown at him. "Hell yeah."

"I didn't know. You hate me."

"Not your music, though," I say without thinking.

Shit.

I start to apologize, but the smile that blooms on his lips makes my cheeks tingle.

"This is great, kids. I'm proud of you. I think it's time we kick it up a notch. Luna, you're going to watch the game, and I want you to be aware of the angles and appear as though you're thinking deeply. Rio, I want you to touch her hand when I say go. After he touches your hand, Luna, turn your head to look up at him slowly. I'm going to count to seven, and you will hold each other's gaze for five seconds like you don't have twenty-five thousand people around you."

I look away as she tells me, and I keep trying to concentrate on counting the seconds, but my eyes focus across the court, where I spot Adina and Thierry sitting together. Sadness takes over me. This is something we would have told each other and spent hours trying to choose the perfect outfit for her. Instead, she's releasing interviews about what she calls my betrayal and staring me down as the players travel back and forth on the court. My eyes begin to burn.

"Go," Maeven orders, and when Rio's fingers slide over mine, I almost jump.

Instead, I force myself to focus on the task at hand, turning slowly until I'm staring into the brown haze of his eyes. My pulse quickens, and my lips drift apart. He smiles at me, and I can't help but smile back.

And then he leans in...to kiss me?

Oh shit.

Rio

Luna's warm breath brushes over my lower lip, stirring an ache inside my chest. Her lips are so close that I can almost taste them—I'm thinking a mix of her cinnamon gum and sweetness.

"Luna," her name slips out like it does in my dreams, and her lips part.

She wants it. I want it. Badly.

"Don't kiss her," Maeven whispers in our ears.

The need is so strong I inch closer. Luna licks her lips. It's subtle, but the darting out of her tongue...that flash of pink stirs every inch of me in an invitation I can't refuse.

"Do. Not. Kiss. Her," Maeven snaps this time, her voice louder. "It will be more powerful if you don't.

I want it so bad I can't think straight. Luna has to decide, and I urge her with my eyes to greenlight me. *Say yes.*

Her eyes drift to my lips, but then she presses a hand to her forehead and tilts her head down as if she's blushing.

Except, she's not. She's flustered but not blushing.

Disappointment settles in my belly anyway. She didn't want it as much as I did. I lean in to ask, but Esme tugs at her hand, whispers something in her ear, and they both spring to their feet.

Luna turns to me. "I'll be back." Her gaze lingers on my face for a breath. Then, she shakes her head, pivots, and follows Esme.

I'm left to stare after her even as Tito asks if I'm enjoying the game. It occurs to me I haven't paid him any mind this whole time. Now, his voice is faint because my ears are still ringing with Luna's little gasp, the surprise at our almost kiss. My eyes are filled with that bombastic body covered in innocent pink because there's nothing pure in that. That body is not made for purity. It was made for *perreo* and worshiping—with my tongue and definitely with my dick, which I'll probably never get to do. *So dejate de eso.*

Before she disappears into the crowd, she looks back and shoots me a smile over her shoulder. I can't help but return it like teenage Rio used to with my *noviecita en la escuela.*

"Rio, get up and follow them. Wait outside the bathroom, and then you'll both walk out together but take separate cars. When you get home, post the messages I'm going to send you. Good job, kids."

I almost shake my head but do as she says. When Luna comes out of the bathroom with Esme, her smile is nervous, almost sheepish. But as we walk to the car, I don't get the chance to ask her because Esme and Ty are there, and so is Tito, flanking and ushering us out.

When I open the door to the car, I'm close enough to ask. I open my mouth, but there are flashes of light and people screaming my name. She leans in and presses her lips to my cheek. Without a word, she gets inside the SUV. On my ride back to my place, I still feel her lips on my skin. This shit just got weird and complicated.

But fun.

On the way home, the text messages start coming in. The first one is from Niko.

> NIKO
>
> You and Luna? Shit. Te lo tenías callaito.
> Congrats, my boy! She bad.

The DJ from a popular radio station contacts me.

> SENSACIONLIVE
>
> Something's obviously going on. Let me
> know when you're ready to talk.

ZAO

Pero por poco te la comes ahí mismo,
Manin.

He's not wrong. *Yo le hubiera comido esa boca*, if she had let me. And I still want to. So fucking bad.

That's why this is not fun. This chick is crazy and she hates me. She's playing a role too freaking well. We both are. My body doesn't know it, though. Neither does my brain. It keeps replaying every moment of tonight over and over. It keeps begging me to ask questions. *Was it all an act? What if it was? What if it wasn't?*

I pull up her name on my phone, start typing a "Hi," but hit backspace and exit. No, this is what it is, and I'm not going to push that. I'm going home to sleep.

On the radio, the Niko block is on fire. They're playing his third album, the one where he experimented with sounds that normally don't go with reggaeton. The track I'm listening to, '*Biología*,' is a chill, lo-fi type of song with soft lyrics. As the song plays, new lyrics sprout in my head.

I wish I didn't get in my head
Me convierto en científico and dissect
Every look, every breath
Under the microscope in my brain
This should be simple
Tas soltera y yo I'm also single
We should let our bodies mingle
But we're not normales
We act like breeds of different animales
Si fueramos planetas
Yo sería Venus y tu fueras Marte.
Are we going to keep circling the wagon
Or move on to the good parte?

I jot them down quick to make sure I remember. Hmm...I think they're kind of fire. I switch to my messages app to message Niko.

ME

Listening to Biología. You got a remix in the future?

He responds almost immediately.

NIKO

What are you thinking?

I copy the lyrics I just wrote and shoot them his way.

NIKO

Uff. 🔥 🔥 🔥

Hitting up Vampiro. Stay tuned.

And that's how I find myself wide awake at three in the morning.

Sleep won't come. No drugs, not even a painkiller. Dulling the pain never makes it better in the long run. So, I'm sitting in the dark with this hole in my stomach, but my thoughts are on Luna's smile and her parted lips. My mind is stuck on replay, watching her walk in her pink dress and sneakers, looking beautiful, earthy, and thick. I know sleep won't come tonight. So, I flip the night light, grab my notepad and pen, and pour out my thoughts.

No queria verte así
I don't even dare to fantasize
But it only took a touch
A turn of your head, widening of your eyes
A smile that reached and grabbed me by the throat

I can't swallow
I can't breathe
Solo quiero una cosa

The taste of your lips

Mami, sueño con desnudarte
Con morder to cuello
Y los senos chuparte
Perderme en el valle entre tus piernas
But in this moment, it can wait
Cause I have something else on my mind.

Nada mas te quiero besar
Sentir tu aliento mingle with mine
Don't lean into me if that's not what you want
If you don't open your mouth, me puedo controlar

Pero apretaste mi mano
And parted your lips
That little catch in your throat
Demanded my kiss

The world filtered through, like always
Y me quede con las ganas
De probar el sabor de tu boca
Y saciar el deseo que me azota

Until the next chapter
Espero que estes ready
Because you can't put the genie back in the bottle.
Es Rio

The lyrics make me shake my head. I call her crazy for the way she's always acted toward me. But I'm the one reading a million things into an almost kiss. She's probably long asleep, and I'm writing about her.

Si ella es loca, what does this make me? A fucking mad man.

10

Luna

"I'm going to be sick."

My mom looks up from the garment she's sewing, needle in hand, to stare at me with a calm-down face. "You're going to be just fine."

"How?" I ask.

"Maeven set everything up, and she's extremely thorough. You see people are already talking about you and Rio. The last two weeks since the Knicks game, you've been in everyone's mouth. The two of you are naturals at this." She finishes and goes back to sewing.

"He hates me."

My mom snorts. "No, *ese muchachito* doesn't hate you. Just like you don't hate him. I thought the flowers were a nice touch. Shows he can be sweet even though he sings *esas freaky frescuras*."

Her wording always makes me chuckle, but my eyes drift to the peach rose and eucalyptus bouquet sitting on our dining room table.

"Mami, the flowers were Maeven's idea."

"Except, it wasn't. She was surprised when I mentioned it, so make sure you thank him."

Oh man. He sent them to me. I don't need more things to be conflicted about. I tinker with my hair, making sure my edges are tight.

"I'm spending the night at Darren's tonight. If something happens, call me."

I can't help but tease her. "I'll be okay. Go be with your man. Get it, girl."

"*No seas atrevida.* I can still give you a few *nalgadas.*" To prove it, she swats my butt.

The doorbell rings, surprising both of us. My mom hands me the t-shirt she finished hemming, and I throw it on. "Don't fight at Yankees Stadium. Don't have deep conversations either."

"You sound like Maeven," I say as I kiss her cheek and head for the door. When I open it, Rio is standing outside, filling the door frame in jeans and a baseball jersey. His smile is instant.

And so is the rustle of butterfly wings in my belly.

"Hi." He leans for a kiss on my cheek, and then his gaze darts behind me. "*Buenas tardes, Doña Raquel.*"

He goes around me to shake her hand, but my mom gives him the customary kiss on the cheek. "Take care of my *mariposita,* and no fighting," she says to him.

He pauses and then says, "*Lo prometo.*"

His manners are so sweet, my mom blinks a few times, and I can't fight the grin that breaks over my lips. Then we rush out the door without talking.

We get into the car, the radio playing '*No Más Guerra*' by Belú "*La Teniente.*"

I love this song. It's high on my Spotify playlist. "I should've known you listen to Belú."

Rio frowns. "Who?"

I point to the speaker. "*La Teniente.*"

"Oh," he says and shakes his head. "I don't know much about her, but she's with *Ficha* like me."

"You should hear her whole album. She's awesome. They call her the daughter of *El General* and she lives up to the name. Her music is fire and real, a call back to the beginnings of reggaeton. This is her love letter to him, a thank you for putting the genre on the map. You know?" I tap my chin. "You and her on a song would be hot."

"I'll listen." It's noncommittal, and we're silent for a while.

Now I'm thinking about everything that's going to go down today, and I'm anxious again.

"You okay?" he asks.

I finally look at him and shake my head. "I'm nervous."

"Don't be. Just remember, we can't stand each other."

I roll my eyes. "But we're supposed to be falling for each other. What if the kiss falls flat?"

"*Mami,* we almost set The Garden on fire just looking at each other." The smoldering look that follows makes my entire body flush.

He's not wrong. We've been feeding social media with an almost kiss.

"It's all people have been talking about. Well, because we have not been seen together since, today one of your *Sirenas* wondered if you dumped me for being a *sosa*."

His bark of laughter is so sudden it startles me. And it doesn't stop. I don't think I've ever heard him laugh so hard.

"Stop laughing."

He presses a hand to his belly. "I can't. Where do people get this stuff?"

"They said I always acted like a *sosa* when I was hanging with Adina. So that's my personality anyway. Meanwhile, you're so *bellaco,* their word, you got bored quickly when I didn't grope you at MSG."

He laughs all over again then stops, and his gaze narrows on me. "I think that's how you had to act. I don't think Adina could've handled it if you were spicy on top of looking spicy."

What the hell?

I rear back, frowning at him. "What is that supposed to mean?"

"Come on, Luna. You know all eyes were on you, right? You just tried to make yourself invisible around her. You're in the background in all the photos, like anyone was looking at that skinny *sosa*. See? The word really applies there."

I so don't like the way that sounds. "She was my best friend. We rode for each other."

I also don't know why I'm defending Adina like a *pendeja*.

"You rode for her."

I don't know what hurts more: that I did ride hard for her or that the whole world knows, and now I feel stupid. "Rio, don't start with me. Just because we are not friends anymore doesn't mean I'm going to shit on her."

"No one is asking you to shit on her. Just be honest with yourself."

"Stop. We have a plan for today, and we told Maeven we don't need her in our ear. We can't kiss if we're arguing."

He scoffs. "Speak for yourself."

"Oh, because you're a great actor?"

He shakes his head. "No, I don't need acting skills to execute what I've thought about doing for a long time."

My brain goes blank, and my mouth goes slack. His eyes are round, and he looks away.

Did he mean that? Wait, what did he mean?

The car plunges into a thick silence, and just when I'm ready to ask him, there's a cough from the front of the car.

"We're here," Tito says. I tear my gaze from the back of Rio's head to look at him.

He ducks his head, but I see the small smile.

Rio turns his head in my direction but doesn't look straight at me. "Are you ready?"

"Yeah." I don't know why I whisper it.

The next second, Tito opens the door, and Rio steps out first and then helps me out. We rush through the entrance.

"Rio brought her to the game?" someone yells.

"Yooo, that shit is on and popping. Way to land on your feet, Luna," a woman yells.

I stop dead in my tracks and am about to turn around and give her a piece of my mind, but Rio's hand clamps on the small of my back and keeps me moving.

It's not until we're at our seats that he leans to whisper in my ear, "What were you about to do?"

I give him a pointed look. "It's the Bronx. You *know* what I was about to do."

He smiles, and before he looks away, I reach to place my hand on his cheek.

"Thank you for saving me from myself." His smile deepens, and I can't help but look at his lips, and the words are out of my mouth before I can fully think them. "I'm curious too."

He opens his mouth.

"Rio!" someone calls out from behind him. I look up as two girls stand there smiling a little nervously at him. "Can we get your autograph?"

He nods. "Yeah."

Their faces light up. I look away and exhale.

Rio

I'm curious too.

Her words keep repeating themselves in my ear as I sign the autographs and stand and pose with the two girls.

"Let me take your photo so the three of you are together," Luna says, and I get to gaze at her and smile as she angles the camera to snap a couple of photos. She's beaming too, stretching those glossy rose lips. I wish I could see her eyes. I want to know if, behind the shades, she's affected like I am.

When she hands the phone back, one of the girls asks, "Can we take a photo with you too?"

And now it's my turn to take their photo, and we snap a group selfie of all of us together.

"Thank you," they say, and the other girls lean in and whisper to Luna, "Fuck those bitches online. And way to go." She tilts her head toward me when she says it.

Luna laughs, and we take our seats again.

"They're sweet."

"Yeah," I say, wanting to get back to our conversation.

"I'm surprised they didn't want to snatch my face off. The *Sirenas* are super protective of you."

I chuckle. "That they are, even when I'm a mess, but I think you won two over."

She shrugs. "I think we are all messes at times. I think they understand you and who you are. That's a testament to your branding."

"You sound like Maeven."

"Dude, I want to be Maeven when I grow up." We both laugh.

The game begins, and we settle in. After a while, her gaze shifts around us. Tito, who is sitting close by, is doing the same.

I lean in. "Forget they're here."

She turns her face toward me. "How? They're taking photos and videos and constantly talking about us like we can't hear them."

"Imagine walls around you wherever there's a person. Once you're enclosed behind them, they don't matter. I'm good at blocking the noise, not letting it touch me. I can be in a stadium full of people and be alone."

She nods, and just then, Judge hits it out of the park, and we stand to watch the ball sail away into the stands. The stadium erupts in cheers.

When we sit back down, Luna places her hand over mine.

"I get why you block the chatter. You need to stay sane, which I don't know how you do it with everyone always watching you. But who reaches out?"

I frown, and I'm glad I'm wearing shades too, because her question hits too close. Dr. Jacinda asked something similar last week.

"I have friends."

"I know. But sometimes even our friends don't fully know what's going on with us because we just don't go telling everyone. It takes someone to reach deeper..."

"And ask the right questions," I finish.

"Exactly."

"Tito's my cousin and best friend." I hook my thumb toward his seat. "Niko and Zao keep an eye on me. El Flaco can sense my SOS moments. My family in DR and PR do a good job of checking in on me, but they're far away."

"Which side of your family are you closer to?"

"Both. Neither would have it any other way. My dad used to take me to Guánica, his hometown, when I was a kid and taught me so much about the land."

"And your mom?"

The flare of pain in my chest is so fast and potent that my throat clogs. "She's gone. A year and a half ago."

She releases a wounded sigh, shoulders drooping. "Oh. I don't think I knew that."

"It wasn't public. I didn't want it to be. I couldn't deal..."

I trail off because the heavy weight I carried on my chest during those days is back sitting over my heart. I felt like I died too, but everything they told us was a lie because, in my death, there was so much agony. I have to close my eyes and breathe. Because I can do that now. I can feel the air flow through my lungs. *When will I be able to talk about her again without my insides caving?*

Luna's hand closes around mine, and in that moment, I need something to hold on to, so I lace my fingers through hers and squeeze.

Someone taps my shoulder. "You're on the jumbotron."

I look up at it, and yes, both of us are there with the words 'Kiss Cam.' It's our signal to go. I turn my face back to her, but I'm frozen.

She takes her other hand and presses it against my cheek, pulling me closer while tilting her head up.

"I'm sorry," she says as our lips press together. In the background, there's noise and people. In my chest, there's pain. But my lips are coated with sweetness. And in my hand, there's another to keep me anchored.

When we pull back, we are staring at each other, but I can't see her eyes. So I pull my shades off and reach for hers. With her gaze naked before me, I see all the warmth her hand was infusing into mine. I see the welling of eyes who understand loss. I see the smile of someone who sees me, who is reaching out. The lump in my throat is instant, as is the heat in my chest.

And this time, it's me, and not because of a fucking script, or because I'm trying to convince anyone of anything. I take her face in my hands and kiss her, our mouths fusing together. Her hands are on my wrist, like she's trying to secure me there. And that tiny moan when my tongue flicks over hers fills my ears and my chest. And I flick her tongue again and press small kisses in sequence.

My phone rings, jolting me, and I reluctantly pull away. It's the confusion in her eyes followed by her tongue swipe of her bottom lip that intensifies the beating in my chest.

"Answer the phone," she says.

I do, and Maeven's voice comes through. "That was gold. Now, control yourself. There are children around you."

Is she laughing?

"Okay."

"I got you into the after-party. All the players are going. Party, but focus on her. Remember the rules: two drinks max. I think Adina will be there. Keep Luna away from that clique. I'm sending the info to Tito and Marco. Gotta go."

I open my mouth to ask if we have a VIP area, but she hangs up before I can ask.

"We got yanked back?" Luna asks.

"We're doing too good of a job, I think," I reply.

Her gaze lands on my lips. "We really are."

"And now we have an after-party to go to. I think she wants us to keep it up there too."

Something crosses over her eyes, an emotion I can't pinpoint, but as she looks away, she bites her lower lip.

11

Luna

I sip on my bottled water, dancing in my seat while Rio spins in the DJ booth. Some of the Yankees players are in the same VIP section. Their spirits are high after today's sweeping victory.

"That color is really beautiful on you," Leisy, one of the players' wives, says to me. "I'm low-key obsessed with it."

"Thank you," I reply, looking from my royal-blue plunging neckline top to her outfit. "I love your top too." The one-shoulder lace bodysuit is gorgeous. She's stunning with beautifully golden-brown skin, and tall —at least 5'11".

Her eyebrows knit together. "How are you faring?"

I shrug. "I'm good. It's been six weeks of people coming for me. I'm almost getting used to it."

"Girl." Her hand smacks my arm like we've known each other forever. "It's only going to get worse now that you took a hammer to all these girls' hearts today."

I flip my hand in question.

She tilts her head to the booth. "You and Rio on the kiss cam. You've been trending all afternoon and evening."

78

My lips are still tingling from that kiss, so I only smile at her, and she chuckles.

"It's so good to see. Enjoy it. It's always so fun, and I think you both deserve it." Her smile wavers. "Going against the Belmonts in New York is no joke." Her gaze drifts to the other side of the club. In the VIP area, Adina is with her friend Carrie. They're staring right at me, pointing and giggling to each other.

My spine stiffens. But I force a breath. I'm not letting them get to me.

"I'm not going against anyone. I'm just living my life." I turn to her. "Enjoying my relationship."

She high-fives me. "I know that's right. The best revenge is to never let them see you sweat."

"Okay, I'm getting off this booth," Rio says into the microphone.

"Noooo," the crowd yells.

"I'll see you at the concert. *Los amo.*"

When he steps off, Carrie rushes to him. She goes to say hi to him, and he stops for a second. She points to Adina at the booth, gesturing for him to come with her. He shakes his head, points my way, and walks the other way.

He stops to take photos but moves quickly, reaching me in a couple of minutes. Leisy winks at me and moves over so he can sit next to me. "Sorry about that. It took longer than I expected."

His scent is stronger now. It's hot in the lounge, and it feels like it's activated the notes of his cologne.

"It's okay. Everyone's so happy to see you. And you seem to be having a good time."

"I am with only one drink. Do you want me to make you something?"

I shake my head. "No, thanks. I don't feel comfortable drinking at clubs anymore."

He touches my cheek. "I get it. What happened to you was horrible, but you know me and my people will keep you safe, right?"

My fingers caress his hand. "I know. I don't want to drink tonight. Besides, the music is good, and I'm feeling it."

He studies me for a few seconds. "I think we should probably talk about the kiss."

"Kisses," I correct him.

He chuckles. "Yeah, kisses. The first one was the one we had agreed on. The second was because we wanted to."

I stare into his eyes. "Really wanted to."

"Are you okay with that?"

"I...don't know... I think it's setting us up for failure."

He frowns. "How? *¿Porque se va a terminar?*"

"Yeah, Rio. We have an expiration date."

He nods, his face growing serious. "Then let's drink the water until it runs out."

Now it's my turn to frown. "I don't know if I'm capable of that. I don't think I'm built for casual."

"It doesn't have to be that. Think about it."

I open my mouth, but the *boom boom boom*, and the beat drop.

"Rio is dedicating this song to the beautiful Luna. I better see you two *perreando* together."

I laugh as his voice blares from the speakers, and the whole club sings along with him.

Dime Mami que te doy
¿Te doy el mundo?
No mejor te doy
Pa bajo pa bajo

Rio stands and extends his hand. We step down onto the dance floor, close to the VIP section, pausing by a pillar. He stands behind me as I level down — crouching with my feet planted on the ground with my hands on my knees as I grind circles on him to the tempo. His arms go around my waist, his body bucking against mine, and I let my head drift back against him.

"I've never dreamt of *perreandote* like this." His hips rock against mine, his dick brushing my ass.

I'm hot, fueled by the energy emanating from him; By remembering the way he kissed me at the stadium, and I grind harder.

"Do you want this?" he asks, and I know I need to stop. We are getting in too deep, with everyone probably watching our every move.

He kisses behind my earlobe, my body shivering. My eyes are about to drift closed when I spot Adina and Carrie heading our way with their entourage of *lambones*. They're arguing with Tito and some of the players' bodyguards. If Rio sees this, it's going to be a mess.

I can always ask to leave, but he'll notice. And it will ruin this night and how good the day has been. I decide then: I won't let her.

Adina and her crowd have already ruined too many nights for me.

So I turn around, push Rio against a pillar, then position myself between his legs, and hook my arms around his neck. "This is how I like it."

And I roll my hips against him, our bodies pressed tight together while the music reverberates over our skin. His face is on my neck with his breath fanning over my skin while he moves against me, brushing me in all the right places.

I can see the argument. The fight that breaks out after. But I keep on grinding against him, and when his head lifts, I don't let him turn toward the mess. I offer up my lips for him to kiss and he indulges me with *gusto*. His groan vibrates through me, and his tongue slips into my mouth.

It's not until the lights turn on, and Tito is there, next to us, that we realize the party is over. Tito ushers us out of the room and outside through the back entrance to the club.

"What happened?" Rio asks.

"People can't hold their liquor. Shit went south."

And it's on me since I made things real messy for us.

Rio

"Hold on," Maeven says on the other end of the line. "So you're telling me that you didn't see or hear the fight? I mean, that's what it looks like in the video, but I don't want to assume."

"Yeah." I'm feeling dumb too. The whole crew was in a scuffle, and I was in the back, oblivious, while completely wrapped up in Luna.

I'm still waiting for the regret to kick in.

Maeven chuckles. "I love Luna. She's a fucking dream in this relationship."

"What? You think she knew?" I ask because I don't think she did. We were both so wrapped up in the dance.

"I can almost guarantee you she knew."

"She did," Tito confirms from behind me.

"Why didn't she tell me anything?"

Maeven hums. "She was protecting you. If you knew there was a fight, you would've jumped in there. The talk would have been about how you can't stay away from trouble. Instead, everyone's talking about you almost burning down the dance floor with her. Good job."

We wrap up the conversation.

"You sure Luna saw it?" I ask Tito.

"I know she did. I was standing by to make sure no one got close."

I throw my hands up in the air. "Why would you not tell me?"

He shrugs. "Rio, you drool for this woman. You're mad slick with every other girl, but this one makes you say cornball shit. *Tu ta aficiao de ella.* She was letting you *perrearla y chulearla.* I wasn't going to cock-block that."

I stare at him for a bit, and then I laugh. "I owe you, man."

"Tell her to bring her prima around, the one she's always with on Instagram."

I nod. "You got it."

He leaves me alone. Like I do every night before bed, I look at the butterfly on the glass pane and then head to my room.

My notepad is on the bed, and I beeline for it.

Tenemos que hablar
Yeah, we have to talk
I don't know what you're doing
This is not part of the plan

I don't think you know that was my soul
That thing you touched with your fingers, with your warm gaze
Or did you?
Es Rio, Mami.

You had my soul in your hands
Y no debio pasar
Solo nos estamos conociendo,
Yeah, we're just getting to know each other
And you got that deep
When you kissed me, it was more than mouths
I could see it in your eyes
All of me was in there

Baby, yo se que me ves
Cuando bailamos, you gave me a little taste
Del daño que tus caderas pueden hacer
De tu boca
Y ese culo como lo sabes mover
And then you go home
Dejandome con las ganas
Corazon, you're a mindfuck

But I don't want you to stop
I need to see how far we can go
Your body needs to see como te puedo castigar
Comer, morder, besar
I want to mindfuck you too
Until you think of only me

Baby, te quiero poner como me pones a mi
It's only fair
It's not that I want you to stop
I just want you to feel me too
Still waters run deep
Rio

12

Luna

I am screwed.

The consequences of my actions are *seriously* chasing me—the headlines in newspapers, posts all over my social media feed, the calls and emails for comments. All of it is distracting, and it feels like a condemnation, which makes it difficult for me to focus.

I made the decision to distract Rio and myself from the presence of Adina and her crew. Now, we are all people can talk about.

I mean, it's fine. I'm getting used to being online fodder. When no one's dragging me, I start getting paranoid. The issue—no, the problem—no, the disaster—is that people keep sharing the videos and images from yesterday. And every single time, I'm transported to that moment.

Our first kiss at the stadium, which was scripted in most ways, ended up being deeper, more intimate, and especially touching. When he mentioned his mom and revealed she's gone, it shattered me. Now I can't put away the pain in his face, the darkening of his skin, and how his jaw worked.

It hurt me to execute the plan when his heart is clearly broken. And if that wasn't deep enough, he took our glasses off and kissed me again with the *ganas* he spoke of earlier in the day and the heat I wasn't prepared for. He burnt himself into my lips, which did not stop tingling until we were at the club, when our mouths meshed again, and this time our bodies joined.

Dios mio, what did I do?

There are so many things about him that have taken me by surprise. He's really sweet to me and protective. After everything that happened between us the first time we met, he didn't have to help me at the Coliseum. I know it's human decency, but still, not everyone is decent.

I don't think I ever thanked him.

The flipping of the deadbolt makes me snap my gaze off my computer screen to the hallway. The door opens seconds later, and Sel walks into my living room. She's wearing shades of blue, jeans, a blue hoodie, and a Yankees cap, accompanied by her signature Air Force Ones.

Bronx girl core if I've ever seen it.

"Good morning." Her smile is bright, exposing the two hundred thousand Dominican pesos worth of perfect dental work. In her hand are two bags: one small and the other very large.

"What you got there?" I ask.

"In this one, our bodega orders." She holds up the smaller bag and then points to the larger one. "That one is for you. The delivery guy handed it to me."

I'm not expecting anything, but I stand and take it from her. It's from Faye & Fleur, one of the clients we do social media for. Their products are extremely expensive, so we don't order from them. "I wonder if they sent us this to celebrate their one million subscribers."

Inside, there is a large hat box, along with a note that reads, *Remove gently.* I take it out and place it on the table. When I remove the lid, we gasp in unison.

It's a flower arrangement in the shape of a large moon formed from pink blush roses and small flowers for the crater details. It's backlit, illuminating the bed of indigo roses that make up the night. The bed of greenery it sits on is colored like a night sky full of stars, with a note on the side of the moon's crescent.

Gracias por tu ternura y protección, Diosa Luna. — Rio

My chest squeezes, and I'm frozen, reading the sentence over and over, hearing it in his melodic voice.

"Thank you for your warmth and protection? And he called you a goddess?" Sel walks up to the couch and dramatically lets herself fall, crossing her arms over her chest like she's lying in a casket. "I'm dead."

But it's my heart that threatens to give out. "It's so...wow."

"Yeah, the boy is in deep."

I guess I'm not the only one.

I keep staring at the full moon, the conflict brewing between the heart that won't stop pounding and the logic that tells me we are going too far off the deep end.

"Okay, talk."

"I don't know what to say...scratch that, this is the most beautiful thing I've ever received. It's so thoughtful, you know? And this is the second time he's sent flowers. The first time, I didn't think much of it, because I thought Maeven asked him to. I just found out yesterday that it was all his doing."

"But?"

"I don't know, Sel. It's getting out of hand. I don't like this man. We don't like each other. And now reality and pretend are blurring."

She presses her lips together. "Girl, that you-don't-like-each-other ship has sailed. It's somewhere off the coast of Alaska, fishing for shrimp. The kisses at the stadium were one thing. Me and your mom were squealing."

"You watched that with Mami?"

"We always watch the Yankees. Btw, she loved it." Then she laughs. "Anyway, that club footage was *everything*. You may need to take a pregnancy test because *ese hombre te pintó* two babies with *esa perreá que te dió*. His primo was standing like a third wheel in the back—a *fine*-ass tall drink of a third wheel, I must say."

I don't know which of the statements makes me laugh more. "Next time, you're coming with me so you can help me stay out of trouble. You can chat up Tito."

"I'll come, but I'm going to push you to get yours. This is obviously meant to be, because no matter what the Crypt Keeper and her mom tried, bro is obviously after you like a heat-seeking missile."

He asked me to think about us, and it's all I've thought about, but if it goes south, it's bound to be an epic wreckage.

"And you want to, Luna."

"I'm confused."

Sel rolls her eyes. "Bitch, stop. *Tu te lo comes con los ojos* like he gobbles you with his eyes. Go sell that confusion story to someone who doesn't know. If you're scared, say you're scared, but you know what you want...a lot."

"Shut up. I need you to be the one with common sense and steer me away."

"From what?" she yells. "A dude that wants to put it on you. Steer you away from dick you're dying to sample? No, ma'am. You got the wrong one. And you know he would do a great job, because Perla is still singing about him and giving scorned-ex interviews. That bitch is two seconds from recording *una bachata* with Joe Veras talking about how he left her behind like a small-town girlfriend and never looked back."

I laugh so hard I have to sit down. "You are fucking insane."

She shrugs. "That's why you love me."

I do, because if there's a war, I don't need an army, just Sel. "*No puedo contigo.*"

We both cackle this time.

She sobers up. "Listen, you should give it some thought because we're not kids and cannot jump into shit blind. But it's going to have to be some fast thinking since you have to be around him, and after last night, it's only a matter of time before he backs you into a corner, giving you that Alexis y Fido '*Mala Conducta*' treatment."

The butterflies in my belly are instant as the vivid images that song conjures. I see him *castigandome* in a bed, against the wall, everywhere. My mouth drops open. "Sel, stop."

She grows serious and stands. "I'm sorry that was insensitive of me. I'm acting like he's not the king of *bellaqueo*." She bends her knees and places her hands on them, pointing her ass my way. "It's more like, *Te doy pa bajo, pa bajo, pa bajo.*" She quotes Rio's lyrics while leveling down and winding her hips, dropping her butt three times.

I laugh again. "Let's get to work. You're too wild this morning."

She nods to the bag. "Let's eat and talk because my chopped cheese is waiting for me. Btw, Manolo hooked up your ham and cheese with tomatoes, mayo, grilled onion, salt, and pepper. He threw in your favorite kettle cooked sea salt and cracked pepper chips."

"Yas. Pull it all out. I need to thank Rio for these flowers."

She turns and grabs my phone from the table. "Let me take a pic of you with the flowers so you can send it to him."

"Oh no. I'm not even wearing a bra or makeup." I put my hands up to cover my face.

"First, you don't need makeup. Second, the man got you the most beautiful arrangement we've ever seen. The least you can do is let him see the girls fall naturally."

I start to protest, but her judgment is never off with men, so I let her snap a few photos. We pick the best one. Me, leaning in, looking at his flowers. And the camera doesn't lie. My face reflects how happy they make me.

Me

Thank you. These made my day. They're so beautiful.

But I promise myself that I'm going to give this the right amount of thought. I won't jump into this without being completely sure. No matter how much my body is pressuring me.

Rio

Patience is one of those things that won't come easy to me.

But as Dr. Jacinda loves to remind me, if I push, I'm going to make Luna run. Except for the past week, since the club...that seems to be happening anyway. We text, but I haven't seen her. We both know things are turning between us. My tour rehearsals have started, and I don't have much time to hang out, but every time I try to set up a meet —I won't call it a date to not scare her—something always happens. I'm even cursing Maeven for finding her work.

I'm left like a fucking *pariguayo*, looking at our conversations and waiting for the next text in between rehearsals.

I go back to the photo she sent me with the bouquet so often I should just make it my screensaver. She looks so sexy and earthy in it. It is my favorite since her hair is loose and untamed, and she's just beautiful in it, with no makeup or anything. But, I was conflicted when I got it because who took the photo?

ME

Coño, Mami, que bella te ves así. The flowers can't compare. Come here and dame ese besito.

LUNA

ME

Who took the pic?

LUNA

My enforcer

ME

Who's that?

She followed with a photo of her and Sel working at a table. Luna is pointing a thumb at her cousin.

My relief was instant.

Me

She's got to come hang with us. But next time, I want to be alone with you.

She kept going between typing and not that day. Until finally...

LUNA

I would like that.

But it's been a week, and I can't get away from the images of the club. My beat-off playlist is my hands on her ass that night and her tits in that tank top from the photo with the flowers.

It's ridiculous. I've got women throwing themselves at me, but I don't want to fuck any of them. I only want the girl who has me listening to Aventura on a loop. I even play *'Dime Mami'* so I can remember her smile from the first day I met her, and I'm back at the club, *perreandola,* while the venue was practically coming down around us.

I try not to think of the warmth of her hand against my cheek at the stadium. Or the tears in her eyes after I said my mom was gone and then froze. No, not going to think about that.

My phone pings, and I rush to check.

MAEVEN

Niko is coming into town next week. We scheduled the Limerancia video shoot. He wants to direct, and FME is going to let him.

Ficha Mundial Latin Entertainment, our music label, would do anything to please Niko. My friend's talent and influence grows by the day. I'm excited to see what he can do.

MAEVEN

Btw, we need to put you and Luna in the same room before people start speculating. So...she's going to be your love interest in the video. You're welcome. 😊

Excitement shoots through my veins. It's probably the sexiest song on this album, and I'm going to see her there.

ME

You're my everything.

MAEVEN

Don't you ever forget it.

I chuckle, switching to my chat with Luna, and there are messages I missed. WTF.

LUNA

Thanks for being my coworker today.

The text is followed by a photo of her YouTube, playing one of my fan-made playlists.

ME

Where's the photo of you dancing? I know you're not just sitting while all that is playing in the background.

Btw, you're going to be in my video next week.

LUNA

I heard! I'm nervous.

ME

Don't be. We got that chemistry. And you see? I'm a prophet. Niko's directing the video, so you are one of his models.

It's a callback to the first time we met.

LUNA

Omg. Now I'm double nervous.

ME

It's going to be epic. Headed to rehearsal. Maybe we can chat later.

She doesn't respond for a while. When I get in the back of the car, I get a message from her.

It's a still of her in a tight shirt and sweats with her hair in a ponytail. There's a play button in the center, and my finger rushes to it. The music blasts, and '*Dime Mami*' plays in the background while she rocks to it. In the *pa bajo* part, she bends her knees and rotates her hips in perfect low circles. But it's her face, how into it she looks, that makes it the sexiest. Then she turns her back to the camera and ticks her hips. My eyes follow the movements—left, thrusting her ass at the camera, right, ass back to me—like it's trying to hypnotize me.

I watch it again and again.

ME

Jesucristo. Dame que yo quiero. 😩

And I go back to watching.

"Rio," Tito yells.

"What?" I look up, confused.

"We're here. I've said it three times." His voice is laden with annoyance, but I smile, because I have one more track for my playlist. And because...it's only a matter of time until I have her moving like that against me again.

13

Luna

"Girl, the way these people can't stop talking about the two of you the past two weeks...these blogs will be eating off your back for months," Breya, the makeup artist, says.

Chris, the hairstylist, chuckles as he applies moisturizer to my curls. "I mean, it was epic, and that footage is everything, honey. That club could have fallen apart, and neither of you would have noticed."

Except, I did. I noticed the fight, the yelling, and everything else. I just made a choice. *One that has haunted me since.* Ever since that night at the club, I feel like things are coming to a head. I've made a couple of excuses not to go out, but the text messaging is worse.

The photos of him lying shirtless in bed is bad enough. But the bedhead or wet-from-the-shower selfies have me engaged to my fingers at night. How long will I be able to control myself?

I couldn't avoid today since I'm going to be in the music video. We met here instead of arriving together, and he has been busy working with Niko on the details. The hello kiss was brief because he was helping set up some equipment. I've been in hair and makeup, avoiding the constant thinking and overthinking—or trying. I wish Chris and Breya would stop reminding me about all the online chatter.

There's a knock, and the door opens. Rio stands there in his baggy cargo pants and tank top. The wing on his chest tattoo peeks out toward his shoulder. He walks into the room, and immediately the air goes out. My gaze meets his in the mirror, and it's the edge in his gaze that latches onto my ribcage, squeezing tight.

Something's happened. Something that rattled him and is slithering up my spine, even though I don't know what that is.

Still, he says nothing, and I'm too afraid to ask.

Breya puts down her brush and clears her throat. "Come on, Chris. Let's go check out the buffet."

Chris doesn't move but looks between Rio and me. "Um, girl, I'm gonna stay. I want to make sure her curls fluff some more."

Rio's gaze doesn't move from mine.

But Breya moves quickly and grabs Chris by the arm. "We're going."

I'm barely aware of the closing of the door, because Rio's gaze is so intense, so heavy on me that it weighs my shoulders down. After the morning I've had, I don't think I can take any more bad news, but I still ask.

"What's wrong?"

"I'm annoyed," he answers.

I smile. "That's the understatement of the year. What's the reason for your annoyance?"

He shrugs. "I don't really want to talk about it."

I tilt my head and purse my lips. "Yet you came into the room and scared glam away."

"Fine, I'll go." He turns to leave.

I spin around and latch on to his hand before he can go. "Stop. Just tell me what it is."

"There are a couple of interviews out there today."

My stomach sinks a little. "What about?"

"Me. Us. A lot of bullshit."

Oh, just people talking shit like always these days. I release a breath. "Ah. What are they saying?"

"One is Perla talking about the mess I've been and how I hurt her and shut her out."

My heart softens. "Everyone has a *despechado or despechada* ex out there. She's been telling her story to any channel or paper who will listen since you guys broke up. What else you got?"

He shakes his head. "It's more than that. She knows what I was going through back then. It's like I didn't know her at all. Anyway, they're also comparing me to Niko. Song for song—"

I don't wait for him to finish. "You win."

And I mean it. His music is so much better, heartfelt, and evolved.

He rears his head back. "What?"

"Did I stutter? I said you win that battle. Easily."

"Are you high?" he asks, the frown deeply etched in his face.

I chuckle. "I wish." I'm not into anything mind-altering, but it would probably take off the edge of the last couple of months. "You don't think your songs beat his?"

"He has more songs. He's a lyrical genius."

I scoff. "So are you. Your music has everyone shaking their butts and swaying even when they don't want to. It's more versatile because you don't just do *perreo y bellaqueo,* you do actual romance that makes girls go gaga. You use themes and incorporate culture into your work. And do you know how beautiful your voice is?"

He smiles—like really smiles—just like the first time I ever saw him in person. I knew what that smile looked like on TV, but I wasn't prepared for the damage it would cause to my chest when he's across from me.

"Thank you, but I don't deserve all of that, Luna. Niko is my friend, my brother. We grew up together personally and in the industry. Our collabs are the best because we get each other. I hate when people compare us. It's never a good thing. Shit like that destroys friendships. You can tell he's pissed about it."

"I love that you think about it that way. You're a good friend. But you're both in your own lane. You shouldn't be listening to these dumb radio shows or reading internet comments when you're working on your art. It's never productive."

The smile slips from his face. "It pisses me off."

Because there's more.

"What else are they saying?" But I'm already reaching for my phone and opening the *Tlk Bout Me* app, which tracks my mentions and his.

My score is at 92%. It means everyone is talking about us. *Fuck.*

He sighs and takes one of the chairs. "They're saying I'm a fuck-up and a liability. That I'm latching onto you because of the scandal. That you're finding something to hurt Adina with, and you always want all the men she touches."

My face tingles. *Jesus, when is this going to stop?* But I can't let this get to me too. He's already feeling it. We need to be strong and not react to everything. It's my turn to be strong for him.

I push off the chair to go stand in front of him.

"So what if they're saying that? We are two people anchoring each other through a bad time. You're trying to find your way back after a hiatus. I'm not trying to hurt Adina, but my life is not about her. People fall out as friends all the time. I don't even care what she does anymore."

He nods, his hands shooting out to yank me closer, ripping a little gasp from my lips. His hands go to my face. "Promise me you'll hold on to that."

The dip in my belly intensifies. *They're saying other shit.* That's why he's so affected.

"Okay..."

His jaw works. "Perla and Noryel released a song together. It's a diss track. His verses are for me, and hers are about you."

"What?" My mind can barely wrap around the idea. I'm on a diss track? WTF is this timeline? "What does it say? What is it called?"

But I'm already searching on my phone and find it easily. It's called *Sosa*, meaning bland, and I can already imagine what it's about. It's what one of the *Sirenas* called me online.

Rio reaches for my phone, but I step back and hit play. It opens with Perla.

Al que le guste la comida sosa, ahí se jarta.

"If you like bland food, I'm a feast?" I almost yell the words, and his face goes dark. I can't let this get us off focus.

I force a laugh. "It's kinda funny. Why are you that bothered?"

"I don't want anyone to say shit about you. It makes me so angry. But Maeven has already got this."

"I'm a big girl, Rio. This song is not even that bad compared to some of the shit people have already put out there."

"I know. When I see him, I'm going to beat the shit out of Noryel again."

I laugh, but he doesn't, and the glint in his eyes tells me it's not a joke. He would do that.

"No. It's not worth it. You can't afford bad publicity with this concert so close. What if they think you're a risk and don't let you perform at your concert?"

He rolls his eyes. "Who cares? You sound like Esme and Maeven."

I take his face in my hands. "You don't like to be called a liability, so stop trying to use me as an excuse to act like one."

His gaze hardens, and he tries to push away from me.

I hold on, stepping between his legs. "You're doing so good. Everyone's talking about your music. The concert is almost sold out. I'm not going to let you fight someone for bullshit and ruin all that."

"It's not bullshit."

I push even closer. "It is. They only matter if we let them. And right now, you're so close to your goal. The album is at the top of the charts. Your concerts are going to sell out. This is going to be the summer of Rio."

He grimaces. "I just want people to lay off you, Luna. I want us to win."

My chest goes warm, my breath catching in my throat. I smile and press my lips to his. "You can be so sweet. Who knew?"

"You could've found out, but you didn't give me a chance."

"I'm learning." I smile.

"I wanna learn you, too. But I can't if you shut me out."

My face starts to tingle. "That's not what I'm doing."

"That's what it seems like," he insists, adding, "We get hot and you disappear."

"That's not true. We text. If you wanted to see me in person, you could have insisted."

He shrugs. "The ball is always in your court, Luna."

His voice is soft, brushing against something inside my chest.

"It's a two-player game. Not just what I want, but what we both want. You have to tell me."

"I asked you to think about us."

I brush his hair back with my fingers. "I am thinking."

He nods. "While we wait, do you want to know what I'm thinking about?"

"What's that?"

His gaze drifts down my chest. "I'm wondering what you're wearing under that robe."

My pulse quickens, but I scowl at him. "Really?"

He laughs. "I'm sweet, but I'm a *fresco*. But I'm half joking. I don't want to compromise that good-girl image."

I don't know why that feels like a dare. I should just tell him to leave if he's feeling better. But that's not what I do. I want him to see the red lace I'm wearing underneath. At this moment, I want nothing more than to watch his eyes move over my body, because I can almost feel them.

I untie the robe, staring into his gaze. His eyes round when he sees my intent. And then they dip to my bra and lower, burning a trail. His mouth slackens, and when I lean forward, his bottom lip catches between his teeth, and he swallows. It sends currents of excitement through me.

Back off, Luna.

And then his head presses against them, and he brushes his lips over my skin from one mound to the other, brushing his way back with his tongue. He sets off my desire trigger, and I press forward against his mouth, offering him my breasts, begging him to flick my nipple.

And he does, brushing it over the lace, sending currents through my pussy, making me so impossibly wet.

"We can't do this." My breath is choppy, but I lean forward, sending my hair around us like a curtain.

"Is this your spot Luna?" he asks, closing his hands to grab them and putting one nipple in his mouth. A moan forms in the back of my throat.

I take one of his hands and place it between my legs.

"*Coño, estas mojadita.*"

I lower my bra for him, and he latches on while pressing his fingers on my clit. I'm going insane with need and wind my hips, grinding against his fingers with my eyes closed until stars burst behind my eyelids. I sag forward. His mouth captures mine, our tongues brushing each other.

Then the sound of voices filters through. That's when what we just did hits me.

"They're talking to their lawyers on the phone," Tito says loudly. "Give them a minute."

"Oh shit. Oh God. They're coming back." I run into the bathroom of the dressing room.

I'm freaking out. *What the fuck are you doing, Luna?* You just almost fucked this man in the dressing room. God. *Haven't you been cancelled enough?*

I take off my panties and rinse them, then dry them with the blow dryer and try to get a hold of myself. I fan myself and use the blow dryer to fan my bra. When I feel more put together, I walk out. Rio is gone, and the hair and makeup artists are back.

"They're ready for you," one of the assistants calls out from the door.

But the knowing smiles are there. *How long until I see the comments on social media?*

It's not like I can do anything about that. I put on my robe again, and we head into the set. I get to shoot a scene by myself. He's standing across the room, watching me. I follow Niko's instructions and roll on the bed with my hair brushing over my face while staring at Rio.

My body is on fire, and I'm wetter under his gaze than before.

After, I go back to the dressing room and change for my scene with Rio. This time, I get to wear jean shorts over my panties and a barely there crop top with knee-high boots. *Thank God.* I don't trust myself around him without layers of clothing.

Rio is already in the middle of the floor. It's a club scene, and thank God for the leather jacket I get to put on top because my nipples are hard as rocks.

When our gazes cross, the heat from his eyes makes my heart pound in my ears. Niko places me on a stool, and when Rio stands between my legs as he sings to the camera, goosebumps break all over my skin and warmth pools in my belly. The heat of his body and his scent create a heady combination that makes me almost lightheaded.

It feels like it's all for me. When his hand touches mine, I tremble. There's a part where he buries his face in my neck and whispers, "*No puedo dejar de oir the little noises you make cuando te vienes. Me tienen loco.* I want to make you come with my mouth. I want to worship you como *la diosa que eres.*"

My pussy throbs, my hips grinding against the seat.

"Rio," I say breathless.

My brain is muddled and fuzzy. I can't think because my whole body is aching for him, and to have him so close between my legs without being able to rub this *ganas* off, is killing me.

"Cut," Niko yells. "That was good. That was a good call saying his name, Luna. We can use that with his voice for the ending of the song."

When we're walking back, Rio turns to me and says, "Let's get something to eat, and we can go hang at my place tonight."

"Hang?" I ask, my eyes on his.

"We don't have to do anything else if you don't want to."

I blow out a breath because it's time to stop running from it. "Who says I don't?"

And I go inside the dressing room and close the door.

Rio

Maldita sea.

Nothing is going like I planned. We had a good afternoon, visiting some shops and getting a bite to eat at *Sabor de la Calle,* an indoor food truck venue.

People recognized us but mostly stayed out of our way. We laughed at those trying to angle their cameras discreetly to take shots. Everything came to a halt when I got the text message in my group chat with Niko and Zao.

NIKO

Bring your ass home. Zao's in town.

ZAO

The party is starting without you.

Fuck.

"Zao is in town. Him and Niko are at the crib. They want to party. I'm sorry."

She hesitates but smiles. "It's all good. I wanna see how you behave with your boys. I'll call Sel to come by."

Tito smiles and gives me a thumbs-up behind Luna.

In twenty minutes, we are on the Upper West Side, walking into a house full of people. Niko is already spinning in the DJ booth. Zao, with his bigger-than-life smile and personality, hugs me and then jumps on Tito. I introduce him to Luna, who's smiling next to her cousin.

"*Mas linda en persona,*" he says to her.

Yeah, she's definitely more beautiful in person.

Her smile mirrors his. "Thank you. *Me encantan tus dembows.*"

He looks at me and back at her, pursing his lips. "Which one?"

"'*La Ducati.*'" And she and Sel break out into the viral dance and singing Zao's first hit.

He claps and waves his hands, egging them on.

"We're keeping her," Zao declares after the dance.

I keep my eyes on her. "I'm trying."

"Good to see you smile, *Manito,*" he says, and I nod because he was there for me the last two years. He kept trying to pull me from the hole.

"It feels good to have reasons."

He looks at Luna and Sel. "That's a lot of reason. Got *el manganzon de* Tito smiling con la *muela de atrás,* too."

I laugh. "He's trying too."

"I got a song I want you and Niko to jump on. A *los Domi* anthem. Dembow y Reggaeton."

I nod, because I don't need to hear it. What Zao says, it goes. "Vamos."

Niko is in a mood tonight because he's playing old reggaeton. I get to watch Luna and Sel sing Ivy Queen and yell that just because they like to dance sexy, doesn't mean they're trying to sleep with anyone.

I'm happy to just watch her, but when Niko spins Tego's ode to Dominican women, I grab her and grind on her.

"I swear he wrote this song for you," I whisper in her ear, wrapping my hand around her belly.

She tilts her head up, and I peck her lips.

Damn, I wish all these people weren't here.

We get pulled apart after the song, and while she chats it up, I go around the room making sure everyone is enjoying themselves. She's in deep conversation with Tito, her cousin, Niko, and Zao.

I sit on the couch, watching her with my people. It's as if she's known them forever, and they love her. All these days of wanting her here, and now she's here. After how hot she was in the video today, it's annoying having to share her.

I don't want to be the one to break the party, because she's enjoying herself, but man, I'm tired of all these people.

Luna

I spot Rio on the side and on his phone. Everyone is partying around him and doesn't seem to see him there alone, so withdrawn.

His words from the stadium play in my head. *I can be in a room full of people and be alone.*

I cross the room and go sit by him. "What's wrong?"

He looks up and smiles, shaking his head. "Just tired."

"You need to go to bed."

"I don't want to be the *agua fiestas*. If you weren't here, I would just go to my room."

I stand up and go to the DJ. "Wrap it up."

"But the party is not over," she protests.

I pin her with a look. "It's over now."

She tells the people twice that they need to go home, but no one answers. I extend my hand, asking for the mic. "Hi, everyone. Niko's gone. Zao went to bed. Rio has rehearsals tomorrow. You need to find another place to party. Tito, hit the lights."

He walks to the far end of the room and works the digital light panel. The room is flooded with harsh white light.

People turn to Rio. He chuckles and shrugs. "You heard *la jefa*. Party's over."

I don't miss the angry glances from some of the women—and even some of the guys—toward me.

"You see how easy that was? I don't mind being the bad guy for you."

He laughs.

"I should go too. You need to rest." I kiss his cheek and turn, but he latches onto my hand.

"Don't go. I'm not sleepy, just tired of all those people. I didn't plan on all that. I was planning on bringing you here and chilling with you."

Warmth spreads through my chest as I sit next to him. "I don't think any of the things you had planned can go down today."

He purses his lips. "So we can't pick up where we left off this morning?"

"Not with your boy in the guest room and my cousin and yours in the rec room."

"Tito's probably in heaven."

My gaze sharpens.

He raises his hands. "Not like that. He just asked that she come around more often." He shakes his head. "I'm not implying anything about Sel."

"Good."

"Damn, that look was something. You looked ready to black out."

I nod. "Sel is more than my cousin or a best friend. She's my sister."

"Same with Tito," he says. "I trust no one like I trust him. He's not a *sucio*."

"Right..."

"I mean, he's a good guy. Anyway, you want to watch a movie?" He turns on the TV, but it's set to YouTube. His home feed catches my eye, and I stop his fingers from clicking the home button.

Mukbang compilations. Ocean geography previews. 4K Fly-over videos.

Nothing I would've expected to see.

I point at the screen. "This is your feed?"

"Yeah, why?"

"I don't believe you. Where are the music videos with all the *culonas*?"

A grin stretches across his face. "Somewhere in there. I've been watching more of these."

I narrow my eyes on him. "Are you sure?"

"Yeah. There's only one *culona* on my mind these days. I'm starting to think she's the jealous kind."

"Maybe a little." I show him a space between my thumb and index finger. "It's crazy that you're a fly-over video buff."

"I love watching the places I've been to and where I want to go. Lately, I've been watching the ones from Puerto Rico. I've been falling asleep to drones flying over *El Yunque*. It's a rainforest and a national park. My dad and I used to camp there when I would go visit him."

I have so many questions, but I start slow.

"Is your dad still there?"

"No," he says, softly. "He died when I was younger."

There's an instant pang in my belly. "I'm sorry."

His smile is sad. "It was a long time ago."

I feel it in my soul and point to my chest. "Yeah, but it's still there, right?"

He nods.

"Let's watch it. You can tell me all about it."

The tour starts at the entrance to the park, flying over the visitor's center, but Rio starts talking, and I teleport there, in the heat and with the misty rain falling over my face.

"*Mi viejo* had stories for days. He was a musician, a college professor, and a history fan. As *Mami* would say, he considered himself a *dique cultural anthropologist.*" He laughs, and the light in his eyes is so bright, like the memories are coming alive, playing in front of him. "Papi was very much into *Taíno* mythology, and he would take me all over the island, showing me all the places where our people began. He would tell me all the stories. Every summer, we would go camping at *El Yunque*. It was so beautiful, *pero* the mosquitos would have a feast with me..."

The drone flies over the green jungle and pauses over a river where people are swimming, and he points. "We swam out there. When we were in front of the waterfalls, I would get the full lecture about *Taínos* worshipping Atabey and how the moon goddess was the guardian and protector of the jungle. And don't get him started on the two observation towers. Every year, he would grumble and complain that the Mount Britton tower wasn't named Guacar after Atabey's other son. He would say, 'We could've had Yucahú and Guacar towers watching *La Selva* and the crops with their mother. And of course, there was a lot of shade to that raping thief, Columbus."

The warmth in his voice is so palpable. He loves to tell the story, and I don't want him to stop because he seems so happy.

"What's the story of Yucahú and Guacar?"

He shakes his head, still smiling. "How long do you have? Roberto Armando Castillo would have loved to be here and tell you this story. But you'll have to settle for Riomar's version."

That's his full name. I don't think I knew that. I love it.

I kick off my heels and crisscross my legs on his couch, settling comfortably. "Hit me."

He nods with excitement. "Atabey is the mother goddess. She gave birth to herself and the world. She was lonely, so she had two sons Yucahú and Guacar."

He goes through the whole mythology, and I'm in awe of how much he knows and how he relates it to the images on the screen, the earth and rivers.

"This is so good. My limited Taino knowledge is about the five *Cacicazgos* of Quisqueya and, of course, Anacaona. You should do a project with all this knowledge."

He shrugs. "*Papi* left a binder with all his notes. Maybe someday I'll go through it." He leans closer and brings a hand to my cheek. "I'm sorry this ended up different than I planned. I have to travel with a lot of people constantly, and my friends like to party—"

I place my finger on his lips. "Don't apologize. Today was great. All of it. Niko and Zao are really cool, and I got a whole history lesson. Who knew this *muchachito fresco*, as Mami calls *reggeatoneros*, had so many different sides to him?"

"Still waters run deep, *Mami*," he says, using his catchphrase.

"No, you didn't." I roll my eyes at him but end up laughing.

He takes my face in his hands. "Thank you for kicking everyone out and spending time with me." His eyes bore into mine, so deep my breath catches in my throat.

"Luna," Sel calls out from the hallway, breaking the spell of his gaze. "Let's go before Tito gets crazy ideas. Good night, Rio."

"Gotta go. Thank you for sharing with me. I press a kiss on his mouth and push off the couch.

"Marco will take you ladies home," he says, leading us to the car. He wraps his arms around me, molding our bodies together. His sigh fills my ears and the warm scent of his boy mixed with his cologne envelopes me. We cling to each other but reluctantly pull apart.

Sel and I keep it light in the car, but buzz with excitement. She decides to stay over, and the minute I close the door to my apartment, we giggle and cover our mouths.

We lie on my bed and debrief.

"Tito says Rio's gaga over you."

"Really? He's probably being a good wingman."

She scoffs. "You do know I'm better than all the government letters, right? The CIA, FBI, and DEA have nothing on me. I grilled him like a perp on Law & Order."

I laugh. "You're crazy, Sel."

"But effective. Tito said Rio was put off by all the people there. I think he wanted to be alone with you. I think he's trying to get in there..."

"And I might just let him." I don't know why I'm playing coy, because I would definitely let him—not in a house full of people like today, though. I don't like people in my business like that.

"No, duh. I'm surprised it's taken you this long. What were you guys doing while I was emotionally going John Wick on Tito?"

I almost spit out my water. "Watching TV—well, YouTube. He knows so much about *Taíno* culture, and he was telling me about his time in Puerto Rico. It was a lot like the first time we met, minus the Adina part."

"Ugh. Don't mention that Crypt Keeper. She might show up like a minion from hell."

I lie back against my pillow. "Other than emotional torture, what else did you talk to Tito about?"

She takes off her hoop earrings and puts them on my nightstand. "Bro is in awe of me. I told him not to catch feelings."

"He won't be able to help himself," I declare. Because Sel is a bad bitch, and guys go crazy for her. "Hey, I was thinking... You know that song they released today?"

Sel's face twists. "Yeah. Add Perla to the on-sight list with Adina. If I see that bitch, Imma beat the bricks off her."

I shake my finger. "No, let's do even better than that. Let's use it for our own gain."

She frowns. "How?"

"You know that scoop neck shirt with the peonies we just got in? The one we're not that excited about?" I wait till she nods. "Let's call it the *Sosa* shirt."

It takes a couple of seconds for the meaning to dawn on her. Sel's eyes go wide, and she hops off the bed. "Girl. That shit is diabolical and genius! Let's put up the preorder."

We head to my desk and pull up the site on my computer. It takes us only fifteen minutes and we giggle the entire time.

When I lie back in my bed, my phone pings.

RIO

I can still hear those little moans. I can't wait to hear them again. Good night, Diosa Luna.

ME

Good night, Riomar.

14

Rio

I stare at my notepad, eyeing the blank page, begging for words to come. I don't know what's wrong with me. Tomorrow's the day. I go back to the stage on my own. It's the day I've been waiting so long for, working hard toward.

But I'm restless, and my heart is jumping in my chest. Dumping my thoughts onto paper has been calming me down for months but the well is dry.

Everyone, from Niko to my elementary school teacher, has been sending me messages of encouragement. Even the impossible-to-please trio—Maeven, Esme, and Kresh—have told me today they're proud of me. I feel the support, but something's wrong or off. Luna comes to mind. The way she sensed I needed to be away from those people the other day. The fact that she kicked them out.

I push off the bed because I do know.

I don't mind being the bad guy for you.

Her words plague me, like her kindness and her eyes.

And then I see the butterfly on my glass pane. Luna's mom calls her

Mariposita, and I haven't been able to get it out of my head. Because this one butterfly calls to me.

"You're everywhere but by my side," I mumble.

And I hear Mami's voice, exactly a month before she was gone. I see her sitting up in her bed with my head in her lap.

I'll always be there, mi niño. Like a butterfly in the dark of night, under the moonlight, over the water. You won't see me, but where you go, Riomar, I'm always there. With you.

I told her that her lyrics were better than mine. She laughed so hard. It was the last time I heard the sound. Shit, I would give anything to hear it again.

My eyes well up, but I blow out a breath to stop the emotion. Tonight is not the night for it. I plop myself back on the couch and grab my notepad. This time, I don't let myself think. I just write what comes.

Es la historia de un amor,
a love story for the ages
One that ended way too soon
Porque como todo en la vida
Cumplio su curso

Lo unico es que no estaba listo. No, I wasn't ready
Mi mente no computa
Mi corazon no accepta
Mi alma llora

Soy un niño perdido
Vagabundo de dolor
Calling out
Llamandote

El silencio me mata
La soledad me ata
Tengo que llenar el vacio
Con lo que sea
Alcohol, nalgas, tetas, peleas

Pero nada calma mi angustia
Y te termino llamando
A Dios le estoy rogando
Tu ya no me oyes
El ignora mi canto

Es Rio
Hay perdidas que no se olvidan
Amores que nos marcan para siempre
Te digo, still waters run deep
Y las turbulentas, tambien.

The words on the page are horrifying. They're in the wrong place. I should be writing about rehearsals and the road to tomorrow. But the past week and a half have been kicking my ass. Every night I come home, I'm so tired, like I've been beaten up. I should be happy since there's plenty of reasons to celebrate: sold-out concerts, the album went number one, and things with Luna are going well...kind of. I've been busy with concert prep, and she has been doing some influencer work that has been coming her way while working on her business.

But something's been bothering me, and all roads lead to Ana Fernanda Castillo. The part of me that I buried with my mom.

I miss her so much. It's painful, and all I want is for it to go away. Why is it happening today? It's the eve of my comeback and...

It's because it's tomorrow.

I push to my feet. I want to talk this out. I need someone to listen.

I grab my phone to call Dr. Jacinda. But I stop, because I don't want her, or Tito, or anyone.

Except one person. The one that brought on this feeling because she did what *Mami* would have done on the day of the video shoot. She called me out and *me cantó mis verdades*. Yeah, she told me the truths I didn't want to hear. She held me, distracted me, and sent people away when she sensed I needed it.

I need to get out of here.

I grab the keys to the car and head down. I yell at Tito that I'm going out.

He's in front of me in the blink of an eye. "Where the fuck are you going by yourself?"

"A dar una vuelta."

His mouth falls open. "To drive around? Are you nuts?"

"I need to get out of here," I say. "I'm not going to do crazy shit. I just need some air."

"Let me go with you. I'll keep my mouth shut. I'll be in the front without saying anything." He's already slipping his feet into his shoes by the door.

"Okay," I say. It's easier than arguing.

I drive myself this time, and Tito doesn't ask where we're going. He doesn't even comment when we park outside Luna's building.

We sit there in silence, with me feeling like an idiot. *What am I doing here?* I haven't heard from her in a few hours. I haven't even messaged her. Her living room light is off, and I'm sitting here like the creep she called me that day in the park. I feel so fucking stupid. I reach for the shifter to pull into drive, but Tito's hand stops me.

I look at him.

"Call her," he says. "You came all this way."

"No, she's probably busy or talking to some *macho*."

He scoffs. "The only *macho* that woman has got on her brain is you. Just like you're not chasing any other *culo* because you're stuck on her."

"Shut up."

He sighs. "There's nothing wrong with it, Rio. The two of you are circling the wagon and living the dream."

I frown. "What dream?"

"You get to play kissy face with the chick you like."

"Veta pal carajo," I tell him.

He outright laughs, but then his face goes all serious. "Call her. You need her."

"I don't need her."

Fucking liar. You just don't want to admit you do.

"Maybe not," Tito says. "But it's different with her. And I don't have to tell you how many dudes want to trade places with you."

"It's not that..." I trail off because what am I about to say? That she's a million more things than the body all these men want to fuck?

That when she smiles, my anxiety ebbs away? That even though I want to pick up right where we left off in the dressing room, I'm happy when she doesn't look like she wants to throw a brick at me? That sitting with her in my living room, talking about my vacations with my dad, and watching me geek-out over videos meant so much more?

I contemplate for a while, not ready to put myself out there, but he's right. *I need her.* Maybe if I just hear her voice, I can go home and sleep.

If she doesn't pick up, I'll go home.

Luna

"Diablo, que bruta es esa tipa." I stare at the telenovela's main character in disgust. I can't believe she was dumb enough to give up her big modeling break to help her friend break into her ex-boyfriend's house to spy on him.

My mom snorts. *"Pendeja es lo que ella es. Coje ahí. Novelas* are here to teach us about real life and not about being punks."

"Mami," I say, shaking my head. "You know this is not real."

"No?" My mom turns her head all the way around to look at me. In her sleeping bun, the glare in her eyes makes her look harsher, like a stern *doña* and not my sweet mom. Her gaze holds mine, making my stomach sink. I just know she'll say something I'm going to hate. And the lady doesn't disappoint.

"You've done stuff like that for Adina. And before you ask when, let me tell you. You passed on Cornell to stay in the city and close to her because she wanted you both to go to the same school. Then, she failed anyway. You didn't go out with that player from the Mets because she liked him and pouted about it."

I roll my eyes. "He's a cheater, and we hate the Mets in this house."

"But you didn't know he was a cheater back then. And for the right *novio,* we can overlook the blue and orange." She places a hand on my thigh. "It's my fault. I took you there, as if you were her hired play partner. I regret that."

I cover her hand with mine. "Don't. I loved being her friend back then. It was innocent."

"No, it was never innocent, *mi Luna*. Bethany thought you would grow up to be only her kids' companion. Maybe you would take over for me when I'm too old to take care of her household. And Adina is a leech, like her mama. *Pero le diste un galleta sin mano.* You're the real deal, everything she wishes her daughter could be—smart, beautiful, and with talent they'll never have. I can't wait for your reputation to be fully restored and for people to see you for who you are. It's working too."

It doesn't erase the way Adina turned on me and not once tried to defend me. I'll never forget she was the main one throwing mud my way. But I think of the call with Faye & Fleur and the offers for me to sponsor products and smile. "Yeah—"

My phone buzzes with a call from Rio.

"Your new *novio* calls," Mami says out of the side of her mouth. I don't miss the crooked smile. "Go take it in the living room. I don't want to miss any part of today's episode. Joaquín is going to find out that his evil twin brother, Salazar, married Mari Carmen, pretending to be him."

I hop off the bed and answer, closing the door behind me.

"Am I interrupting?" he asks, his voice low.

"I'm just watching a *novela* with my mom. She's addicted."

The quick intake of breath and the silence that follows weighs heavy on the line.

"Is something wrong?"

"No. You should go back to spending time with your mom. That's precious."

I chuckle. "Are you serious? You know *novelas* are on every night, and she watches from 7-11 pm? Hell, if it was up to these channels, they would air them Saturday and Sunday, and Dominican moms would never leave the house at night."

He laughs a little. "Yeah, but this is your time with her. I used to watch *Corazón Salvaje* with my mom."

My phone buzzes with a text.

TITO

Look out the window. I never told you.

I frown and cross the distance to look outside my apartment window. And there's a black SUV parked across the street.

He's outside?

"Go back to your mom. I'll call tomorrow."

"No, wait. I have questions," I say as I cross my living room and head for the door. "The old *Corazón Salvaje* or one of the newer ones?"

"The old one. My mom hated the newer ones."

"Because the first one with Palomo was so good." I sprint down the stairs.

"You saw it?"

"Have you met Raquel? She's a straight-up *novela* aficionado. It's how she would bond with my grandma after work. When she goes out with Darren, she records them. I remember being little and the three of us piling up on my *Guela's* bed to watch. *Toque de queda,* they used to call it. Because it was exactly like a curfew. Everything stopped."

"Yeah, *Mami* and me used to watch the nine p.m. one together over the phone if I was touring, or she would wait for me if I was performing that night. When I couldn't record it, she would fill me in. It was our quality time."

There's something so sad in the way he says the words. *He misses her.*

"Which one was her favorite?"

"*Sortilegio.* Listen Luna, you should go—"

While he talks, I cross the street and knock on the driver's window. Rio turns to me with wide eyes.

"What are you doing down here?" He's a little flushed, like he can't believe it.

I point back at my window. "I could see the car. Come upstairs for a bit."

He shakes his head. "You and your mom are spending time together."

"Sir, we live together. Come on, open this door."

He unlocks the door and steps out. I hug him, and his arms wrap and tighten around me, squeezing me. Tito is already coming around.

"I'll call you," Rio says to Tito, who leans to kiss my cheek and gets into the driver's seat.

I take Rio's hand in mine and lead the way back to the building. I walk fast. He's silent up the steps and through the door. My mom walks back to her room in her big blue robe over her night shirt, holding a glass of water.

"Hi, Rio."

He steps forward and offers his hand. "*Disculpe la interrupción y la hora.* I'll leave soon."

She kisses his cheek and smiles. "You're okay. It's normal for my daughter's *novio* to come calling."

My mouth goes slack, and I give her a pointed look. The respectful version of what-the-fuck.

Her smile only brightens. "I'll see you later." As she closes her bedroom door, she yells over her shoulder, "No funny business."

Rio flushes. "*Yo...Yo no le faltaría el respeto.*"

She laughs. "I'm teasing you."

I want to die. "She's in a weird, funny mood."

He stands there, as if he doesn't know what to do.

"*¿Qué te pasa?*" I ask.

He says nothing.

I close the distance between us and take his hand again. "I know something's wrong."

He squeezes my hand. "It's tomorrow."

I frown at him. "What about it? You're ready. Rehearsals are perfect." The videos he's been sending have been amazing.

"I know..." He breathes out. "It's her... I'm ready to talk about her."

And it's the somber light in his eyes that brings me back to his earlier words about how precious the moments I spent with my mom are. My heart shatters for him so fast.

His mom.

I want to hold him, but I hold myself back. I don't want him to clam up. He needs to let it out. I guide him to the couch instead.

I tuck my legs under me and pull him to sit beside me. "Tell me. I want to hear it."

"It was cancer. I found out two years ago. I had just finished a tour and she was here in New York. She found out before but didn't tell me, waiting until I was done with that fucking tour to tell me. She waited about a month to go to the doctor, where they told us her days were numbered. We headed to the DR, and I took care of her until her last moment. I couldn't be away."

The flash of pain punches through my chest. He had to watch his mother die. I bite the inside of my cheek to stop the surge of emotion.

"Watching her fade away was as bad as losing her. She used to be active and lively. She was kind of like your mom, but a lot feistier. It hit me today after we got home from the last rehearsal." His eyes turn cloudy, like a storm coming closer and closer. "The concert opens tomorrow, and I'm not going to hear her voice. *Ella siempre estaba ahí.* Before every concert, I got a call from her. But this time, she won't tease me about *chiviricas* throwing their panties at me onstage. She won't give me her blessing and send 25-30 saints to stand behind me, hold my hand, or go in front of me. There won't be candles on anyone's mantel tomorrow or a mass offered with gratitude after."

Tears glisten in his eyes, a knot in my throat. His hand tightens around mine. I'm impotent as the tears drop down his cheeks, and mine fall just as fast. My mom is my everything, and to think of him living my worst fear is just devastating.

"I don't want you to cry," he says.

"I can't help it. I don't want you to hurt like this." I can barely get the words out because my throat hurts so much.

He covers his face with his hands, leaving the tears that keep falling as the silent sign of his pain. *How many times can a heart break?*

I pull him close, pressing his face to my chest, and hug him as tight as I can.

"Why did he do this to me?" he asks, and before I can ask, he adds, "Why did He take her? She was so good. She helped everyone. I needed her. I don't have my dad anymore. *Me dejo huerfano.* He left me alone."

Orphan.

I'm desperate to help him, but I don't know how. I breathe and hold on tight. I let him cry and let my own tears cloud my eyes, fall, and clear my vision again. He's not alone. Doesn't he know that?

Maybe you need to say it.

"I'm here, Rio. I'm here with you."

He pushes back, lifting his head from my chest. His red-rimmed eyes are moving all over my face. "*¿De verdad?*"

And I know what he's asking. *Do I mean it?* The words came out of my mouth so fast, in a way that only the truth can. Because I do mean it. I'm here. I don't want him to be alone.

"Yes, because…"

"You feel sorry for me, and you're nice—"

I press my fingers to his lips. "I'm falling in love with you."

His eyes round. "But you said…"

"I know. My mouth says a lot of things, but…" I can't seem to get all my words together, so I just press a hand to my chest.

He sits back on my couch with his hand tight around mine.

My heart pounds its way out of my chest. I just confessed I'm falling for him. I put myself out there when he's confessing about his mom, and I don't know if he feels the same.

I look toward the other side of the room and swallow. *What the fuck did you do, Luna?*

"Thank you," he says.

My stomach knots, and fear settles like a puddle. He's grateful. *Shit.*

"I don't trust people, and I haven't even been able to talk about *ella* with anyone. *Ella* es sacred."

His mom.

"Why do you say *ella*?"

His whole body tenses again, and I squeeze his hand.

He breathes out. "It's easier to say her or *ella*. I don't trust myself to say anything else."

"You talked to me about her."

He lifts his free hand and settles it on my cheek. "I trust you *con mi Mai* and you're the only one."

The warmth floods my chest, and it's scary how much I want to take his pain away. "Thank you for trusting me. Now you can say mom, *mamá*, or *Mami*."

"*Mami*." He pulls me to him and presses his lips to mine.

I sit back, and his head falls onto my shoulder. We stay in silence, and his breath evens out.

He's asleep, but I'm wide awake and panicking.

Luna

I'm happy he opened up to me, and I'm there for him.

But now I'm in knots because I put myself out there, and shit like that changes things. Now I don't know what this means for us. But part of me is at peace because he let it out. It also explains so many things about him, all the trouble he got into, the anger.

When the door to my mom's room opens again, he sits up, as do I. *Mami* stands there, looking at us with concern.

"I'm sorry." He stands. "I'm leaving. We were talking, and I fell asleep. I'm tired and..."

"We have to call Tito," I say.

He looks at Mami. "I can do an Uber. I didn't mean to keep you up—"

Her hand shoots out to touch his shoulder. "You're tired, and tomorrow's your big day. It's late, and you shouldn't be out and about. *Lo malo*, evil stuff, is always out to get you before your big victory. You can sleep in Luna's room. She can sleep with me."

I'm stunned. He's frozen.

"Let me get you some towels." But as she walks away, worry clouds her eyes.

How much did she hear?

"I don't have to stay." He looks almost panicked, and it makes me smile.

"My bed is really comfortable. I have a soft mattress pad. I mean, not like what you're used to, but it will be a restful night."

"Stop messing with me. I don't want to disrespect your mom." He's whispering, and that makes this even funnier, which I feel he needs in order to lighten up the heavy stuff he shared.

I lean into his ear. "Then don't think about the fact that my panties are only a few feet away while you're in there."

My mom returns before he can answer and hands me the towels. "Help him settle. *Hasta mañana, Rio.*"

"*Buenas noches,*" he says, and I show him to my room. "This is not how I pictured your room."

His eyes are everywhere—the mauve walls, my corkboard with my to-do list, and my bed.

"How have you been picturing my room?" I pause to look at him.

"Red silk sheets, low lighting."

"That sounds like it would be your room more than mine."

"So you try to picture my room too?"

I already told him that I'm falling for him. *What's one more confession?* "Yeah."

"I'll have to show you since I already know what yours looks like."

"I would like that."

He smiles so wide, like his normal self coming back to the surface, and my body heats up. Then he brings me closer, whispering in my ear, "When we go to my house, I'm going to kick everyone out *y nos vamos a matar las ganas* in every corner."

Shivers break over my skin, making me shudder. "I'm ready."

"I bet your panties *estan mojados* like the day of the video. I'm dying to check, but...I don't want to be a *falta respeto.*"

I can feel how wet I am from just thinking about him between my legs with his mouth latched onto my nipple. *Mami* falls asleep fast, and she won't come in here. I can turn on the TV and be really quiet.

But no, I can't do that. He's being respectful, and I need to be too.

"Why don't I give you a souvenir?"

"What's that?"

I walk to my dresser and pull out a pair of panties.

"I want the wet ones, not the clean ones," he mutters, his voice deepening.

I hook my finger into my pajama bottoms and push them down my legs along with my panties. I step out as he stares at me, wide-eyed.

Then I put on the clean ones and bend over to pick up my used ones and hand them to him.

Then I pull my pants.

"*Buenas noches.*" I lean and press a quick kiss on his lips.

I walk out of the room fast, as if my nipples aren't hard and the ache between my legs isn't uncomfortable. *Let me wash my face.*

When I finish, I climb into my mom's bed where she's watching the news.

"Is he okay?"

"Yeah," I answer. "He was having a tough time."

"He's missing his mom."

"You heard?"

She turns to look at me. "I wasn't eavesdropping, but his voice carried. You were both crying... But I could tell when he came in. When you lose a mother, you recognize the pain in others."

My heart is so full of love for her. "I love you, *Mami.*"

"Me too, *Mariposita.*" Then she smiles. "Sooo...do you want to go sleep in there?"

Her head tilts in the direction of my room.

"He's *respetuoso.*"

She raises a brow. "I'm glad *he* is respectful. And it's not an invitation for you to go. Not under my roof. I'm asking, do you want to?"

"Yes."

She nods. "And you thought about it?"

It's all I can think about.

"Yeah," I say as casually as I can muster.

"Okay." She turns on her side and lies down.

I lie on my side of the bed, grateful that conversations with my mom put a damper on my *ganas.*

Then I see a notification on my phone. I tap on his name.

RIO

Pilla. Abusadora. Cruel.

I smile until I see the next text.

RIO

I licked the moisture out of it.

And I swear I feel that tongue on me.
He follows with a photo of him with my panties in his mouth.

15

Rio

I open my eyes to tiny slivers of light filtering through the blinds. I sit up in bed, confused. The warm pink walls with the emerald accents are a stark difference from the dark-blues in my bedroom. The feminine furniture, the massive mirror in the corner, the vanity desk with the corkboard behind it.

In her soft sheets, I'm surrounded by a scent I would know anywhere. Luna's perfume. Luna's room. Luna's panties—the ones that got me so turned on it took me forever to go to sleep— lying near my face. No, it wasn't her panties. It was the way she took them off and handed them to me. Then got dressed and walked out. I had to take a cold shower for my body to settle.

She teased me. She held me. She lodged herself so deep in my chest. I can't repay her.

Then I hear her clearly. *I'm falling in love with you.*

And my heart speeds up because I'm crazy about her. I don't know when it happened.

The whispers reach me. I hop off the bed and get dressed. I need to head out soon, but maybe I can take her and her mom for breakfast. It's the least I can do. I step out of her bedroom and into the living room. Her mom, in the same robe as last night, settles something on the table.

"*Buenos dias*," I say.

Her eyes are on my face. "*Buenos dias*. How did you sleep?"

I smile. "Very well. Luna's bed is comfortable. Thank you for letting me stay."

It's her turn to smile. "Sit down. I have breakfast ready."

I look around, and she seems to read my mind.

"Luna will be right out. You need to eat so you can sing and dance tonight."

I look down at the breakfast and blink. She has the Dominican *tres golpes: mangú with eggs, cheese, and salchichon*.

"Wow, I haven't had this in..." I trail off because I remember the exact time. Sick as she was, my mom had still insisted on cooking for me. Love surges through my chest. "This was one of the last things *mi mamá* made for me. She loved to feed me."

"It's how we show love to our kids. Nothing makes you feel better than a good meal."

I chuckle. "When I was with her, I would always have to work out twice as hard."

"That's why weight loss in this house is impossible," Luna says, stepping into the room.

She's wearing a white tank top tucked into jeans. My eyes feast on all of her — bare face, curves, and thick, bouncy curls. She's breathtaking.

"You don't need to lose an ounce. You're perfect."

A grin brightens her face, and she takes the chair next to me. Her mom hands her coffee.

"You're not eating?"

"I don't eat this early." She places her hand over mine. "How are you doing?"

She's watching me as if she's searching my face for something.

"I'm good. Thanks for sharing your bed."

The twinkle in her eyes brightens.

"I'm going to get dressed. I have to go to work. Luna, make sure he eats everything. He'll need his strength tonight." Her mom heads to the bedroom.

"She's amazing."

"She is. But you're watching my mom like you want to be my dad."

I let my gaze linger over her. "I'm grateful she let me stay. For her kindness. But no, I want to be your daddy *no tu papá*."

Her cheeks redden.

"I made my *negrita* blush."

"It happens sometimes." She fans her face. "I walked right into that one."

I lean closer. "I'm going to pay you back for last night. I'm going to make you scream and cream."

She leans in, her eyes never leaving my mouth. I grab a piece of fried *salchichon* from my plate and place it in front of her lips. She opens her mouth and bites a piece, brushing her lips against my fingers.

"*Malvada.*"

But I kiss the grease smeared on her bottom lip.

"Luna, your phone is ringing off the hook. It's Maeven." Her mom calls out.

I manage to sit back before she comes out and hands Luna the phone. "The warden of Rikers calls."

Luna laughs and picks it up. "It's FaceTime."

Maeven's voice rings out, "Hey, I don't blame you for not picking up the phone. I'm so sorry this happened, and I'm looking into it."

My ears immediately perk up.

"What do you mean?" Luna asks her. "I left my phone in *Mami's* room, and I haven't been on it today."

"Oh God. You don't know." Her voice is rushed. "There's no way to sugarcoat this. It's everywhere, and the video is getting released shortly. Rio was apparently out with Adina last night and went to her place. I don't know the details, but he's not answering my calls. And Tito won't tell me where he is. If this is all true, I'm going to tear him a new asshole before he goes onstage today and he's going to crawl through every single set. I'm just so pissed—"

"Maeven," Luna says, pressing her lips.

"What?"

Luna turns her phone to face me.

I wave. "Hi, boss."

"You're with Luna." I'm not sure if it's a question or a statement. Her slacked jaw is almost comical.

"Been here since last night."

The flush on her face is priceless. "Oh." But in true Maeven fashion, she recovers fast. "At what time did you get there?"

"Is that mangú on his plate?" Esme's voice booms in the background. "He's living the J Cole song. *Breakfast after sex is like a reward—*"

"He slept in Luna's room, and she slept in my room," her mom yells, stepping back into the room, now dressed in black slacks and a cream blouse.

"Yeah. It was all respectful," I say. "So what the hell is happening?"

"Seems like our good friends, the Belmonts, are playing games. Supposedly, there's a video of you taken in Adina's living room." Her gaze narrows. "Bethany can go play the lotto, but she can't play me. Luna, take the phone to your room. Rio, come along. I was going to save this for later, but I won't have people thinking you're a cheater."

Luna does as she says, and I follow. She turns the camera around to show her.

"Got it. Rio, when you're exhausted, what position do you sleep in?"

"On my belly, arms down."

"Take off your shirt and get into bed in that position. Luna, I want you to take an angled selfie at your desk, and I want you to get his arm and face. I don't want Rio to be the focus. I want him to be in the background, discreetly but visible. We may have to move the desk. Wait, no. How about if you take one and get the mirror and have him reflected there?"

Luna angles the phone up. "It works."

"Okay," Maeven says. "I'm hanging up so you can take the photos and send them to me. Take a few photos. Don't jump on social media if you haven't already today. I'll call you back after examining the photos."

"Lie down." Luna waves me down. "I'm going to do a burst and maybe a little video."

Before I do as she says, but, a little idea comes to me, and I grab her panties and put them right next to my face.

When she's done, I get up and throw my shirt back on while Luna steps out of the room when her mom calls. I shove her underwear under the pillow as her mom comes knocking on the door.

"I'm leaving for work. But I wanted to give you something." She's staring at her hands, not directly at me.

Maybe she wants to tell me to slow down with Luna or stay away from her. Maybe she thinks I'm too much of an issue. "Okay."

She takes my hand and places a chain with a medal in my palm. "This is Our Lady of Mercy. She will take care of you tonight. I'm going to be praying for you."

A surge of my emotions rushes up my chest, clogging my throat. I barely manage to say, "Thank you."

"I...I also wanted to ask if I can *darte mi bendicion* before I go."
She wants to give me her blessing.

If she sucker punched me, it wouldn't have doubled me over like this does. My face tingles, and my heart quickens. Because the only thing I want as much as I want Luna's mom's blessing...is her daughter.

"I nod."

She hugs me, gives me her blessing, and is gone before I can catch my breath.

I look up at the ceiling. "Thank you, *Mami*. I know you did this." And I crash onto the bed until Luna walks in.

"What was that about?"

I show her the chain in my palm.

She smiles. "It's her medal. She doesn't go anywhere without it."

"And she gave it to me."

"She must think you need it. You want me to put it on you?"

I bob my head up and down, not trusting my words.

She places it around my neck. I turn to her, the words—how much she and her mom mean to me—inching to the surface but her phone rings.

"I love when people know how to follow directions," Maeven says on speaker. "These are perfect. And the video too. Btw, gorgeous mirror."

"It was a birthday gift from Bethany Belmont," Luna tells her.

Esme cackles in the background.

Maeven smiles like the Cheshire cat. "Oh, we are going full-on petty mode with the video. Luna, post it with the caption, *getting a little work in before heading out to our concert.* By the way, Tito is on the way to pick you both up. He's going to come upstairs to get you. Two girls are going live right now, in your building, Luna since they saw you both going in last night. If they engage, acknowledge them. I have to hop in an interview with The Lowdown Lounge. They're going to ask me about the video circulating. Good job, you two."

She hangs up.

"Shit, she gave me a compliment."

We move to the living room. Luna is posting, and I turn on the TV, browsing until I find Maeven's interview.

"Speaking of learning how to handle clients, tonight is Rio's opening concert to kick off the tour next week. But it seems like your boy can't escape controversy."

She smiles. "Whatever do you mean?"

"Come on, Maeven. He can't stay away from Adina Belmont while being seen out and about with her former friend, Luna."

"That's ridiculous. Rio hasn't been around Adina."

"Tell it to the footage," the host says, and he plays a video shot through a window of Adina with a man as they're touching each other.

Luna laughs beside me. "He looks nothing like you."

"Is that the video you're talking about?" Maeven laughs too. "Anyone could see that's not Rio."

"Looks a lot like—" He presses the earbud. "Well, apparently, you're right. He just looks so much like Rio and with their history...but it seems like Adina Belmont is hanging out with the Temu version."

"Stop," Maeven admonishes him. "I, for one, am happy to see Adina move on. The relationship with Thierry seemed to be taking a toll on her. I'm glad she valued herself enough to know it wasn't working. I think last night was all about her and had nothing to do with anyone else. And listen, I'm here for girl power."

"She used to date Rio, didn't she?"

Luna stiffens next to me.

"She did not. Rio was never after Adina. If anything, Rio has his sights set on the sky."

The host chuckles. "I see what you did there. What can we expect to see from him tonight?"

She smiles at him. "*Calor, sazón y perreo.* The Rio the world has been missing."

I switch off the TV.

"She did really good," I say.

Luna nods. "She's a bad bitch. Always."

"I was never interested in Adina. I think it was all a bad misunderstanding." But she doesn't look at me.

She nods, peering up at me. "I believe you. You're not a liar."

I shake my head. "I wasn't even paying attention to her. She's not my type anyway."

"What is your type?"

"*Morenita,* with the kindest and warmest heart, great boobs, and a break-the-internet kind of ass."

I lean in to kiss her, but then my phone rings, breaking the moment.

"I'm outside. Let's go," Tito orders.

Luna grabs her things and takes my hand. I lead us down the stairs, ignoring the smile on Tito's face.

When we get to the car, someone screams, "Luna, tell him to say hi to us."

Before Luna gets in, she looks up and points at a window.

There are two girls there, just like Maeven said. I blow a kiss at them. "*Las amo.*"

One of them squeals, and we are off to my concert.

I've been held to the fire
With everything building inside
Time flies or drips like honey
And I feel it all rise

It's the pain

The loneliness relegated to the bottom
The fear
The work that doesn't stop
Hope that trickles in a sliver of moonlight
It's all starting to boil

Burning my feet
Spreading through my body
The old feeling is back
My heart is roaring

The call of the stage is strong
Savage beyond my control
And I need to purge it all
I have to let the ardor out

There's no anchor point from the fire
I just let it out
Before it consumes me
The walk is not gentle

But your hand in mine is pure courage
I can walk through fire and not be burned.

A hand presses over mine. I look down to delicate fingers with burgundy-colored nails and then back to Luna's face.

Her warm smile sends a flare through my chest. "I'm going to go to my seat because it's almost time."

For a moment, I'm lost. She's been sitting by my side while I write my ideas. I never do that. *Why am I doing it with her here?*

She leans close and kisses my cheek, then brushes her lips to the side of my mouth. "You're going to kill it."

She stands, and I can't help but watch her walk away in her jeans and sparkly white halter top.

At the door, she turns and mouths, "*Rompe.*"

Then she closes the door.

And I'm left staring, thinking about last night and today. What does it all mean?

I'm falling in love with you.

Her words bring back the familiar warmth into my chest. And then my shoulders slump.

I didn't tell her I feel the same.

I need to tell her how I feel. I push to my feet, race to the door, and swing it open, but the stage manager is there.

"Fifteen minutes."

And everyone rushes in. The hairstylist pushes me back into the chair to retouch something.

It will have to wait until after the concert. But she'll know. I have to let her know tonight.

16

I'm scared. I feel it with every step I take toward our seats. I didn't want
to leave the dressing room. I stayed as long as I could.

Does Rio realize he rested his hand on my thigh the entire time?

I concentrated on my phone and tried to send him good energy as
he scribbled away. We were left alone for a while. I don't know what he
wrote. Just that he kept going, and I posted some of my get-ready-with-
me shots. Lost in today's worries is that I got ready with beauty and lifestyle influencer Bougie Girl and Lauren Guerrera, owner of *Autumn
Lush*, my favorite online clothing subscription. It's another collaboration that Maeven secured from me. It's exciting because I'm such a big
fan of both and my whole outfit is from their collab.

I feel good and comfortable as security takes Sel and me to our seats.
People scream in the crowded arena but unlike before, I don't really hear
their words. I guess it's like Rio told me the other night. You can isolate
yourself to the point you don't hear them. Because I have bigger things
to internalize, like the fact that he's about to step on this stage alone for
the first time in almost two years. And his world is different. When I get
to our box, Esme and Maeven are already there. We hug and exchange

131

one look. My nerves are reflected in their faces. Sel sits to my left, Maeven is my right, and Esme next to her.

"He's got this," Maeven tells me.

"Yeah," I reply.

She smiles. "You two..."

My chest squeezes because her thoughts are written all over her face. Just like mine, too. "I...I think so. I don't know what he thinks."

"Girl..." she says and outright laughs. "There's nothing more certain than what he thinks. It's all over your faces."

Is it really over his face? I don't know...

But he's shown you.

"I'm not going to assume."

She nods. "I get it. You need the words, and that's fine. As your publicist, this is both a dream and a panic attack."

"Does this always happen?"

Her hand waves from side to side. "No. Mostly it's purely transactional. Sometimes people get confused because the lines are blurred. I don't think this is the case. I think he's been attracted to you for a long time. You were too."

"It was the Adina thing. I couldn't..."

"I would never touch fire for a client, because I've been burned so many times. Fucking Mateo." She rolls her eyes. "But if there were a moment where I would for Rio, to say he never hit on Adina. He doesn't lie. Even when he fucks up, he comes clean. She was after him. That's why her mother wanted me to set them up together, but I wasn't going to hand that grieving man into Bethany Belmont's web."

My mouth falls open. I want to shake my head, but the shock renders me still. "Adina couldn't have known. She would have told me."

"No, she wouldn't, Luna. This is the type of thing that requires an NDA, which they had your mom sign, but not you, after you became of legal age."

"I wouldn't have. What kind of friendship requires an NDA?"

She points her hands. "They're vultures. You were there so she could copy your style and use you. That's what they do. Remember when you were interning for me, and I told you the things you needed to keep to yourself like details for negotiation and who you're interviewing with?"

I nod. "And I did."

"Oh, I know. If you had not, you wouldn't have gotten the Elevate job, because they would have stepped in front of you. It's what happened with Bonita. She made a call to them."

The floor almost gives way beneath me. Bonita Global was one of my dream companies. It promotes a clean lifestyle, and its practices are humane, helping to build small communities in third-world countries. After the interview, and out of pure excitement, I shared with Adina and her mom that I had done a great job. I expected the offer. It never came and that devastated me.

They cut me at the knee and the sting of their betrayal threatens to cave my body.

"Why would they do that to me? I never hurt them in any way."

Maeven shrugs. "Except, you did a lot. You have all this potential, qualities, and abilities Adina doesn't. She won't ever apply herself. Part of that is a testament to you, but the other part is that you were not born with a silver spoon in your mouth. Your mom worked like crazy for you and taught you to do the same. Shit, you make your own clothes. Beautiful things too."

Someone brings us the feature drink of the night. I look at it and place it on the holder.

She points her chin at it. "You can drink it. We don't have people doing fuck-shit here."

"I'm just...I can't believe this. How could Adina do this to me?"

"Jealousy. Envy. That's why we're building you back. You always had great things going." She tilts her head to the stage. "When we accomplish that, you need to stand firm and not make the girlie mistakes we all do. Trust only those who have shown they stand behind you one hundred percent and are not threatened by who you are or what you attract. Don't compromise your career for anyone. If someone loves you, they'll find a way to support you without being jealous or crazy because you're winning."

Before I can reply or thank her, the lights drop and, along with them, so does my heart. A crowd of twenty-five thousand people begin screaming his name.

"Rio. Rio. Rio." Chants rev the air.

As if triggered by the fans, his name made of thousands of light-bulbs, shines on the stage.

Maeven's hand latches onto mine. Her fingers are cold.

Yeah, we're all dying right now.

"New Yooooork," his voice croons in his signature sexy voice. Then the beat drops. "Are you ready to shake it?"

"Yeeahh!" we all scream in unison.

"*Vamo a romper.*"

The spotlight focuses on the middle, and when he steps out, the arena erupts into chaos. My face splits into a smile. He opens with "*Cuando la noche llega,*" and the audience answers, "*I only got you on my mind.*"

I'm transfixed. He's swaying his hips in a sexy way only he can evoke. His stage presence, the way he commands attention, the lights playing with the shadows over his face and body, all create an immersive experience. I'm captivated by his movements and how he lures our eyes to follow the outline of all those muscles and the new tattoos that I've yet to fully see. The butterfly on his chest curves under his arm and his ribs and ends on his back. His silken and soulful voice sends goosebumps over my skin.

And the arena is there with him, singing along at the top of their lungs without missing a beat—enthralled, just like I am.

Happiness swells in my chest. Tears fill my eyes, and when I look at Maeven, she is teary-eyed too. As is Esme. We exchange looks and laugh because he did it. He filled the arena and kicked off his tour.

Thirty minutes before the end of the show, Maeven leans over. "When he says goodbye, they're going to come to take us to go backstage. Be prepared because it's always a rush and a mad dash."

I don't take my eyes off the stage.

"New York. Thank you for all the love you've shown me and my new album. It means the world to me. But now, I want to go back in time so I can play Luna's favorite song." He's looking around. "I want to see her dance on the screen and all of you along with her."

The blood rushes through my head as a collective gasp echoes through the arena. The trumpet sounds in, and then the medley of instruments kicks in, and he gyrates his hips. *"Dime Mami, que tu quiere que te haga."* He points the microphone to the audience.

"Que me des duro por la noche y la mañana," the audience yells back.

And before I know it, I'm shaking my hips along with everyone. During the *pa bajo pa bajo pa bajo,* we dip it low as he asks and pick it back up. Hands point to the screen, where I'm magnified for everyone to see.

And his eyes are on me, fanning the heat up my chest. I place my hands on each side of my head and roll my hips in that sensual way he likes.

Maeven leans over. "Are you sure you don't know what he's thinking?"

My heart hammers against my chest. By the time he begins to say goodbye to the audience, I'm so amped to tell him how good he was. Most of all, I'm bursting with excitement to hold him.

The guard comes to escort us to the back, and as Maeven says, it's a mad dash so we can beat anyone trying to leave early. Rio starts singing *Si tu me dejas* with the audience, and everyone sings along with him—in the hallways, the concession stands, and even as we make it backstage.

"I want you close to where he will come out. He'll want to see you," Maeven tells me.

But not even two hundred feet from me is Adina and her friend Carrie. They begin to walk toward us, but there's a rush, and my eyes focus on the muscular build toward me.

Rio passes a bunch of people calling his name. Before I can form a thought, his arms are around me, his sweat-slicked skin warm against me in a tight hug.

"You were amazing. Omg, I'm so proud of you." I'm almost screaming the words.

Then he pulls back, takes my face in his hands, our eyes clashing as a myriad of emotions swirl in his eyes. My throat closes, the air fails me, and I can almost see his intention right before his lips descend on mine. There may be twenty-five thousand in the venue, but in this moment, it's just us. And I'm drowning in my emotions, in him, in us, because I've been wanting this kiss so badly. I let him engulf me in the heat of his body, his natural scent mixing with his cologne, overwhelming me.

He pulls back, and we're staring at each other like it's the first time, even he's tugged into a round of congratulatory hugs.

Niko bear-hugs him and they clap each other in the back. Chico Sparx follows with a tight hug. Then Adina and Carrie step forward.

Adina throws her arms around him, but it's the smug look she turns my way that sets me off. The anger rises from my chest, over my neck, to my head. I flush like a geyser, almost violently. I picture myself snatching her by the hair off him and slapping her right across the face. I take a step forward but a hand wraps around my wrist, pulling me back.

"I have someone I want you to meet." Maeven pulls me away from the crowd, and I let her because if not, I'm going to disgrace myself in front of them.

She waves to a couple of people and pulls me into Rio's dressing room. People are waiting inside. The minute they see Maeven, they scram and close the door.

"I want you to breathe, Luna."

I stare at her but don't say anything. I don't trust myself to open my mouth.

"If you go after her, she wins. We have to keep hitting her where it hurts."

"And where is that?" I yell. "Because she's still winning. In minutes, that image of her hugging Rio will be everywhere, and people will still find shit to say about me."

She holds her hand up. "The tide is turning, and it will all the way. You're winning. You don't see that, but you are. He's putting your name out there as his girl. And you have some deals and offers. She hasn't killed your career."

"But she's got her hands all over him, and he's letting her." I want to stop talking but can't. "After what she tried to pull this morning, trying to have people believe she spent the night with him and now this? I'm so fucking pissed I don't know what to do with myself. We can't even celebrate his triumph without her and her *lambona* ass friend. I know I need to calm down because this is his night." I try to breathe, but it's as if gasoline is being poured up my nose to keep fanning the anger. "How can he be so clueless? Or does he know exactly what he's doing?"

She grins.

And that makes me even angrier. "What the fuck are you smiling at?"

"Babe, you got it bad."

I blink a few times, stunned. "What are you talking about?"

"Let's recap quickly before he gets here." She turns and locks the door. "One, you're mad she's touching him. Because he's yours, that's how you're thinking, even if you don't admit it to yourself. Then, you're trying to fake the funk not to ruin his big night."

"Well, this is not about me."

She rocks her head side to side. "It kind of is. But I need you to calm down because you're bound to say or do something that may give us a lot to clean up."

"I'm not stupid, Maeven."

"You were about to snatch Adina by the hair."

My hand goes straight to my forehead. I was. "I never fought anyone in my life, and I was about to. God, over a man."

"In your defense, she has it coming, and it's not only about him. This woman has been manipulating and fucking shit up for you for a while. I would want to snatch her by her lace front, too."

"I'm so embarrassed I could die. I bet you someone caught that shit on video."

She chuckles. "Stop worrying about dumb things. You got me. If someone saw that, I can make people forget they did. Now, go to the bathroom and freshen up before he comes in. He probably noticed you left."

"He's too busy with—"

The banging on the door makes us both jump. Maeven points to the bathroom. "I'll stall for you. Press a cold towel on your neck. Remember, he ran to you. You were the first person he wanted to hug after his concert. You."

I run to the bathroom and lock myself inside.

"Where's Luna?" Rio's voice thunders through the door.

"Retouching her makeup," Maeven replies.

My heart triples, like it's trying to carve a hole through my throat. I sit on the bench to try to calm down, setting my timer for two minutes, closing my eyes, and breathing slowly.

I'm safe.
He's safe.
Adina is not a threat.
Maeven is right.
I'm at peace. I'm at peace. I'm at peace.

By the time my watch beeps, my heart rate evens out. I stand and look in the mirror. Reapply my lip gloss and reapply it. After one more deep breath, I open the door to find Rio standing right on the other side.

My heart flops, but I push a smile on my lips. "Bathroom's all yours."

I try to move past him, but he blocks my way, forcing me to retreat a step. And another until I'm back in the bathroom.

"I don't think it looks right that we're in here."

He waves a hand. "I don't care. Why are you upset?"

"I'm not."

"Don't lie to me. You walked away from me, and now you're trying to act like you're not hiding—"

"I'm not hiding. I needed a minute, so I took it."

Fire roars in his eyes. "So you took your minute. Now tell me so we can talk about it."

"What is there to talk about, Rio?"

I move toward the door. He leans against it and crosses his arms. "You tell me."

I sigh. "Can we not do this now? Today?"

"If we kill it now, it won't fester."

"It's your day. I want it to be perfect."

He moves from the wall, and now we are close again. "How can my day be perfect when you're not happy?"

His soft tone makes me feel so dumb for thinking about all this shit with Adina, but my feelings are my feelings. "I hate that she walks into our spaces so easily. No one questions that she's here after what she pulled this morning. Not even you."

He opens his mouth, but I stop him with my hand in the air.

"And I'm fully aware that you're in an impossible situation. They came like every single one of your fans, to support and show you love. And that's good for me. I'm just annoyed that I'm annoyed."

"Luna, I don't want her or her people here. This is the fucked-up thing about the business. We have to play politics and sometimes pretend, but I don't forget. The fans mean the world to me. They really showed me love." He rests his hands on my shoulders and pulls me closer. "But you...you've been my support, my anchor, everything."

The air escapes me. Words won't form, so I just shake my head to try to break myself from the spell of his eyes on mine.

He leans and brushes my mouth. My breath becomes one with his. "Before I took the stage, all I could think about was you. Your confession last night. I was so caught up in my feelings that I didn't tell you my truth. I didn't say that I'm already in love with you. I've been fighting these feelings for a long time. The night we met, I instantly felt that connection, but then you turned on me. I forced myself to hate you because you've mess with my head and my heart after you blocked me."

"Rio—"

He shakes his head. "No. Let me finish." He pushes me against the wall and trails kisses from my ear to my chin. "Every song tonight, I kept looking into the audience, around where you were sitting, trying to make you out in the crowd. I didn't see you, but I felt you. It made me so happy when they put you on the Jumbotron. You looked happy and so fucking hot dancing. Tell me you believe me."

He says all this between kisses, with his hand on my waist. His words are making me drunk. His heated touch gets me high.

"I believe you."

I crush my mouth to his, and he presses himself against me. My nails dig into his skin, and I buck against him.

He groans, pulling back.

"I need a shower."

"Okay," I say but kiss him again and don't move.

"You're going to join me?" He tilts his head to the shower.

"Not here."

"Come home with me tonight when we are done with the after-party."

There's enough space for me to breathe, and I'm clear-minded when

I say, "Okay." Because I'm sure this is what I want. No, not sure. This *is* what I want.

He leans into my ear. "It's going to be messy and sexy. You know I'm going fuck you until you're limp."

"Promise?"

He licks my bottom lip, and I open my mouth and catch his tongue, swiping it with mine.

"Go *o te cojo* right here."

I walk out in a haze, the smile so wide it hurts my cheeks.

Maeven and Sel exchange a look, but they smile right back.

"What happened to your lipstick?" my cousin asks.

Rio must have kissed it right off.

I shrug. "I think I forgot to apply it."

Maeven chuckles. "First-world problems."

"Raquel's little saint fucking men in a public bathroom," the familiar voice singsongs from behind me.

We turn to face Bethany and Adina. Huh? *What the fuck is her mom doing here?*

"Fuck off, lady," Sel tells her.

"Watch how you talk to my mom, ghetto bitch," Adina spits at my cousin.

"I'll show you ghetto if you really want to see it," Sel says, moving toward Adina.

I place myself in front of her. "You are all swearing like sailors and lying on my name, but Sel is the one who's ghetto?" I take a step forward, and Adina takes one back. "All of you need to leave me the hell alone."

"Leave. Don't make me have you escorted out." Maeven signals for Tito.

"We'll leave. We came to support Rio. I hope you enjoyed that." She tilts her head to the bathroom. "Because that's all you're going to get." She points at Maeven. "That one's the master of making shit that isn't real look so much like it that it confuses the eye."

"Which is why you and your daughter want my services."

Bethany goes beet red. "You don't want to fuck with me, Maeven. I'll destroy you and this little ungrateful bitch that I helped build."

"You helped build me?" my voice rises.

Adina smiles. "If it weren't for us, you would be nothing."

"If you built her, how come you couldn't do the same for your daughter? Luna got straight As and graduated at the top of her class." Sel throws a finger toward Adina. "That dummy can't even follow simple instructions on a hair color box. You're all just mad because she's doing well, and now she's got Rio while your daughter is still sniffing around trying to get a smile out of him."

"Sel—"

"Luna, hold back your pitbull before we put it down," Adina screeches.

Anger flames over me, and I take a step toward her. "If you touch my cousin, I'm going to forget we were once friends and give you that real Bronx experience you always wanted."

Her eyes go wide.

"What the hell is going on?" Rio asks from behind.

I can feel the weight of his gaze on me, but I keep looking at Adina, daring her to step up.

"Well, the Belmonts want to convince the world that you and Luna were getting down in the bathroom."

He scoffs. "We were there for, like, five minutes. I need more than that."

My gaze snaps to his, and the crooked smile on his face stuns me. The way he's looking at me leaves no room for doubt.

"Good for you," Maeven adds. "I'm waiting for the greatest hits, like how you snuck into Adina's DMs before you hit on Luna."

"That again?" He looks at Adina. "Can you all stop it with that shit? It didn't happen." He turns to me. "Luna knows it, too. She saw the text thread."

I'm confused, but the way he's staring...it's obvious he's trying to communicate something to me. I nod.

"You know those are private conversations," Mrs. Belmont tells him.

"Go ahead and sue me. We'll release everything and see who's got more to lose."

"Go. I got it from here." Maeven waves a hand in the direction of the bathroom.

I take his hand as we walk away, and the minute he closes the door behind us, I square up on him.

"Show me the thread."

"Luna, I shouldn't have said—"

"Show me, Riomar."

My use of his full name makes his jaw go slack, but he grabs his phone from his pants pocket, and hands it to me. "I'll go finish my shower."

With his Instagram DMs on the screen, I scroll all the way back. The conversation is full of Adina fangirling over him. Rio's responses are cordial. I stop at one message where he asks if she's bringing me to Niko's private concert. He continues, mentioning there was a misunderstanding, and he wants to clear the air with me. Adina tells him that I have a boyfriend who's jealous and felt guilty about the flirtation.

I pull out my phone and match the dates. This was the same night I told her about him hitting on me and her freaking out. It was the first time she had ever turned on me like that. She knew it too, because the next morning, she showed up at my house apologizing and admitting that I would never stab her in the back.

The conversations go back and forth. Adina openly declared her interest, but Rio never did or led her on. For months, he asked why I'm so cold to him.

This bitch played me the whole time.

17

Rio

I wrap a towel around my waist and get out of the shower. Just having Luna this close, twice in this bathroom, and controlling myself has been tough. And there she is when I get out, still looking through my conversations. This time, she has her phone, looking back and forth.

This is not good.

"You okay?" I ask.

"She played me." Luna shakes her head. "She told me you were trying to go out with her, but it was her the whole time. My best friend."

"She was fucking Chico before, even that night, in one of Niko's bedrooms. I don't have that many people I call friends, and the ones I do, I would never disrespect. She's not my type. I like thick chocolate and curves for me to crash no matter where my tongue goes."

I say it in a joking-non-joking way just to make her laugh because she looks fit to kill. And she turns those eyes on me, looking as feral as she did when she blacked out. But fuck if I'm not excited.

"I'm pissed the fuck off. Don't catch a stray, Riomar."

"*Coño Mami,* how can I be serious when you say my name like that? Like, *castigame, dame con la chancleta.*"

Her mouth goes slack, and then she starts laughing. She drops her phone. But the sound makes me laugh too.

"*Estás loco.*"

I stand in front of her and reach for her face. "Crazy for your mouth. *Por comerte enterita.*"

I kiss her, and her hands go to my waist. "Me too. But I need to go outside before I get accused of fucking you in here again."

"I think they're daring you. You shouldn't back down and do it. Show them you mean business."

Her bottom lip disappears between her teeth, and my dick springs to life again. She doesn't miss it and hooks a finger on the waistband of the towel and pulls it, freeing my dick in front of her face.

"You should get dressed."

But she takes me in her hand, skimming over my member with her delicate fingers. I follow the trajectory of her pretty pink nails from tip to base.

"I knew it was long, but I didn't know it was going to be this thick." She closes her hand over it.

"Luna—"

She leans, and her breath washes over me, spreading warmth and making me desperate for contact. But she presses kisses all over it. Not just any kisses, wet noisy kisses combined with savoring moans that make all my blood rush down. I need to be in that mouth so bad it's painful.

"*Abre la boca,*" I demand.

The banging on the door has me jumping back, grabbing my pants, and rushing to the shower stall to dress with a raging boner.

She goes to open the door to Tito.

"Are you guys ready? We need to vacate, and the car is here."

"Pretty boy is not ready," she says, tilting her head toward me.

"I'm just throwing my shirt on."

"What the hell is taking you so long?"

I look at Luna, and she has a half-smile on her face.

"Oh," Tito says. "Table that for later. You need to get out there and help Maeven because Sel is dying to lay one on Adina."

"Why are they still here?"

His gaze drifts toward Luna. "They were invited to the after-party by the label."

Luna's face tightens, but she shakes her head. "We're not there for them. Let's go celebrate you."

I put on my shirt and watch, and then I grab her hand.

As we meet our group, someone yells, "After the after-party, we keep going at Rio's place."

Everyone cheers.

I want to yell *fuck no* because tonight is not about all of them. After I get done with this shit, I want to be alone with Luna. But now that I think about it, my place was never going to be the right one. I have my entourage with me. We were not going to be alone, and we need to. I don't want to expose her. I want her to be there just for me.

Take her home.

The thought makes me stop in my tracks. Home. My mom's home. Samaná.

Do I dare do that?

The quickening in my heart, the image of her by the water, the warmth that follows...all of it spells a resounding yes. I don't have my next concert until next week.

When we climb into the car, she turns to me. "Is everything okay? People were talking to you, and you weren't answering."

I nod. "How do you feel about getting away tonight?"

"Where do you want to go?"

I smile. "Home."

She smiles back like she understands. "Okay."

The world sings with me
And I'm back in my own skin

Standing, though still missing a limb
In the moment when I felt alone
In the glare, watched by vultures in the sunlight
I felt your gaze like a warm light shining on me

How does that happen?
How does the light in the dark become balmy on my face?
How do I hold it in place so I can keep basking in it?

Your warm hand anchored me in moments of doubt.
Tus besos strengthened me for the battle.
Tu lengua me tiene prendido.
I want to ride your body hasta caer rendido.
I want to give you so many Os
Hacerte que te vengas
As much as your body can take
I want tears of pleasure running down your cheeks
I want you to fade screaming my name.

I put my pen down, stare at my words, and then close the notebook and tie it up. Next to me, Luna sleeps with her hand on my thigh. We'll be landing soon, but there's a burn in my chest, a roaring I can't explain. It was there last time I came home. It didn't go away until I found my center, but to get to that place, I have to face my demons and giants.

18

Luna

From the moment I woke to the flight attendant coming around to tell us we were descending into El Catey Airport, everything felt different. The smell of humidity was in the air, and it wasn't cold anymore, even with the jet's air conditioning still blasting. The warmth clung to my skin, and excitement, pride, and emotion flooded my body.

I'm here. I'm home.

Sel and I clap as the wheels hit the tarmac, as is tradition. Rio and Tito laugh, but do the same.

After-party, we boarded the flight at 3:00 a.m. We are all tired, but now, everyone is wide awake, taking photos as we ride to Rio's hometown, Las Galeras. The bright sun rises on the horizon, and I take pictures of everything because I don't want to miss a single detail.

Rio is unusually quiet. He hasn't said much since we landed. There's something tense about him, but I don't want to press him. Sel and Tito are in their own world, whispering to each other.

"It's not just us," Rio whispers in my ear.

I look at him and shake my head, touching his cheek. "Let me in."

He kisses my hand. "You're already in."

There's that sadness in his gaze, and I just want to kiss it away, but I hold myself back to give him space.

"We're here," the driver calls out, and we stop in front of a large gate, which opens up.

Rio lowers the window and leans in, yelling, "Julio!"

"*¡Muchacho!*" the guard at the gate yells back. "Bienvenido a casa."

Rio sticks his hand out the window to shake his. "*No vemos mas tarde.*"

We drive down a long driveway that curves around a line of palm trees. The water comes into view, an intense turquoise segueing into teal and aqua, forming a gradient that fades into the sand. It is gorgeous beyond anything I've ever seen, and when we reach the house, it's like a dream in white. It's the type of house you see in a magazine or the movies with two floors, balconies, terraces, and windows so wide you can peek inside from where we stand. It also brings home something I haven't stopped to think about. He's rich.

"What do you think?" he asks.

"It's so beautiful." I look from the water to him. "How do you leave this place?"

He chuckles. "Reluctantly."

We pull up to the front, where security guards walk around. One of them comes to open our door, greeting Rio with a warm smile and a hug. Tito climbs out first and helps Sel. We are the last two to get out, and there's the joy every Dominican experiences when our people come home.

Warm hugs and tight handshakes.

A petite older lady rushes out of the house. "Mi bebé."

Tito rushes to her, lifts her like a feather, and rocks back and forth with her. The noisy kisses he places on her cheeks have my face hurting from smiling so hard.

When he puts her down, she turns to Rio. She's half his size and practically disappears in his arms as he hugs her.

"*Tía* Chelo."

She starts to sob, and my heart doubles because Rio holds on tighter, but the pain is there in his gaze.

"*Te extrañamos mucho.*"

She's telling him how much she missed him without being able to see the agony reflected in his face.

When she pulls back, he wipes her tears so gently. She hugs him again, and then her gaze drifts to me, her eyes widening.

He steps back, his hand reaching for mine. "*Tía*, this is Luna."

Her gaze follows the movement of his hand, and the raised eyebrow says it all. She's questioning who I am and why he brought me here. But she moves forward and kisses my cheek.

"*Mucho gusto, Luna.*"

"*El gusto es mio,*" I say.

Her smile brightens. "Oh. *De la mia.*"

One of mine.

That fills my heart. She meets Sel next and immediately hooks her arm around her elbow, ushering us up the stairs lined with roses and hibiscus. Inside the house is an open-plan area with a direct view of the water.

"Waking up to this view must be amazing," I whisper.

"It is," she says. "Go settle on the terrace. I'll get you some coffee."

"*Tía*, come sit."

"*Después del café.*"

Rio takes my hand, and we go to the terrace where we settle into rocking chairs. Tito and Sel go with his aunt.

"She wants to know who I am."

A smile spreads across his face. "She said it. *Tu eres mía.*"

You're mine.

My pulse quickens, and I force myself to tame it. "She said *de lo mio*. Not specifically to you."

"Tell yourself that." Then he chuckles. "She liked you. If she hadn't, I would have gotten a look. She has been very protective of me since *Mami* died. *Tía* moved down here when she got sick to help me care for her. After, she couldn't go back to New York. She kept my mom's house. It's on the other side of this one. We can walk there later so you can see the entire property."

"Why doesn't she stay here?" I ask without thinking then almost kick myself. He brings girls here. "Privacy."

He shrugs. "Yeah. I need my space to write and make music. I like having people over and partying here, but once it's over, I need to recharge."

"And women," I say, because we are not children, and he's being super coy.

"Not as many as you think. It's a new build."

"How many am I thinking?" I don't know why I'm asking these questions.

He's serious and pinning me with his gaze. "One."

Probably his ex, Perla.

I'm saved from saying anything by his aunt's return. They start catching up and talking about family and the property.

I excuse myself to go to the bathroom and grab a moist wipe to freshen up. When I come out, he's waiting for me in the middle of the living room.

"Let me show you around."

He shows me the rest of the first floor. In addition to the rooms, there's also a bedroom. "Tito's room."

As if on cue, Sel's laughter carries out.

We chuckle and move along. He walks me up the stairs, and it's just as breathtaking as the downstairs area with three rooms, including a studio and an office. Then, he opens the door to a bedroom toward the front of the house.

My breath catches. It's an indoor-outdoor room where the panoramic glass doors have no frames and fold open to create a seamless transition. It's warm, but there's a great breeze. The massive bed, with its two nightstands, faces the water. There's a couch and a sitting table along the far wall.

"Wow. This is so amazing."

"Thank you." It's so cute how bashful he is, or maybe it's more. He seems nervous, his jaw tight, his shoulders tense. *Is it regret for us coming here?* It's kind of soon.

We go stand by the railing, looking out, and for the first time, I reach out, my arm on his back. "Why do you look so uncomfortable? If this is too soon, we can go."

He brings his arms around my shoulders. "Coming back—

"Rio, can you come down?" Tito calls out.

He sighs but presses a kiss to the corner of my mouth. "I'll be right back. I'll explain. Lay out or look around."

He heads back through the room and down the stairs. The sky is quickly turning gray, with storm clouds hovering in the distance over the water. Lightning flickers like a flash of a camera, making me flinch. It's going to rain. That sucks—I was hoping to go to the beach today. There goes that idea.

I walk to the other end of the balcony, which is furnished with an outdoor bed, a breakfast table set, and a fire pit. The balcony panoramic glass doors are open, and on the other side of the wall, there's a huge spa bathroom with a large oval freestanding tub and a standing shower. It's all modern, including the rainfall shower.

Everything is impeccable, as if new.

Man, he's rich-rich.

On the other side, the double-sink counter spans half the wall. There's so much space and perfect lighting, thanks to the window between the sinks. It's a makeup girlie's dream. I'll need to try getting ready here. Through the window, a *bohío*, a small house in the native island style, catches my eye. The teal siding with reddish frames around the windows and door gives it such warm appeal. The roof is made of zinc planks, reminding me of my grandma's house in the *campo*. It looks like...wait, there's a photo of that house at Rio's place in New York. He walks through the door as I wave an imaginary makeup brush over my cheeks while staring at the little house.

"I love your bathroom. It's like a dream."

He walks up behind me and hooks his hands around my waist. "You're a dream right here."

Rio kisses me below my ear, and his body presses against mine. I feel every part of him as he molds himself to me. I let my head fall back and offer him my mouth. He indulges me with his lips, opening his mouth, brushing his tongue over mine.

"Is everything okay?" I ask.

He nods. "The press knows I'm here. They want me to do interviews. Maeven is on the job."

"How did they find out you're here?"

"They always find out, but it's okay. It's more respectful here." His fingers trail along my belly. "What do you want to do today? Do you want to explore the town?"

"I would like that. I wanted to go to the beach, but that rain will be here soon." I hook a thumb toward the water. Then my gaze catches the little house. "Hey, who lives in the casita?"

He lifts his head from my neck and looks at it. "It's my great-grandmother's house. She was the original owner of all this land. When she died, it became my grandma's. Mami was born there."

His voice is soft and colorful as he says it, the tenderness clear.

"It's beautiful. It reminds me of the colorful traditional paintings similar to the photograph at your place. Which is beautiful by the way."

"Thank you." He stares at it for a minute, and shifts in his gaze when it meets mine. There's something turbulent in his eyes, reminding me of the storm looming outside.

"Do you want to see it?"

"Yeah, I would love to."

He takes my hand, and we walk down the stairs. Sel waves from the pool. Tito walks over with two *Presidentes* in hand to join her.

His aunt is in the kitchen with another woman who is prepping food.

Rio blows her a kiss. "I'm going to show Luna *Abuela's* house."

"*No se estén mucho. La comida va a estar lista a las doce en punto.*" His aunt tells us.

Tito pauses to look at us, and then he keeps going. His aunt's eyes are rounded, but she smiles and nods.

Rio leads me out the back of the house. I want to ask what that weird reaction was, but along brown lizard, nearly as long as my arm, slithers quickly across the grass. My heart lurches and I almost jump on Rio's back.

"I hate those things."

He laughs. "*Mariguanas*? They're harmless."

"But creepy AF."

"Don't worry. I'll keep them away from you."

"My hero," I say, breathless, without losing sight of the demon beast."

When we reach the door, we pause, and the two red *cayena* bushes are so charming, they look like a painting. Rio tugs at the chain around his neck and removes it, taking out the charm. He uses that key to unlock the door. I knew it was a key, but I thought he meant symbolically.

And then I remember his words. *It's the most valuable thing I own.*

He opens the door and pushes it, and it's like stepping back in time. It's small, but it has a traditional small mahogany living room set, a settee loveseat, and two individual armchairs. The oval mahogany table is topped by a doily in the same shape. In the middle, there's a vase with roses.

In the corner, there's a seamstress' dress form mannequin with a wire on the bottom with an old measuring tape draped over the neck. On the other side, in front of a tiny kitchenette, is a wooden table and two high-back guano chairs. The embroidered white tablecloth frames the table and features a fruit bowl in the middle, filled with real-looking mangos, oranges, and cherries. He closes the door, and I get a whiff of sweet, ripe mango fragrance in the air.

The fruit is real. So are the roses.

"I love this," I say with my eyes on the black and white and vintage photo on the wall. The bride's long white veil trails down and out onto the floor while the much taller groom holds both her hands as they face each other, smiling on their wedding day. Both resemble Rio but that pales in comparison to the next photo. The young woman in the flowery sun dress standing next to the sewing machine could be his doppelganger.

His mami.

"God, you look like them." I turn to look at him, and I'm caught by the way he's staring at the photos.

And then he exhales.

I touch his face. "What is it?"

He kisses my wrist. "I'm always scared of entering whenever I come back."

"Why? It's so peaceful here."

"It's a long story."

The patter on the zinc-plank roof has me looking up, and then the rumbling of rain outside begins. "I think we have time. If you feel up to it..."

He shows me toward the back, which is sectioned off by a curtain. "I remember so vividly my first time coming here after *Mami* died. I was a wreck. Wherever I went, I felt anger. Here, I felt a presence I couldn't see."

My heart knots as I cross the threshold and blink, because even though the same traditional wood planks are all around, in this room, there's a modern bed, and on the wall, a framed TV displaying traditional Dominican art. It's probably sixty inches. Under the TV, there are video games. On the opposite side, the king-size bed is made with dark-blue bedding and nestled between two nightstands, lamps, and a charging station. In the bathroom, there's a clawfoot tub with a curtain around it on the far end. Lounging clothes—like the sweats and tank tops he likes— rest on an armchair near the bed.

Something occurs to me. "There's air conditioning."

"Yeah, I had it installed because when the sun hits the roof *es un infierno*."

He's here a lot.

"Rio, this is where you stay. This is your real room."

Yeah, he nods but doesn't move from the middle of the room. "This is where my peace is. I just have to get through the first few minutes. I'm always worried I won't feel her, like she's really gone. But once I settle down, I remember: she will never leave. Especially now with you. Thank you for coming with me."

I move to him, wrapping my arms around his chest.

"Thank you for sharing it with me. I'm never going to forget this."

He holds me tight. "We can go back to the main house. I know you like the view, and that's better for a getaway. It's more romantic."

I pull away. "Are you serious? You just opened your heart to me. The only view I need is right here."

His head rears back, his eyes lingering on mine for a few ticking seconds.

"Luna, I love you." His eyes go round as if he didn't know he was going to say that. But he did, and now my heart is racing as if it's trying to escape my body.

19

My heart is in my throat. That's not what I was going to say.

The words echo over the drumming of the rain on the roof. I could try to pretend that I got caught in the moment, but it feels right. *This whole thing feels right.*

And I want to be here with her in the place that means the most to me. I want her body here. I want her. I love her. The feeling is so strong it almost strangles me, and I step back, staring into her eyes.

Without missing a beat, she reaches for the hem of her tank top and flips it over her head. My eyes dip to her tits encased in a lace bra—just the way I like. I can still feel them in my mouth from the effects of the video shoot in my mouth. She shifts her hand, trailing her fingers over them. My dick is so impossibly hard, but I keep perusing down her body, and her hands follow my gaze over the plane of her belly to the button of her jeans. She undoes it and pushes them down past her knees, bending over, with her ass in the air.

"Fuck," I groan.

She slides her panties off next and stands in front of me just in her bra, and it's almost perfect, except for her hair. With one look, Luna reaches up and removes the hair tie, flinging it on top of her clothes.

Her thick curls tumble on her shoulders, her lips parted with want, the thirst in her eyes growing, and her skin glistening. I just stand there, taking a mental photo. I want to hold her in my memory like this.

Then she sits on the bed, pushing back until she's in the middle, and runs her hand down her chest, over her torso, between her legs, and reaches out to me. I kick my shoes off, take her hand, and climb on the bed. The room smells like her, that sweet and tangy fragrance that has imprinted on my nose. I put my knee on the bed and beeline for her pussy with an open mouth and a grateful heart. Because I get to be the one to sucks and fucks her. When my lips touch her folds, she rocks forward, seeking closeness. I flick my tongue against her, and she grabs my hair with both hands.

I swirl my tongue, and she presses my head down, holding me in place and rocking her hips, fucking herself against my mouth. I grind against the mattress, emulating her rhythm, needing the friction.

Her breath grows as loud as the rain and every swipe of my tongue. When her thighs start to tremble against my hand, I hold her wrists in my hands and yank them off my head.

I want to be buried inside her when she comes. I pull back and yank my t-shirt over my head. Her trembling hands try to help me remove my jeans, but I take over and undo them, pushing them and my boxers past my hips. My cock springs out. She licks and bites her lips, flooding me with urgency and I'm ready to explode.

I don't even finish kicking off my jeans. I hook my hands under her knees and pull her closer so her legs are on either side of me, and I spread her. But as I lower myself, I pause.

I don't have a condom. My mouth falls open because I'll die if we have to stop now.

"We're good. I'm on birth control." She's breathless, her tone colored with the same urgency flowing through me.

And I push through her tight heat tunnel, which sends me into a desperate state. I lift her hips, sit back on my knees, and thrust over and over until her head drifts back into the pillow. I'm pounding into her while studying her reactions, letting her body speak to me.

She squeezes her tits, dipping into her bra to fan one nipple with her digits. My mouth should there, so I lean forward and lower the bra on her other tit. When her nipple springs out, I flick it with my flat tongue. She presses it into my mouth, and I suck it, recreating the pressure that sent her over the edge last time. I'm at the perfect angle to give her what she wants and pound her with my cock.

I've got my rhythm going, and as much as the pressure builds, I can't let go. Her nails dig into my shoulder. A guttural scream falls from her throat. It's primal, forcing my gaze to her as she falls back against the mattress. Her body goes still as her pussy contracts at a maddening speed, like she's begging for my cum. That makes me thrust her faster, like I'm losing my mind and all my faculties until a shudder tears through and I explode too, and now I'm the one pulsing into her, giving her every last drop of me.

I lift my head, and she smiles a little.

"Ven," she says, pulling me closer and kissing my lips when I'm on top. "Let go. Let me feel your weight."

My heart goes insane as it pounds in my ears. Her fingers trail circles on my back. And we stay connected until I'm spent and my heart evens out.

I go grab her a wet towel, and Jesus, I'm never going to forget how she looks naked, spread out, with my seed smeared on her pussy.

I drop the towel in the bathroom hamper and come back to bed. Her eyes are glossy.

"The rain is so loud, like a storm."

I drag her against me, and she leans on my shoulder, with her hand on my belly, and falls asleep.

My body begins to follow her, but I'm afraid to close my eyes because I'm at peace and sated like I haven't been in years.

It's all because of her. Because I love her.

And love is the door to losing someone.

Rio

I shower and put on the fresh clothes Tia left me on the chair. Luna is still out. Sound asleep like a lion after the hunt. Mane for days, beautiful, savage, lying on my bed. It's scary how many emotions flow through me. I want to climb into bed with her, but I need a few minutes, or I'll end up waking her up by putting my mouth all over her.

I grab the notepad from my drawer and sit on the armchair, staring at the rain falling. It's always like this. It rains as if it will never stop, and then the sun comes out. I'm relaxed. My heart is at peace. I even slept for a bit. But my mind is a battlefield, and scars are beginning to show.

I put my mark on you.
Etched and sketched on your skin
Drew imagenes de placer
Y luego les dí vida con mi pincel.

Eres la santa en mi escapulario
Y me he convertido en tu mas fiel devoto.
I worship at the altar
Of your face, your mouth, your nalgas, tu toto.

But you're more
You're the storm and the storm master
A word from your mouth calms the waters
A look from your eyes makes my body rage again.

Me muero de miedo
No se que vas a hacer conmigo
Nunca te conviertas en cruel
And leave me without sin tu Abrigo.

Encontrarte no ha sido facil, Mami.
Y me asusta pensar que no te pueda tener.
Pero eres mia
No te suelto sin pelea.

You know who it is.
Still waters run deep
Rio.

I stare at my words, contemplating as I always do when I write, and *shit, I got a lot of feelings.*

The rap at the door is soft and barely there. I close the notepad and place it on the coffee table next to the flowers, then rush to the door so whoever it is doesn't knock again and wake Luna up. I open the door to Tito.

My cousin stands under the rain with a tray of food in his hand. "*Mami* sent this. She wanted me to get you, but I told her you're probably staying here."

I nod, ignoring the knowing smile lingering in the corner of his mouth.

"*¿Y Luna?*"

"Sleeping. Hold on." I take the food and place it on the table, then step out, closing the door behind me. "Where's Sel?"

"With my moms."

"Be careful with her, Tito. She's not a groupie."

He grows serious. "I know. Me and Sel know what's up. Do you?"

"What is that supposed to mean?"

"You brought Luna to this house. The two of you are...chillin', but if she's in there..."—he points to the inside of the house—"it's more than that."

I stare him down, not in the mood to be analyzed. "What are you, my therapist?"

"*No me comas tampoco,*" he says, raising his hands.

I shake my head. It's not his fault I'm feeling some kind of way, and though I am thinking I'm getting too deep, I want to get back in the room and be alone with Luna.

I sigh. "Nah, bro. I'm still tired."

"She's good for you. You're smiling again—and not because you're fucking drunk or high. I haven't seen you like that..."

He trails off because he was there. He knows.

"Since before *Mami* got sick."

He blinks a couple of times and then nods. We haven't talked about her since the day I buried her. Tito was the one who dragged me from the graveside and brought me here. He and Tia sat on the chairs and watched over me for days.

"She's special because you brought her here. Did you tell her what that means?"

I shake my head. "I don't even know what it means yet."

And my face heats up because I'm lying to the best friend I have in the world. But I can't tell him that I love her. I'm not ready to tell him that she fits in there like she belongs. Because right now we're hot for each other, but how long is that going to last? How long until I say or do the wrong thing, and she walks away? How long until my pain is too much for her to bear? *Like Perla.*

Tito makes me look away with the all-too-knowing smile playing on his face. You can't lie to the people who know you best.

I'm about to tell him to fuck off when footsteps approach, and we both watch Sel make her way with two cell phones in her hand and a bag on her shoulder. She's in her bathing suit top, and Tito's eyes bounce along with her curves. He smirks in the same way I do when Luna is near.

"You were saying?"

He doesn't even bother to take his gaze off her. "Not the same."

I chuckle. "You should see your face."

"Shut up."

Sel reaches us, rolls her eyes at him, and looks at me. "*¿Y Luna?*"

I put my hand to my cheek in the universal sign for sleep.

Sel smiles like Tito did a few minutes ago. "You put her to bed, huh?"

I gape at her.

"She's like a guy, I swear," Tito tells me.

"But with all the right parts, right?" She puts her hand on her waist. "Anyway, your mom is mad because you're taking too long. She asked me to bring Luna's bag and your phones. And we need to hurry back so we can eat."

She hands me all of it.

"You're getting in good with the *suegra*," I tease.

"I love her. She's a savage, like my mom. But he doesn't want anything permanent with me," she says, looking at Tito. "I'm not Luna. I'll chop your balls off and feed them to you and your homeboys for sport. Anyway, Maeven wants Luna to call her when she has a chance. Doesn't need to be right away."

"What's going on?"

"Her favorite family is back *jodiendo*. I'm telling you, no one fucks with my cousin. I wouldn't hit the elderly because my mom raised me better. But Adina's gonna catch a fade. She doesn't know it, but she got a date with these hands." She flexes her fingers. "Go make Luna smile. She's been through it." With that, she turns around and shoots over her shoulder at Tito, "Hurry up, your mother is waiting."

"She said so much in one breath."

"*Esa es una sicopata terrorista*," he says, watching her walk away. "Shit, maybe I'm in love too."

I laugh. "You better go. I don't think she's playing. Let's take them out on the town and to the beach tomorrow."

He nods and runs to catch up to her. I go inside and place the food on the table. Then I walk into the room as Luna steps out of the bathroom, her hair dripping, and wrapped in a white towel around her body.

I know my mouth is slightly open, but I can't seem to close it.

"Did I hear Sel?"

"Um. Yeah. She came to bring your bag and our phones. Tito brought the food. You hungry?"

"Yup." But she drops the towel and crosses her room barefoot and naked. "But it can wait. I woke up alone, and I was planning something."

My dick springs in my pants, and I drop her bag on the side and throw the phones on the chair next to me. "It's not too late. *Dime.*"

She moves to the foot of the bed. "I almost got myself off in the bathroom."

"That would have been cruel. I want to be the one to get you off every single time."

"Apágame el fuego entonces."
Put out my fire. Jesus.

I pull off my shirt and pants and sit against the headboard. "Use me like a hose and put out your fire."

She places a knee on the bed and then the other, crawling toward me, wild-haired like a beast on the prowl. She moves between my legs and bends to kiss the inside of my thighs. It sends a spark of electricity through my skin. My eyes begin to flutter until I catch a reflection of her ass on the art TV. The sliver of pink makes my heart lurch and my cock twitch.

I grab on to her hair with both hands, dragging her up my body. But she pauses and takes me in her hand, licking me from base to tip and then tipping me into her mouth. Her mouth is so wet and hot I hiss when she sucks me.

"Así, Mami. Take more."

She mmms, like she's savoring every inch, and goes deeper.

I massage her scalp and try to control myself, but I want to thrust, but I don't want to hurt her. It feels so good. I need to go deeper, and I do. She lets me, but I go harder this time and hit the back of her throat. She chokes, the sound echoing in the room, threatening to undo me. I have to hold on to the sheet so I don't come on the spot.

I pull her face up. "Come ride me."

She lifts herself and straddles me. My hands go to her tits, massaging them as Luna positions herself, and then she lowers herself on my cock, slow and measured.

"Así, cójeme entero."

"Mm-hmm," she moans.

Her eyelids drift closed. Her lips are swollen and wet.

Her hips rock back to front as her hands palm my chest to steady herself. I hook my hands around her lower back and push her to me. Her tits are hovering in front of my face, and I take one into my mouth.

"Suck me harder," Luna begs.

"Lo que tu quieras, mi diosa." I suck and bite her as her hips roll faster.

She grinds hard, taking her pleasure. I feel her eyes on me, and when

I look up, she takes my mouth, and we're a knot of bodies, arms and tongues who become tighter until she explodes and goes limp against me. The clench and release of her walls makes me shudder and robs me of everything.

20

Luna

"I'm not getting on that thing," I say, shaking my head and staring at the motorcycle.

Hell no. I'm not that adventurous.

But Rio smiles. "Trust me. It's the fastest way, and you'll love it. I swear."

I shoot him a doubtful look.

"Come on. I want to show you *El Cabito*, but it's hard to get there by car. You can hold on to me real tight. I'll go slow unless you want me to go faster. You know, like last night."

I shoot him a death look, but then laugh. Yesterday was so good, even thinking about it makes me hot and tingly between my legs.

Tito and Sel will go on one motorcycle, and we will go on another. His security follow us in the Wrangler behind and in front.

We ride at a slow pace at first, but when it starts to feel like we're dragging, I yell for him to go faster, and we do. I'm holding on to him with all my might. Then we get to the treacherous road. I can see why a motorcycle is easier to ride there, but Rio seems so adept, so I put myself in his hands and just concentrate on the *platanales* and all the green trees. We pass houses and muddy areas, but it's obvious they do this all the time. He doesn't even seem fazed at all. We go up hills, and my stomach flops, but he yells, "*Mami, mira pa lante y agarrate fuerte de mi.*"

Look forward and hold on to me.

And I do, plastered against his back with my face against his shoulder, until we make it up. The sound of waves crashing are mermaid cries calling for us to come closer. He speeds up, and we finally arrive at the top of the hill.

When we get our first glance of the sea, I smile, and we stop and park. We enter the restaurant and order *Presidentes.*

Sel and Tito go over to the side terrace, where local art is on display, to take photos and check out the inventory. Sel wants to buy some pieces. I decide to wait until we go into the town.

I look over and see people jumping off the cliff into the water, and I turn to say they're crazy for doing that, but I catch the smile on Rio's face. It's wistful, maybe a little lost in thought.

"You've done that before?" I ask.

He turns, leaning into me, and nods. "Yeah, sometimes. I was a crazy-ass kid. One time, I jumped face-first. I thought that was the scariest jump I was ever going to take in my life." He laughs. "I think my balls shrank back into my body."

I look at the drop and how far down people fall, where the last jumper's head looks like a marble. My stomach takes a dip. "What is it like?"

"Your heart is like a sledgehammer trying to knock out of your chest. The first time, I just jumped. Then, I developed a technique. First, I position myself at the edge of the cliff. I like to visualize where I can land. Then I jump and let myself be still on the way down. Don't fight, just let the water swallow me, and I open my eyes. You're surrounded by this beautiful world of turquoise blue, where it's quiet, and for a moment, you drift down, and then your body pushes you back up."

There's something so magical in his description and the marvel in his eyes. I can almost see it in my mind's eye.

"You make something petrifying sound so amazing. I've never done anything that scary. What can be more terrifying than that jump?" I ask, looking at the insane drop.

He grows serious. "Letting you into the casita yesterday."

The intensity in his gaze breeds a lump in my throat, and I have to swallow to breathe.

"Why was that so scary?"

"It's my sanctuary, the most precious thing I have. Not everyone will understand. It's hard when you've opened the door to someone, and then you have to close it. Would they use it against you?"

I think about his ex. The way Perla talked to the media about his struggles.

He's not the person he used to be, and that's a real shame. I couldn't fix him and wasn't going to drown with him. He needs to fix himself.

I swear to myself in this moment that no matter what happens between us, no one will know from my mouth about the casita or anything else he entrusted me with.

"There are doors that are not meant to be closed once you open them," I say, looking from him to the cliff and back to him. "I would be petrified to jump off that thing..."

"Yeah," he chuckles. "It's cause you're smart. That's not for sane people."

"...But I want to jump...with you."

His eyes go round, and his head shakes. "Luna, it's dangerous. I...I don't want anything to happen to you."

"I'm scared, but you'll be there. You won't let anything happen to me." I take his face in my hands. "I want to see what you see. Experience what you do down there. Share it with me."

He starts to shake his head, but lets a couple of breaths pass, then finally nods. "Okay."

Ten minutes later, I question everything—my choices, the power of my intestines, my sanity, and his. *What the fuck are we doing?*

"We're going to jump together. When the man says go, we push at the same time from our knees. Do not lean forward. We want to go straight down. Point your feet. When you hit the water, don't flail, just go with it and let yourself sink. And then open your eyes. We will swim up."

I swallow and nod, not trusting myself to speak because my heart is pounding in my ears. If I don't die from the fall, I may croak before I jump. But I'm determined to do this.

We remove our clothes and stay in our bathing suits. One of our security collects everything. As we are walking to the ledge, Sel screams my name.

"What the fuck are you doing? Come back. Both of you."

I wave at her like I'm brave and fun and not about to lose my breakfast. "I'll be back, Sel."

"You're fucking insane. Did you convince her to do this shit?" she asks Rio.

"Nope. My idea. Hey, if I die, you can have my clothes, my room, and all the custom jewelry."

"That's not fucking funny," she yells.

"It's really not," Rio agrees.

"Come on," I tell him, like the panic is not climbing the walls of my chest the closer we get.

He squeezes my hand so tightly and lets go as we take our places on the edge. One look down at the drop, the water so far away like a galaxy, and my stomach turns. My heart punches my chest, and my throat is closing by the second. *What if I die?* I've never jumped this high. He's done it a lot.

"Ready?" he asks.

I nod. And I suddenly need to say something to him.

The other man is going to do the countdown.

"One...two..."

Before he says three, I turn to Rio. "I love you."

"...three."

I push off hard from my knees. It feels like an eternity, yet at the same time, like a blink of an eye. I experience everything: the wind coursing through my body, the water rushing toward me, and the inability to open my mouth. I want to scream, but the words don't come out. One second, gravity is dragging me down violently and my eyes are closed as I slide into the water. I count two seconds and open my eyes, expecting full darkness. Instead, I'm surrounded by the bluest, most beautiful silence I've ever known. It's an empty turquoise canvas, and I'm getting propelled up. Just like Rio said.

My heart drops because I don't see him. I whip my head around and he's right there, behind me. His eyes are clear with a smile on his face. He stops in front of my face and brings his hand behind my neck. Bubbles float around us as he pulls me in for a kiss. I wrap my legs around his waist and my arms around him, and we float up with my face on his neck and our bodies entwined.

When we break the surface, I blink against the salt burn, but he's there, and I can't stop staring into his eyes.

"You did that, *Mami*."

With my heart hammering in my chest, I pant, "With you."

"And you said you love me."

"I do."

He exhales and steals my breath with his kiss.

Rio

I speed down the road with the Caribbean Sea straight ahead and Luna's arms secured around me, her hands splayed on my chest, the right one right over my heart. I'm feeling all the things—the adrenaline, the fear, the excitement, and her love.

I love you.

The words followed me down the cliff and under the water. In a world of blue nothingness, she was everything. When I turned, I couldn't help but kiss her and hold her and then let the same gravity that sank us to the deep push us together to the surface.

All I want to do is stare at her, look into her eyes, and see that love. When we climbed back up the stairs, my world already felt different. Even as she got fussed at by Sel, her gaze would find me. I wanted to send everyone away and just go somewhere with her. But it would expose us to people who may want to harm me or get money from me. I don't ever want to put her at risk in any way.

I had planned to take her to Las Terrenas, but I chose Playa Rincon instead. This is more personal, and the people know me. They're more respectful here. Las Terrenas would be too crowded with tourists, and it would turn into a circus. Here we have more control.

When we get to the beach with the soft sand and salty breeze, I'm happy to see there are fewer people than usual. It's a Monday, and not many people come out.

"You know there's a great beach outside your house, right?" Sel says.

"It's different here. You want this experience. There's no *conconete* in the house." And I get to chuckle when her eyes go big. No real Dominican can resist the combination of a coconut bread and a large cookie. The *conconete* here in Samaná is unrivaled, with fresh coconut chunks baked into it.

"Oh my God," Luna squeals, looking beyond us. "LPs!"

LP, short for long play, like the old records, are giant versions of *yaniqueques,* the famous Dominican fried dough sprinkled with salt. They're flaky, crispy, flavorful, and perfect at any time of the day. She and Sel do a mad dash for the vendor like little kids. I signal the security guard who holds the money to go pay for them.

Tito gestures for me to walk with him. The second we are out of earshot, he unleashes on me. "You're a *sicopata*. You know that? You jumped off that fucking cliff again. You know my mom would kill me if something happened to you. How the fuck do I tell Maeven you got hurt when you're supposed to have four concerts next week? And what if something happened to Luna? How would you have lived with yourself?"

All the things I was telling myself. But I know I'll give her whatever she wants. No matter what.

"Relax. Everything's okay. Luna wanted to do it, and nothing bad happened."

"Sel was crying," he says.

I smile at him. "I'm sure you consoled her. She looks just fine now."

His gaze shifts to the ladies, who are now holding more than *yaniqueques.* "Rio, you got something good going with Luna. I like seeing you happy again, but you can't take risks like that anymore."

I blow out a breath. "I won't. I don't think there are any other cliffs we both want to jump off." I look at the women and back at him. His eyes stay peeled on Sel. "What's going on there?"

He snorts. "She's crazy, controlling, and bossy. I don't think I like her."

"Don't like her *pero tu ta aficiao.*"

His face snaps my way, his nose flaring like the warning of a wild horse. Then it deflates just as quick. "Yeah, but I hate when people tell me what to do."

"It's clear you don't hate it that much."

"She's wild," he says like he can't believe her. "She obviously doesn't trust men and already told me she can't be with me because I have to go on tour with you, and she knows you pull too many hoes around. Doesn't trust me or you. She's apparently waiting for you to fuck up so she can lay out."

"*Coño,* she said all that?"

He sighs. "Oh, and it's on sight the next time she sees Adina."

I laugh. I have to, and it comes out louder than I expected, because both of them turn to look at us. Luna holds up an LP and points at me.

"She's bringing you one. Shit, that's real love," Tito says like someone who's convinced he won't get that.

"So you asked her to be with you?"

He shoots me a disgusted look. "Who said I did?"

"You told me she said she won't get with you."

He snorts. "She only said that because she thinks I'm catching feelings for her."

I open my mouth to tell him she's wrong because he already caught all the feelings, but he stops me with a look.

"I know you're my boss and favorite cousin, but I'm going to knock you out if you say anything, Rio."

I laugh again. "I like her for you."

He snorts. "You wouldn't if you knew the plans she has for you if you fuck up."

I don't get to ask, because they reach us.

Luna hands me an LP, and it's still hot and crunchy.

"Let's go for a walk," I say, guiding her in the direction of the river.

"Thank you for my *yaniqueque*."

She laughs. "You paid for it. So, thank *you*."

It makes me smile. "*Mami, yo te doy lo que tu quiera.* I'm happy to give you whatever you want..." I sound so corny, so I add, "And Sel, of course."

Her eyes twinkle. "And Tito. She got him one. We also ordered for the security team."

I throw my arm around her shoulder. "That's sweet."

We fall silent for a bit.

"That's the *Caño Frio.*" I point to the clear water reflecting the sky and the mangrove trees alongside it. "It comes from underground springs. The water is really cold, but it flows over there into *Playa Rincon*. It's warmer there.

"I love it here. A river and a beach in the same place."

"It's a special place for me. This is where my parents met. My dad came on vacation from Puerto Rico, and my mom was here with her friends. Nine months later—don't get hung up on the dates—baby Riomar came into the world."

Her gaze snaps from the water to me. "Wait, this is how you got your name?"

I nod. "My mom was walking down, and they ran into each other where the *rio* meets el *mar*."

"Now *that* is so sweet."

"They both thought so too."

"You don't talk much about your dad, other than the awesome history lessons," she says.

"I spent the school year with my mom, but my summers with him until he died. That man was a scholar and, at heart, a campesino too. He swore Atabey was with him and my mom when they met." I pause and smile. "He was such a great storyteller, had a *cuento* for every occasion. I was ten when he died."

"He and your mom were not together anymore?"

"He loved her, but he was a man of his time with a big flaw: *Mujeriego*. They lived separate lives, but I don't think they ever really got over each other. Then, he died suddenly of a heart attack. We moved to New York when I was fourteen, but she would still send me over to Puerto Rico to visit with the family." I squeeze her shoulder. "What about you? I haven't heard about your dad."

"Long story. He moved to New York because he knew how to use the street drill machine. I was seven when *Mami* and I came to join him. He died the year after." Her words are soft.

"How?"

"He got robbed on the way home. He didn't want to give the guy his wallet. It was payday, and he wanted to come home to us."

"Shit, Luna. I'm sorry." I bring her closer.

Then her fingers flex as they rest on my back. "You know, some days I don't think about him at all, and then something happens that brings him back. When I got drugged, I was dreaming about my grandma, and I heard him calling me. It's like he was behind me, but she wouldn't let me turn."

"Those dreams are fucked up. It's great to hear their voices, but it's the worst waking up to a reality where they're not here."

She looks into my eyes. "Exactly. I missed him like crazy, but my mom is a warrior. She had a kid to feed, so one of my aunts got her a job as the housekeeper for the Belmonts. She didn't clean for long. She became their house manager, and Bethany liked me playing with Adina, so she asked my mom to bring me over often."

Her tone is wistful, like she didn't just go through hell because of that family.

"You cared for them."

"I did. I feel like I've known them all my life and thought it was a genuine friendship, but my mom says I was more like their employee. That hurts like hell but makes it so much easier to accept. You know?"

I nod. "Because it's easier to think of it as losing a job..."

"Than losing someone I thought of as a sister," she finishes.

We are at the edge of the *Caño Frio,* and she puts half her *yaniqueque* in the bag and ties it. "For later. Come on. Show me where the river meets the sea."

We lay our clothes aside, and I get in the water. She puts one foot in and jumps.

"It's freezing."

"*Ven, yo te caliento.*" I hold out my hand, and she pauses but takes it.

"God, it's cold," she gasps, wrapping herself around me.

I cup her ass and press her against me. "I think it's hot."

"*Ni tu te lo crees.*" She goes still with her eyes on mine. "This is almost as cold as the beaches in New York."

I curl my lip. "That doesn't even sound right. A beach in New York."

She chuckles. "Listen, they're the only ones we always have available."

"Well, now you have a place with a beach where you can come anytime."

She smiles at me. "How is this going to work, though? You are always traveling for work. And your tour starts in a couple of days."

"You can come with me," I say, half-jokingly but realizing I mean it.

"I have work too. Now that Morena & Miel is taking off, I want to stay close to it. Plus, I have a job interview coming up with Elevate PR," she says. "But I would travel to meet you."

"You better. I don't want to be apart from you for long." Then, I think of something I wanted to ask her. "Do you really want to go work for someone? I think M&M is a great business."

She shrugs. "Eventually, I want to do that full-time, but I'm young. I want to use my degree and make money. I want to buy my mom a place and for her to quit her building manager job and do something else."

I smile. It's the dream. "It will be the best feeling in the world when you do it. It was the first thing I bought for *Mami* when I signed my first contract. I got it built as a surprise and when she saw it for the first time, her eyes lit up with such intensity. She burst into tears. I'll never forget that... But you know, you don't have to get a new job to do that. You're with me now."

She shakes her head. "Oh no, Mr. Castillo. I want my things, and publicity was my first dream. M&M is a side hustle to use what I learned at home. Plus, *el mundo da muchas vuelta.* Life changes quickly, and we have to be prepared for whatever comes…"

"In case this doesn't work?" I ask, feeling the weight of the words she doesn't say.

"We have to be realistic. I've never been in love like this, but a lot of people who love each other can't be together."

I think back at all the times I've been in love before. The *noviecitas* and then Perla who turned on me when I was already broken. I didn't predict the end until I was almost there.

"You're so proud and smart."

"Let's see what you say a year from now." She brushes her lips against mine. "Come on, take me to the beach side. This is getting colder."

I walk down the river with her until the water becomes shallow. Then I put her down, and we hold hands until we get to the peninsula. The afternoon is fading into evening, and the sun is setting, making its way to the horizon.

"It's so warm." Her smile is brighter than the sun at its highest point.

The guards are following us, and I motion for my phone. Then I take a few selfies of us with my arm around her and then us kissing with the sea as our backdrop.

I point at the moon peeking out, almost blending into the sky.

"That reminds me of the night we first met, when you talked about seeing the two Lunas."

I chuckle and angle us for another photo. "And now I got my photo with the two of you."

Her smile is at odds with her downcast eyes. "I wish I had not fallen for her lies. I'm sorry."

I fling the phone at the guard, and we walk deeper into the water. "Now you're here, and I'm not letting you go anywhere."

We hold each other as the afternoon waves crash against us.

No, I'm never letting anything get between us.

See me
Take me
Make me feel you care
I'm bare
Naked
Exposed to the glare.

The wounds are fresh again—by my choice
Because I put myself out there...again
The pain flares—automatically
The agony is so intense
As I bleed under your stare.

Touch me with your healing hands
Mi Santa
Announce me whole
Mi Angel
Reflect the light so it can reach the dark corners of my heart
Mi Espejo del sol.

Reina de la noche
I bow before you
Perla nocturna
Mi joya mas preciosa
Novia del Cielo
I can't wait for the death of light to call on you.
Faro en la oscuridad
Guide me as I sail this treacherous sea of feelings.

Artemisa de mi corazon
Coyolauhqui de mi espiritu
Ix Chel de mi alma

Mami, eres la leyenda
La mitologia hecha mujer
Still waters run deep
But you shine a light so I can see the way
Never leave me in the darkness, mi Diosa
Es Rio.

21

Luna

I can't take any more photos. I've been capturing the countryside, the coast, and all the authentic sights on the road to *La Capital*. The car is quiet. Sel is lying in the back row, and Rio is sleeping half on me with his hand on my lap. I'm reviewing my weekly calendar to ensure everything is posted as expected and that there are no issues with any content coinciding with negative social media events. It's part of my job to ensure there is no blowback of any kind on our clients.

I post to Morena & Miel, thanking the patrons for helping us sell out of the *Sosa* shirt. It makes me laugh that we were able to sell every single unit except the ones that Sel and I kept. I can't wait to tell her.

"You're not going to sleep?" Rio whispers in my ear, sending goosebumps down the back of my neck.

I turn my head to the side and meet his eyes. Our mouths are so close, and I take the invitation and kiss him.

"I'm too stimulated to sleep."

He smiles. "All I did was lay on your shoulder."

I elbow him.

"You sold out the shirt?" There's laughter in his voice, which triggers a chuckle from me.

"Yup. I bet you they were not expecting that."

"No," he says, kissing my neck. Then he whispers, "I'm sorry we are spending our last day traveling to the city. Zao asked, and it's a good opportunity, especially with the tour."

"It's okay. I haven't been to *La Capital* in such a long time. I can't wait to see Zao again. Plus, it will be fun to see you guys do your thing in the *barrio*."

"He is good to me. When *Mami* died, he came to spend time with me at least once a week while I was here. I didn't want to see anyone, but he would come, and he, Tito, and I would drink beers and talk shit. He was just taking off big time, and he could've been with people who wanted to party and celebrate with him."

"See? Now that you said that, me and Zao are BFFs."

He kisses my temple. "I was planning to lock myself with you in the casita. *Solos*. I have so many things I want and need to do with you before we jump on that plane tomorrow afternoon."

I tilt my head and let him full on kiss me and then lean on his neck the way he was leaning on me before.

"You leave for Cali the day after tomorrow."

He nods against my head. "We are going on the red-eye, and then we have rehearsals for two days ahead of the show. After, we go to Arizona and then Vegas."

"We haven't been that far apart since we started seeing each other."

"I know," he says softly. "When are you flying to me?"

"I have a couple of interviews this week. After that, we can make it work."

"You were only at the one concert in New York, and I feel like it will be weird not to have you at all of them. Like, I don't know how to do this *sin ti*."

He knows how to turn my heart into a puddle.

"You know I'll be watching and rooting for you. I just have to do these interviews. You're going to kill it, and I'll be there soon. I promise."

He hugs me and I end up dozing off.

I wake up to the sound of horns everywhere. I'm disoriented and he says, "Welcome to *La Capital*."

An hour later, after crazy traffic, we arrive at Zao's *barrio*, Buenos Aires. We ride up a hill lined on both sides with houses and businesses. Many home businesses have clothes hanging from the window bars. The *colmados*, convenience stores, are playing music like a club. The kids are running around and waving at the car. It brings a smile to my face. We find Zao at the top of the hill, hanging with a bunch of guys and laughing. He's just a regular guy here, and people leave him alone while keeping a watchful eye to protect him.

When he sees our SUV, he opens his arms. We climb out, and Rio goes to hug him, picking him up off the ground. The little kids come running, and we are soon surrounded by them. Zao tries to pick up Tito, and they both laugh when he can't. Then he comes to hug me and Sel.

"*Bienvenidas a mi barrio*. Welcome," he says, trying his English. "We're filming in the *cañá*."

Rio takes my hand, and we follow Zao through an alleyway between the blue hair salon and the peach façade of the bakery building. Our feet tap against the gray cement road that leads the way into half-paved steps that are partly dirt and covered in moss due to the filtrating water from the roofs. On each side of the steps, there are houses adjacent to each other like rowhomes made of cinderblock and cement, brushed over in more pastel colors that give them personalities like ladies dressed in their Sunday best. On our trek down the steps, we zig zag to avoid the slippery moss.

Rio's hand tightens around mine as he maneuvers us like he does this every day. I'm concentrating so hard on my steps I almost run into his back. When we pause, I look up to find the world has opened up and we are facing a three-hundred-and-sixty-degree hill – a patchwork of yellow, blue, and orange houses like sorbet shades – quilted closely together, some separated by trees and water tanks, and stacked over each other to fill every inch of the semicircular panorama. Beyond are the mountains in their green best.

My breath snags in my throat. This majestic *vista* of humble abodes stitches itself into a tapestry that I'll never forget. I take out my phone and snap photos. It's the only way I can explain to anyone the beauty of this *favela*.

We keep moving down the steep steps down with houses on both sides and people coming out to their porches, yelling for Rio and Zao. We stop in front of a blue house where there's an old lady with the warmest copper brown eyes and a soft smile sitting behind the iron gate that surrounds the porch of her house.

"Fefa," Rio says and goes in to hug her. He slips a hand into his pocket and pulls out some bills and puts them in her hand. He kisses her leathery cheek and then turns around. Zao and Tito do the same. She waves at us, saying, "*Dios te bendiga.*"

"Who is she?" I ask.

"The first lady of this barrio," he says.

I wave back at her, smiling into her bottomless gaze, and her smile deepens. It's another thing that's hard to explain to people who haven't been there. You can sometimes see the love in people's faces without words. How their smiles can fill hearts.

We keep going down the steps until we reach *La Cañada de Guajimía*, a ravine with running water, which has unfortunately also become a landfill. No one seems to notice though. The flat area in front of it is packed with people. Cameras are already set up and music is blasting through speakers.

Zao motions for someone's attention. "*El niño lindo llegó. Estamos listos.*"

"You see?" I say, "I'm not the only one that calls you pretty boy."

"You got your verse?" Zao asks before Rio can answer me, and he nods. "Luna and Sel, you can be in the video in the back."

"When did you write your verse?" Tito asks.

Rio smiles, and it's enigmatic and cryptic. "I sent it to him the other day."

They tell everyone to dance but not make noise as the piano music plays out.

"Zzzzzzao."

"Con Rio," he croons.

They go through the whole song, and then when Rio goes to do his verse, he walks to me, and we flirt as he sings like we did in his video. Then he goes through the lyrics.

They call her sosa
Envidiosas cause they know que es especial.
She's diva
Una fiera
Beautiful, Intelectual
Flat belly, pretty lips y las tetas natural

Cuarto bate, like Judge
Bringing every player home
She's the one to watch, the triple threat
With an ass so epic that it breaks the internet

And everyone goes, "Ooooohhhhhh."

The whole verse is about me, a response to Perla's and Noryel's song.

We have to do the same scene a couple of times so I can stop laughing. At the end, Zao comes to stand by me, and he asks, *"¿Y como es, Luna?"*

As rehearsed, I shrug and go, "Oops," like I did in the video in my bedroom.

After the recording, we go to dinner with Zao, and they catch up while we meet his girlfriend and her friends.

We head back to Rio's. The ride is long, and we are all sleepy. But once we get home, we go to the beach outside his house. It's something we talked about doing before everyone fell asleep on the ride back. I'm on Rio's back, and Sel is on Tito's, and we talk about the next time we'll come here.

We chat and play around for a bit, and then Sel whispers something in Tito's ear, and soon they head back to the main house.

We stay behind, under the stars, and he switches me so we are now face to face with my legs wrapped around his waist and my arms around his neck.

"We are finally alone." His hands tighten on my back, and our lips come together in a carnal way that was inevitable but I've been craving all day. "I haven't had you to myself all day."

"You got me," I say, moving against him.

My head drifts back into the water so I stare at the sky as he kisses his way down my neck. A wave splashes us in the face, and we laugh.

"Let's take this inside." He guides me upstairs to his room inside the big house, and we trickle water across the balcony but go into the bathroom to use the shower. We don't make it there.

We find ourselves in front of the sink, like the first day we got here, but I'm not putting on pretend makeup. I'm pressed against him as he frees my tits from my bathing suit top and rubs them while kissing my ear.

"*Mirate lo bella que estas.* All tanned and wet. Your skin tastes like salt. I'm going to lick every inch of it." His hand sneaks between my legs. "*Si*, so fucking wet."

He kisses the back of my neck, sending a thousand chills over my body. His mouth slides over my spine and down my back. I close my eyes as he slides my panties down to the floor.

"Open your eyes, Luna. I want you to see."

He bends me over the bathroom counter. I almost jump as his tongue slides over my lower back, through the cleft, and parts my cheeks with his hands. My eyes fly open as he licks a trail to my pussy from behind. He kneels, and I tilt my ass up, and he dives in, licking and sucking me until my legs begin to tremble.

"I love it, *salaito asi.*"

He runs his hands up my body, standing, and pushes down his swim trunks. "*Miranos.*"

He pushes his cock inside me and steadies me with his hands.

"*Dime que ese toto es mío.*"

"It's yours. *Cojelo, destruyelo,*" I find myself moaning and trying to brace against the counter.

The sensation is so intense, and I watch the look on his face as he works for it, biting his bottom lip. I'm caught in his concentration, and the orgasm rocks me so hard I let my head hang.

He bites down on the back of my neck and lets himself go.

We shower and put on robes from the closet, and without a word, I take his hand and lead him to the casita.

Crossing the threshold, it hits me that I'm going to miss this place and being here with him, and something cold blows through my chest.

We lie on the bed, naked against each other. I think he's feeling it, too. Then he rolls over me, framing my face with his hands.

"*Dime que soy tu macho.*"

"*Tu eres mi macho y yo soy tuya,*" I say as I nestle him between my legs. "Forever."

22

Luna

"Hi," I say the minute Rio's face materializes on my screen. "I was following the concert footage. God, people love you. How do you feel?"

"Good." His eyes are heavy, like his lids are about to droop at any time. "They showed me so much love in LA. I'm happy. Ficha Mundial is too. They're pulling no stops for the promo and want me to start thinking of the next album."

"That's amazing. You deserve it. But, you look tired, *mi amor.*"

"*Sí.* The jetlag is beating me up." He runs a hand over his face. "But tell me about your day. You did good in the interview. How do you feel overall?"

"I'm excited. I never dreamed that a company like Elevate would want me to work for them. And this is the second time they make an offer."

"Who wouldn't want you, Luna? You're amazing and talented."

My face tingles. "Thank you, *mi amor.* Victor said they've been watching me thrive under the harsh light and carry myself with grace."

"You have. No one has caught those hands."

I laugh. "Not that I haven't wanted to catch a couple of people."

"Right. But your restraint is legendary. So when do you start?"

"This week. They're being super flexible. I'll get to work from home part-time, which will be really good, and I can use the time I would have spent commuting to dedicate to Morena & Miel. Sel will be taking more of the bulk of the business. Thank God she's game. Once I get more experience, I'll amend our schedule as necessary."

"You're going to be really busy." He stretches and leans closer to the camera, watching me with a smile. "I wish you were here."

God, me too. I've been missing him for the past three days like crazy, but can't help teasing him. "Wouldn't that make you more tired?"

A lazy smile curves his full lips, and I feel it deep between my legs. "Yeah, but I would sleep better for the first time since I left you. You knock me out because I work for it. Besides, I would rather make you come than get eight hours of sleep.

I smile back and press my legs together. "That's really good to know."

His gaze narrows. "You sound surprised. I must not have done my job right."

I think about our time in the casita and how he made the stars burst behind my eyelids before leaving while I clung to him for dear life.

"If you did a better job, I would still be lying in a puddle somewhere."

"Yeah? New goal unlocked."

My eyes go to his lips, and my hand drifts down between my legs, spreading them.

"*Que tu haces, Luna?*"

I pan the camera down to give him a full view. He sucks in an audible breath. "*Coño, me vas a matar.*"

I press my middle finger to my clit and rock my hips to rub against it.

"Fuck, baby. I want to be there. You got me so hard."

I tilt the camera to my face. "Show me. I want to see it."

His camera moves down his torso, over the panther tattoo on his belly, to the hard-on outlined on the bedsheets.

"Let me see," I half-beg, half-demand.

He obliges me, uncovering that gorgeous cock, laying fully hard on his stomach. And the flashback is so vivid, so overwhelming, that I can feel it sliding up my walls, digging in, and stretching me.

"Wow. I miss it everywhere, in my pussy, my mouth, even in places I've never had it. God help me." The last sentence comes out hoarse, like a moan, as my fingers circle and press.

"Jesus, Luna." His hand is firm around his dick, sliding down to the tip and back up to the base.

I press and rub on my pearl, transfixed as he strokes himself to orgasm. I'm desperate for more, so I prop my phone against a cushion and rub my clit and my nipples until I come, and my pussy pulses against my digits.

And we both smile at each other.

"Come see me in Miami this weekend." His voice is soft and his eyes glassy.

I nod, suddenly craving him more than minutes before. "I'll be there. *Ahora duermete, mi amor*. You need to be up early."

He yawns and nods. "I can't wait to see you, *mi Luna*."

His. I love it when he calls me his.

It's what I am.

Nothing's ever going to change that.

"*Te amo.*"

Luna

I'm rushing through life today. It's been nonstop. I overslept and had to take an Uber to work with my suitcase because I'm flying out to Miami right after my workday to meet Rio. And that is what's making it all palatable.

Work is a three-headed beast today. Since I arrived early this morning, there has been one issue after another. I don't have an assigned client yet, so they're having me work on ad hoc projects. I've had to write three press releases because the CEO of one of the companies we represent offended their clientele by releasing a statement saying they only cater to certain demographics and their products are not for everyone. All of Elevate has been in a panic since.

A notification comes through on my phone. My boss, Victor, wants to see me in his office immediately. I push to my feet and head to meet him. I knock, and he waves me in while talking on the phone. His square-shaped face is set in a serious expression. His eyes, already too close to each other, but his eyebrows are almost knit together in a frown as he nods and takes notes. Whatever is being said, he doesn't look pleased.

I'm left to look around his traditional corporate office décor, with gray walls and bookcases behind his matching mahogany desk. Awards and books written by some of the authors we represent line the shelves.

He clears his throat, and my attention is back on him. "Thanks for coming, Luna. You're doing a great job so far. You hit the ground running like you've been working at this level for years. It shouldn't surprise me. Maeven Tatis speaks highly of you, but in the PR world, we often make our clients sound better than they are. I'm glad this is the exception."

Thanks? *What in the world of backhanded compliments is happening here?*

"Okay," I say instead.

"All that to say, I have been impressed with your ability to craft messaging and your sound recommendations. Your choices are well-informed, and you keep your ear to the ground. So, I want to assign you a client. It will be under my supervision while you're on probation, but you will be responsible for the portfolio."

A jolt of adrenaline courses through me, making me straighten up even more. *My first client so quickly.* This is great news. I wonder if they'll assign me to one of the female singers. It's got to be Nyxara Solé. I independently drafted a proposal for her and put it on his desk. We can do so much more to further her career.

It doesn't matter, though. Whoever it is, I will make it work.

"Thank you, Victor. I'm so excited. Who is it?"

He adjusts in his seat. "This client has had a challenging history and will require a lot of hands-on guidance for a successful strategic rehab."

My stomach sinks. *Oh crap.* He's going to assign me Killa-Kyra, the boxer and rapper who consistently keeps feuding with everyone online, including friends, while complaining everyone envies her. My hopes are a little beat up but undaunted. I will find ways to channel that fighting energy into pushing her music. Maybe a collab with a boxer or a gym. I could probably also get her to host an episode of *Catch These Hands*, the popular show about sexy street fighters. She would rock that.

"I can work with any client. I won't let you down."

The quick grimace doesn't put my nerves at ease. "I'm glad you said that because I need you to keep an open mind. We just acquired his contract this morning."

His contract? A new client? "I've heard nothing."

Victor clears his throat, the sound causing a weird tingling at the base of my spine. He's adjusting in his seat like the chair is biting his ass. *He's definitely setting me up for something.*

"You see, Luna, this acquisition was kept under wraps. We didn't know if it would go through until the last minute and wanted to keep the media's nose out of it. But now that Thierry Banks is fully part of Elevate, we can share the news with the world. That will be the first task you will undertake under his portfolio."

The blood drains from my face, my fingers shooting to my temples. I couldn't have heard him right. "I'm sorry, what did you just say?"

His face reddens but he clears his throat again. "I know there's a history there, but this is purely transactional. He's a client like any other."

"Except, he's not." My tone is harsh so I pause and take a breath. *Because hell no, this is not happening to me.* "Victor, I don't think you understand. It's not just history. It's deeper than that."

I keep my voice in check, low and soft, trying to find a way to rationalize with him without giving in to the anger that's surging through my chest. Because...*there's no motherfucking way.*

"Yeah, I remember the big public misunderstanding. But no one remembers that anymore."

I remember. I still don't drink in public because I'm scarred by that day. I vividly still hear Adina and her mom telling me to keep my mouth shut, threatening my mom and me. I open my mouth, but he continues.

"Thierry and Adina Belmont are no longer together. You're in a high-profile relationship with Rio. This is a good opportunity for both you and Thierry. Your history puts you at a unique advantage. You have insight into his past, personality, and relationships. It will help you craft authentic content and find him opportunities where he can excel."

This is a hell no. "I understand and trust your judgment, but I think everything you said is the exact reason Thierry and I are not the right fit. We all moved past it, but there's still bad blood with the Belmonts."

He waves a hand. "Don't worry about the Belmonts. They're not going to be your clients. Thierry is. You said you trust my judgment, right?"

No, I fucking don't anymore. But I can't say that to my boss. I nod instead.

A smile flickers and wavers on his lips. "Then trust me. This is a growth opportunity for you. You'll be able to demonstrate not only to me, but also to the agency, that you can handle a challenging portfolio and turn it into a success. You'll have my support and oversight all the way. To prove my confidence in you, I'm also adding Nyxara Solé to your portfolio. I read your proposal and love everything you outlined for her."

The rumbling in my chest, the heat in my skin, the *fuck no* at the tip of my tongue...I stomp on all of it and stay silent. How badly will a refusal affect my career? It's my first assignment, and I'm already telling them that I can't handle it because it's someone I hate. He's going to see me as emotional and take back all those great words he just said. I didn't make it through the last six months only to let the past get in my way.

"I want to say that I have reservations about this—not about my ability to perform my duties, but about the client. However, I trust your judgment here. I accept the assignment, but I will not deal with the Belmonts, only with the client."

Victor nods. "This is a great step for your career, Luna."

And also a pain I'm already feeling everywhere. Rio is going to hate this.

I stand but he stops me. "I'll forward the emails and send the link to the SharePoint folder with the client's information."

I walk in fast steps to my office, not stopping even as someone calls my name. I close my door. My phone, sitting on my desk, lights up with messages. I dive for the first one.

MAEVEN

Call me.

I dial, and she answers on the first ring. "I was trying to catch you before you went in. My contact told me this morning about it and I didn't want you to be blindsided."

My skin is hot as my hands balling into fists. "Too late. I walked into a nightmare, but I accepted that shitshow of an assignment."

She sighs. "As you should. You know I'm not going to sugarcoat this. It's true, you could have said no, but PR companies have a long memory. I knew before you did and I don't work for Elevate, which tells you PR people also have blabber mouths—unless you're me or my people, of course. My point is that you would have immediately gotten a reputation for being too emotional."

"I never saw this coming. Rio is going to flip."

"Yeah," Maeven says. "But he will have to understand. This is your job, and it's just work. You're not going to be out there hanging with Thierry. As a matter of fact, even if you're in the same venue, keep your distance. But on a positive note, if anyone can do this, you can. The last six months have prepared you to handle it. This is the type of portfolio careers are built on."

I nod like she can see me, but I'm not sure. I look around the room, and my eyes land on my suitcase, and for the first time, I dread my trip. Because there's no way Rio will understand this when I don't. I'll just have to explain it to him like Victor did to me.

Like Maeven just confirmed.

But the knot in the pit of my stomach tells me it won't be that easy.

23

Rio

Miami, FL

"Why would you take that assignment?" I say louder than I mean to. My voice carries and echoes throughout the room.

"What do you mean why?" Luna answers, adding, "My boss called me into his office and said he was assigning the client to me."

"They know you have a history with him, and they're making you his publicist. They're trying to capitalize on the whole thing. My real question is why you would let this happen?"

"It's just a job assignment. It doesn't matter who it is. I'm new. I couldn't say no, Rio."

"This is not right. That asshole wants to fuck you. He took the first chance he got—with you almost unconscious and Adina stepping away —to make his move."

What would have happened to her if I had not seen it go down? Why do I even need to explain that to her?

"I understand more than anyone. I'm not going to be alone with him, and even if I am, I'm not getting drugged again. I can handle him. He's a challenge, and it could make my career."

The natural way she responds, like this shit is normal, stings. "Luna, are you listening to yourself? You don't need this challenge. You have so much going for yourself. And you will be alone with him. Maeven is constantly there when there's a crisis."

Why is this so hard for her to grasp?

She crosses her arms in front of her. "It's different. Maeven is personally invested in you. No matter how much of a hard-ass she can be, she adores you. You are family to her. I won't ever forget what happened with Thierry. I don't trust him, so I am not personally investing in him. I am just doing my job."

"It's not that simple, *Mami*. And I'm going to be on the other side of the world. I can't be there to protect you."

She takes my hand. "You don't have to worry about me."

"How can I not? Why don't you come with me? You can do the job from anywhere." It's wishful thinking, but I'm desperate.

She shakes her head. "I can't. I'm expected to be in the office half the time. I don't have the clout of a senior publicist. I still need to run things by a peer mentor in the beginning. I have to earn my stripes.

I close my eyes and grasp at the patience I don't feel.

She tugs at my hand. "I'll fly out as much as I can." She smiles. "I have the money now."

I frown at her. "Do you think that was ever the problem? I could fly you out anytime. If I don't, the label will because you're important to me."

She removes her hand from mine. "It matters to me, Rio. I've never been paid like this."

She doesn't get it. And that's what has me clenching my teeth. "They're using you and what happened months ago to bring them publicity and manage that asshole."

"I'm using them too. I'm building my career from them. I want to see my hard work pay off. I need to make this money on my own. I'm good at this."

"I know. You're amazing at everything you do. I've just been in this world so much longer. Thierry is not the first guy to see an opportunity and try to take advantage. Others have, and they will continue trying. You're a challenge to him."

"He can think what he wants. I'm there to work, and that's it." She runs a hand over her neck. "I don't know what to say to you to make you understand."

A weight falls over my stomach, and I don't know what I can do to make her understand, but I do know this is her career. I know what it's like not to have control. I hate it, but I can try for her. "I don't know if there's anything you can say, Luna. I hate this. I'm never going to be okay with it, but it's your career, and I understand your drive. I'm here for you."

She throws her arms around me. "Thank you."

Her voice shakes, and I press her against me. The knock on the door doesn't tear us apart. Her arms tighten around me.

"I don't want to lose you."

Something cold blows over my chest. "You won't," I whisper. "I haven't yelled, and you didn't black out on me. Is this even a fight?"

She doesn't laugh, and there's another knock.

"One second," I call out.

She pulls back, and there's something sad in her eyes. I can't stand it, so I kiss it away.

"Don't be sad, *mi Diosa*. We are okay. I'm not going anywhere."

She smiles, and as always, my chest tightens. I take her hand, and we head to the door where Tito stands outside.

"Let's go," my cousin says.

But Sel's gaze bounces back and forth between us, with the eyes that miss absolutely nothing.

Rio

There's a nervous energy in the car on the way to the *Ficha* party at Star Island. Outside, evening falls, and the road to Star Island is blocked by fans lining the entrance to the road. It's a beautiful parking lot of luxury cars with access to the view of the sea and million-dollar homes across the water.

Inside, Luna is sandwiched between me and a dozed off Sel in the back of the Escalade while Tito rides shotgun in the front with the driver. Though our shoulders are touching, we haven't said much to each other since we got in the car. Our earlier argument is a ghost, a silent presence sitting between us, keeping us apart—mentally, at least.

As much as I try to get over it, my head is full of Luna's job and her new assignment to work with Thierry. I want to put it away, but it's messing with my head. It's really frustrating because I've been waiting all week to be with her. I couldn't wait for her to get here and be with her, and now we've got this shit to deal with.

Are you going to let that get in the way? She's going back to New York the day after tomorrow. Our time together is short these days, and we won't see each other again for two weeks. I'm going to let this go, because she's mine, and I trust her. No one is going to get in the way of that, least of all that asshole.

I turn, and our gazes meet. Tension is there, lingering in her eyes, and it tugs at my heart because I hate seeing her worried. So, I lean and kiss her lips. A smile curves her mouth against mine, and I drape my arm around her shoulder. Her hand secures me to her as we pepper kisses on each other's lips.

"Damn, Sel is knocked out," says Tito from the front seat.

"She might as well be. We're not going anywhere for a while," adds our driver, an older man with the thickest mustache I've seen in my life.

"So the fans are lining up out here and won't even get to see you guys up close?" Luna asks, looking out at the crowd gathered outside.

I kiss the side of her forehead. "Yeah, *Ficha* wanted an exclusive party with only people they vet. Some artists let *really loose* at these events, and they want to make sure there are no leaks to the media. Phones are confiscated at the door for the attending fans."

"I get that, but these people are here to show their support." She points to them outside. "They should at least get to see you guys."

It makes me smile because her heart is so big. "You're so sweet, *Mami.*"

She elbows me. "*Callate.*"

"You want me to go say hi?" I ask.

I look down, and her eyes brighten. "At least to the little kids."

"Tito, let's go outside."

Tito gets out of the front seat and opens the door for us. "Stay close to the car."

Sel lifts her head. "Where are you going?"

"Go back to sleep. We'll be right back," Luna tells her.

The minute I step out of the car, someone screams, "Rio!"

People rush to us, asking for photos or autographs. I sign a few and take a few photos.

Luna tugs at my hand and points at two young girls holding signs that say: *Lil Sirenas love you, Rio.* They can't be more than ten. I smile and blow kisses at them, beckoning them over. The crowd parts as they approach with their signs. I sign their banners while Luna takes one of their phones and snaps photos of me with them.

When more people begin rushing our way, Tito ushers us toward the car. "Let's go inside. Traffic is starting to move."

Once we're inside the car, Luna takes my face in her hands and kisses me, her lips on mine, hungry, her tongue plunging into my mouth to flick mine. "Thank you."

"*Coño, si te pone asi*, we can just go back out there, and I'll sign more autographs, and we'll go back to the room."

She chuckles and leans against me.

We finally cross the bridge onto the island, and Luna straightens so she can see ahead. The road is lined with palm trees and grass manicured to perfection. We pass mansion after mansion until we reach the massive two-story white structure on a cul-de-sac with 360-degree views of Biscayne Bay, red-roofed massive homes across the water, and the tall buildings that compose the skyline of Miami. There are people milling about on the side of the house, waiting to gain entrance.

Tito parts the crowd for us to get into the mansion. The scent of gardenias is fragrant in the air, I have *mi mujer* with me, and everything is just right at this moment.

Mi mujer? The words astound me. That's what she is, though.

I would've preferred to stay in bed with her, *castigandola* and showing her how much I've been missing her. But I want to do more than just show Luna *cama y bicho*. No, we have to do more than that, like visit new cities and experience the world together. I have plans for when she visits me during the European leg of the tour.

I need to witness her reaction when she sees the Eiffel Tower the first time or walk around Rome with her. She's going to love it, especially when I take her to the stores where she can find a lot of the unique jewelry and pieces she likes. She can curate items for Morena & Miel.

We walk through the gates, where there are dancing lights and loud music playing. Bad Bunny is belting about taking a girl back to Puerto Rico to show her true *perreo,* and the scene inside is straight out of the lyrics. People are *perreando* against the walls and on the dance floor. Bodies are still, but hips are dipping and rolling, as my mom used to say, like food inside a *liquadora*.

I lean and whisper in Luna's ear, "*Ahorita,* we come back here."

"Oh yeah," she yells over the music, her eyes gleaming.

We move to the back of the room, where a massive double staircase leads to a rotunda at the top. Tito leads us up one side. There's a guard who lets us in to the top, and we take a right into the private lounge. This is where artists can greet each other and talk in a more private setting. The second we walk in, a tall man steps up and yells, "*Llego el nene lindo.*"

A smile takes over my face as my friend, Xavier Delgado, known to the music world as *El Flaco,* crosses the room and hugs Tito and then wraps me in a bear hug. He's sporting a buzz haircut and trimmed beard. His eyes are as warm as his smile. One word to describe him is genuine. This dude is the real deal, a friend to the end.

"*Hermano, cuanto tiempo,*" I say, hugging him back.

He looks me up and down and hugs me again. "The setback was only the setup for a comeback, for both of us."

"You look great." I step back and place my hand on Luna's waist and introduce her. "This is *mi mujer.*"

Xavier's grin widens, and he leans to kiss her on the cheek. "*Mucho gusto.* It's a pleasure to meet the woman who made this man smile again."

"*El gusto es mío. Modo Perreo* is still high on my list."

"You're going to like the new one even more when it comes out. I'm going back to the roots." He leans in a little. "You gotta help me convince this one to jump on a couple of tracks."

Luna looks at me and back at him. "I got you."

Tito introduces him to Sel, and Xavier greets her. He then says, while pointing between her and Luna, "*Las primas* that snagged the *primos.*"

We all chuckle.

The women go for a walk around with Tito while I catch up with Xavier.

"I love to see you doing well, Rio. You've come a long way from months ago."

"Yeah, it was a tough road. The thing with *Mami* broke me, but the people who care about me helped me get back." I pat his knee, adding, "Your messages meant a lot to me. I should've answered, and I'm sorry I did not, but I read them, and took those to heart."

"If anyone understands, it's me."

His road to recovery from drugs is well known and praised by all in the industry. "How are things going for you?"

He nods. "Good. Album is almost done, and I hope to be on the road like you. You really are winning, *Hermano.* You're back, filling arenas, hopefully stadiums again, and you got that *belleza* with you."

My gaze finds Luna. She's talking with a woman almost as tall as her with wavy hair and bronzed skin. She's super familiar and then I place her. "That's Belú."

"Si, *La Teniente.*"

Luna is very animated as she talks to her. "My girl loves her music. It's hype and hot, but a call back to the beginnings. We listened to it in the car one day..." I drift off because the idea begins to form in my head along with Luna's words from the that day.

You and her in a song would be fire.

Xavier points at Belú. "She's the real deal. I really meant it about doing a collab for the album, and maybe you can come out to one of the concerts."

"It's been a while since we've done anything together. I wouldn't miss it for the world." I point a finger at him. "Tell me when and where you want me and when I come back to do concerts here, I'll bring you out."

Xavier slaps my shoulder, but my eyes are on Luna and Belú, and I look back at my friend. The idea takes full form. Him, Belú, and me. A marriage of classic and new. A jolt of excitement flows through me.

"Oye," I say. "We can do something really fire with *La Teniente*, incorporating her style El General meets Gen Z. Like something that starts with *Te Ves Buena* segues into 90s reggaeton and mid song flips transitions to Trap and finally Dembow."

His face lights up, eyes wide. "Oh shit. That's next level in the making. Starts slowly and then accelerates rapidly. We gotta do this. Not sure if Ficha is looking to push her that fast since she's still new, but we can try."

"Do you know her?"

He shakes his head. "I was going to introduce myself, but you came in. She's been hanging in that corner the whole time."

"Come on. Let's go talk to her."

We head their way, but as we're a few feet away, Belú turns and walks in the opposite direction.

Luna meets us halfway.

"Where did she go? We wanted to talk to her about a collab—"

"You would have to talk to her manager." Then she grimaces. "And I hope you remember, she's represented by *La Patrona*. Good luck with that."

"This would be great for the culture," Xavier tells her.

Luna nods. "Oh, you know I'm here for it, 'cause I love her. *Pero*, everyone knows *La Patrona* don't play about her clients."

Yeah, Angela Guerra has a reputation for being tough and intimidating. Maybe that's why Ficha isn't pushing Belú like that. Because of La Patrona. The only other person that rivals it is Lucrecia Bravo, my manager. If Angela gets in the way, I'll let Kresh handle it.

I take Luna's hand and head downstairs to the dance floor. Dos|Catorce from Rauw Alejandro plays, and I swear this song is made for us.

"We're like that," she says with her fingers on my face, pulling me closer. "We can read each other. No words are necessary."

I press her closer to me. "I was thinking the same thing. I belong to you, Luna."

"And I belong to you. Nothing and no one is ever going to change that."

And I crush her mouth with mine, brushing my hips slow against hers, and kissing my way to her ear. "We should probably get out of here before this turns into *una porno* like the song hints."

She laughs but abruptly stops and reaches for her purse. The name Victor pops up on the screen. "I have to get this."

Luna steps out onto the terrace, and I signal for Tito. She's on her phone as we walk out of the mansion and get in the car. She's searching for something and then starts typing furiously onto the screen.

"Okay, I sent you a couple of preliminaries. Let me know if you need me to send them too."

She hangs up and looks at me. "Sorry, work issue."

"Everything okay?"

She shrugs. "It's all over social anyway. Adina and Thierry are back together."

"What does that have to do with you?" I ask.

She rolls her eyes. "The Belmonts want a press release."

"You don't work for them."

"I know, but the owner is Bethany's friend, so he's forcing us to do it."

I measure my words. I swore I would be supportive but this is how people in the industry sneak shit in. They start adding things little by little until you get caught up. "Luna, now you have to deal with the Belmonts. Is that what you really want?"

She shakes her head. "It won't be forever."

Just until Thierry creates another fucking mess. But I keep that thought to myself.

24

Rio

I pace my living room.

"When I grow up, I want the mental maturity Rio has developed over the last seven months."

I never wanted to hurl something at my TV screen so badly but my fingers are itching to launch the glass on my coffee table at it. I've been listening to the *Tigueres* and G's podcast for the past ten minutes and growing more aggravated every passing second.

"Shiiiiit, me too, man." The podcast anchor guffaws. "Thierry straight up said he's out to sample the goods first chance he gets."

His cohost pffffts. "And talking about that kiss that everyone saw. I'm risking a relationship for that. That's the type of shit that has all the *tigueres* questioning shit about you."

"Yeah, 'cause Thierry is a big-ass dude. I would think about it twice before I tussle with him. He gets physical on the field. Rio's a singer..."

They all laugh.

"But seriously, he trusts his girl. When you're secure in your manhood and relationship, you don't live scared."

The other man purses his lips.

"Let's recap. Thierry is so bold he knew Luna and Adina were besties, and when Luna was drunk, he made his move, at a concert, WITH HIS GIRL LIKE 200 FEET AWAY!" He yells the last part. "You don't think he'll try to wear Luna down? Couldn't be me." He shakes his head to illustrate the silent hell no.

The heat rises up my neck in waves. I'm so angry I could punch my way through the wall.

That fucker got caught on a hot mic saying if he gets a chance to get into Luna's pants, he'll take it. The convo got released. Luna still feels like this is nothing to worry about. Meanwhile, I'm the fucking laughingstock, a *pariguayo*, trending on all the platforms.

I text Chico.

ME

Where do I find Thierry?

CHICO

At the gym. That fucker is a gymrat, and his team is in a bye week, so he's in town.

Tito is down to go, so we head that way. "Cause fuck this. He's doing too much talking."

"I'm going to make sure he understands Luna is not alone."

Twenty-nine minutes later, we arrive at the gym. Chico lets us in.

Thierry smiles, condescendingly, like he's holding back laughter. "I guess you're here about the sound bite."

"She's not by herself."

"Could've fooled me. She's always on her own when we meet."

The haze of red that rolls over my eyes is strong. "Stay the fuck away from her."

He waves me off. "Tell your girl to stay away. She won't, though, because she's getting paid well, and she gets to stick it to Adina. You probably wonder every day what else she would do for the money and to needle her ex-bestie some more."

"Fuck off. Luna is not Adina, which is why you're after her."

"I mean, I don't have to tell you. But if you keep your bitch close, you don't have to worry about dogs roaming around her."

The electricity that flows through my fist is so strong.

"Big talk when your girl is still in my DMs. Someone should do her a favor because there's no way I'll risk Luna for her. And you felt the same way; that's why you're so sprung after my woman. The only way you could have her is by drugging her, and even then, she was telling you to fuck off."

"Motherfucker." He swings at me and sucker punches me on the lip.

In my mind, I see her that night, out of it, saying no while this asshole cops a feel and kisses her.

It's like he pops me like a balloon, because I lose it and start swinging at him, jabbing him everywhere, the eyes, the mouth, the side. His bodyguard lands a few feet from me, and I'm still punching until someone drags me away.

"*Lo vas a matar*," Tito's voice breaks through, and Thierry is on the floor, grabbing his shoulder and screaming.

Luna

My heart is pounding as I get off the Uber in front of the Midtown police station. There are so many questions and emotions swirling through me. I'm angry that Rio let himself get baited into Thierry and his friends' fuckery. How can he feel insecure about that idiotic fuckboy? There's no way in hell I would ever consider giving him a second of my day other than for work purposes. His asshole friends on the radio are a bunch of loser clout chasers with platforms. They instigate gossip because it's the only way people listen to them. And now Rio is in deep shit.

I'm not worried about the optics. Maeven can create a plan, and I'll do anything to help him navigate through that. It's the charges that concern me. Given his history of fights, the cops and Thierry will likely try to use it against him. Elevate is already creating a plan of action. I sent preliminary statements to my supervisor. While he reviewed them, he asked that I head down here to meet with Thierry and his lawyer.

Maeven is headed this way. We agreed to collaborate for our clients, but I'm still worried. The little voice in my head tells me it won't be that easy.

I walk into the station with the weight of every eye on me. People whisper to each other without bothering to hide it. I keep my face straight and my eyes forward. I spot Hank Brenon, Elevate's chief lawyer, going into a room and move fast to catch up to him. He sees me as he turns his rectangular face with a prominent forehead and geometric glasses to close the door, and holds it open for me. I rush in and stop dead in my tracks. A tall man that I barely recognize as Thierry stands before him. To say his face is bruised would be a gross understatement. One of his eyes is swollen shut, and the other is blackened. His lip is busted. His shoulder hangs in a sling. I gasp, my jaw dropping.

"Jesus Christ," Hank swears behind me. "How are you feeling?"

"How does it fucking look? My arm and shoulder are killing me. That shithead—"

The sound of footsteps echoes closer, and I turn around as Rio is brought in. His hands are handcuffed behind his back. His lip is busted, though not nearly as bad as Thierry's. There's a bruise on his jaw. I don't think, I rush to him. His gaze centers on me, and there's something there. Chagrin? An apology?

"Luna," Thierry calls.

I ignore him and get closer to Rio. "Maeven is on the way with Esme. Don't say anything. I have to go over there, but God, I hate this. Don't talk. Please."

"It's fine," he says. "Go."

I touch his bruised lip. He hisses.

"You need to keep your hands off him," the cop says and takes him away.

I head back as the other two men glare at me.

"Are you fucking kidding me?" Hank asks. He points at Thierry. "You do know *this* is your client, right?"

My spine stiffens. "Yes, I'm aware, and I have already sent statements and a preliminary damage control plan of action. This is your area now."

The look he sends me is of pure disgust. Adina rushes in. "I came as soon as I heard."

Great. *Llegó la que faltaba.*

I take the chance to send a quick text to Maeven.

ME

Are you almost here? He's alone and they put him in a cell.

MAEVEN

Walking in. We got him. HYB.

Handle your business. But how can I? This is so fucked.

As I'm about to turn back to my group, another cop brings in Tito. He shows no sign of having been in a fight. I guess that happens when you're built like Wreck-it-Ralph.

"Hey, Luna." Then he looks at Thierry. "Big as you are, he fucked you up."

"Tito, that's not helping."

He winks at me, and they put him in the same cell as Rio.

My mind races, and when Esme and Maeven walk in with a tall, muscular man, I finally breathe. Both nod at me and the group, and the man leads them to where Rio and Thierry are.

"The shenanigans have already started."

"What are you talking about?" asks Adina. Has her voice always been this fucking annoying?

Hank tilts his head to where they disappeared. "They just walked in with Captain Jamie Byrnes. That Maeven is a bag of tricks."

And you're a nasty piece of shit.

My phone rings, and it's my supervisor, Victor. I pull away and answer.

"Did you forget who you work for, Luna? You ran to the person who assaulted our client," he says.

It's the rebuking tone that strikes a nerve, and I side-eye Hank. "I didn't run to anyone. I went to speak to my significant other, who did not assault anyone. The video clearly shows who threw the first punch."

"Does that mean you can't do your job? Do you need a reminder of what your priorities are?"

I see red but force a breath. "No, I do not. I'm doing my job, which does not require me to believe the BS just to be able to spin it to get Thierry out of this mess."

"Get to it." And with that, he hangs up on me.

The captain steps out of the other room and waves us down. One officer comes and lets Thierry out of the cell. We are all ushered into the room.

Rio and his team are on one side, and we stand across the way. He's staring at me, and I at him.

"I thought you may want a private room to see if you can work this out without police intervention. No one is above the law, but I can see this being a big misunderstanding and the heat of the moment getting in the way. I'm going to give you some time to try to come to a resolution before this escalates."

Once he's out, Esme looks at Hank. "Let's not make this more complicated than it needs to be. It was an angry moment for these two gentlemen, and now it's over. The venue just wants the damage repaired as they're already profiting from today's event. We can split the cost, then retreat to our respective corners of the world. Our two very fine publicists can do damage control."

Hank's laughter resembles a weasel squeak. "You have to be joking. In what universe do you think we would fall for that? Look at what your client did to mine." He points at Thierry. "He won't be able to play for a few weeks. These are charges accompanied by a lawsuit, not a compromise."

Nonplussed, Esme smiles. "We can help with the medical bills if Thierry needs it. There's no need to go to court when the gym is willing to accept the compensation. Plus, do you really want to sue when the silent witness—the camera on the wall—shows your client launching at mine?"

"Yours came to fight and baited Thierry."

Esme's shoulders lift delicately. "Speculation as to motive, Hank?

Rio and Tito went there invited by a friend because they're interested in a membership. It was a misunderstanding at best, especially since Thierry assaulted him first. He felt he had to defend himself. Still we are trying to resolve this amicably. You should probably discuss with your client before you make hasty decisions."

We go outside of the room.

"If I'm not able to play for weeks, that motherfucker shouldn't get to go on tour," Thierry tells Hank.

"We can go ahead with the charges and request that he surrenders his passport. We can drop it later if you choose to."

The flare of red over my eyelids is too intense I need to breathe and force my body to calm down.

"He's a savage. Look at what he did to you, babe," Adina whines.

"He said you were in his DMs. That's what set me off." His tone is downright accusatory.

"Shhhh," Hank admonishes. "Stop admitting to shit."

"It's on video," I remind him.

"Videos can be manipulated."

"It's a lie. He's in my DMs, not the other way around." But Adina plays with her ear like she always does when she's lying.

This bitch. She and Thierry are out to hurt Rio, and with this sleazy-ass lawyer, they may succeed, given how Rio beat him. If he can't leave the country, he'll have to cancel the tour. I can't let that happen. As stupid as he was for not controlling himself, I'm not letting these three play with his career after the comeback he's had.

"I have not told my story to anyone yet."

All three turn to me.

"What story?" Hank asks.

"Tell him to give us a minute," I tell Thierry.

And though Hank protests, Thierry waves him away.

Once he's out of earshot, I say, "You're going to agree to Esme's terms, or I will be doing a little sharing of my own. To be specific, I'll talk about what happened the night of Chico's concert, how you fed me those drinks, and your mom's manipulations, and how this idiot tried to take advantage of me." I look at Adina as I say it all.

"Lulu, you can't."

"Don't fucking call me that," I snap. "And yes, I definitely can. We don't have an NDA, and I'm not scared of what your mom can do to me or my mom anymore."

"This is blackmail," Thierry says through clenched teeth.

I manage a smile. "How can it be when I work for you? Let's recap. You got your homeboys to bait Rio with their shitty podcast, and then you threw the first punch because you got caught up in the heat of the moment."

"Are you crazy? I didn't put those guys up to that."

Adina's hand travels to her ear, and she looks away.

Yup, got her.

"Well?" I ask.

"Fine," Thierry says and calls Hank back.

It takes a few minutes to convince his lawyer, but we go back to the room.

Esme flips her hands and asks, "What did we decide?"

Hank turns a sour look my way. "Go ahead. You seem to know more than I do."

"Thierry will cover his own medical bills. Your client must replace the mirrors and damaged equipment," I say, without looking at Rio. "Maeven and I can prepare twin statements."

I walk out, followed by my group. Hank turns to me outside the room and whispers, "Start looking for another job. Victor will hear from me."

Adina faces me. "We held up our end. Now you keep your mouth shut, *Luna*."

They walk out, leaving me alone. My heart is pounding fast. My decision echoes in my ear, and the consequences are already dragging my body down.

What the fuck did you do, Luna?

What I had to. For him.

And that's when the anger really hits. This is Rio's fault. He couldn't control himself, and I think I just ruined my career to help him.

Because I couldn't bear the thought of this bringing him down.

And now you're the one going down. It will look as if I couldn't cut it. Victor is probably calling for the pink slip as we speak.

Rio and his team walk out. Our gazes cross, and I pivot, heading for the door.

"Luna." He rushes after me. I throw a hand up before he can come any closer.

"I can't talk to you right now. I'll call you later."

I walk out into the summer air. It's hot as hell and feels like I'm in a swamp cloud. I don't even call an Uber as I take the first set of stairs down into the subway.

He knows how important this job is to me, and he let himself get baited into this dumb fight. He doesn't even look like he regrets it, while I'm on the verge of losing my dream job. I didn't think twice about putting myself on the line to defend him, and he didn't think about me once before he got into this shit.

Now I'm pissed.

Rio

I keep staring at my phone, only half listening to Esme's instructions. Sel arrived minutes after we came home. She's alone, and Luna is not answering any of us.

She stands in front of Tito and me. "I'm not sure if anyone told you a million times, but the two of you are idiots."

Tito folds his arms in front of himself. "Were we supposed to let them beat us, Sel? He swung at Rio."

A light crosses over Sel's eyes, but she turns a stone-faced look at my cousin. "Do I look like a fucking cop? No, right? Then don't bullshit me, Tito. Do you think we're all stupid? You morons went there to bait him." She turns to me. "I mean, you did a good job. The idiot fell for it.

But now you got in hot water again." She points at me. "Not only that, but you're probably going to get Luna fired."

"What are you talking about?" I ask.

She rolls her eyes. "Are you dumb? How do you think she got them to drop the charges?"

"She blackmailed them," says Maeven, walking back in the room. "She used the night of the concert."

I swallow the lump in my throat. "They can sue her."

Not that I will let that happen, and if they do, I'll pay whatever I need to. This is not going to bleed on her.

Maeven grunts. "They can, but they won't because there's a little something called discovery, and that's the one thing Bethany Belmont is most afraid of in the world. In discovery, lots of things can come to light. So Luna is safe there, but the lawyer went to the head of Elevate because he realized what she did. Bethany is also moving pieces. They're trying to get her fired and blackballed."

"Blackballed?" I ask, my stomach clenching. If she loses her career, I'm going to lose her.

"Luna is radioactive. No one is going to touch her after this." Esme's lip curls. "She turned on her client to save the person who beat the living shit out of him. In what universe does someone who does that get to keep a successful career?"

The heat settles on my neck. "Whose side are you on?"

"Luna's. My disgust is for the two of you. I feel her. We've all done dumb shit for someone we love." Esme turns to Maeven. "I know you got something up your sleeve."

"Victor's not answering my calls, so I had to call in the big guns. Third time ever, twice today, thanks to you, Rio." She sends an angry look my way. "You're going to make this up to me. Meanwhile, we wait."

Sel looks up. "Luna texted me. She's been called to the principal's office and has made peace with whatever happens."

My stomach constricts. "I'm going to go down there."

"Sit your ass down. Luna is going to yank your balls right off if you show your face while she's fighting for her job," Sel says.

Maeven looks at her phone. "Come on, Mel."

Sel turns rounded eyes on her. "Amelia Solis? That's who you called? Jesus, how do you even know her?"

Maeven shrugs. "Mel and I go way back. She's the only one who can help us right now."

25

Luna

I'm almost done with a handoff list of everything I'm working on. I don't know who I'll be passing my items to, but I want to make sure they know where everything is once I'm gone. I should have probably just gone straight home and waited for the call from my supervisor telling me not to come back. I would have preferred that, but it wouldn't be right for me not to leave things in order. It wouldn't be fair to Nyxara. I still want them to continue pushing her. There's also Killa-Kyra. They assigned me her contract two days ago and she's been so excited about our plans to promote her.

The idea of leaving the work I do with them breaks my heart.

My desk phone rings.

"Victor is ready for you." His receptionist's voice is curt.

I stand, smooth my suit skirt, and drop my phone, charger, and the photos of me with my mom, Sel, and the one I've been avoiding looking at since I got here today—the one with Rio in Miami—into my laptop tote.

I want to make a quick exit after my conversation with Victor and go straight home.

I step out into the hallway and make my way to his office. People turn to look at me as I'm imagining they do when guards are escorting a prisoner to the execution chamber. *Dead woman walking.* I haven't eaten today, so no last meal for me. Across the room, I see Hank, and my middle finger itches to flip him off. I shoot him a smile instead and go into Victor's suite.

His secretary looks at me nervously. I smile at her. "Good afternoon, Amy. Loving the pink on you."

She waves me in.

Victor barely looks up. "Sit down."

I do as he says. He finishes typing on his computer, probably requesting to revoke my building access, and looks up.

"I'm sure it's not a surprise that I called you into my office."

"I'm all ears." I'm not going to make this easy for him. He put me in an impossible situation by assigning Thierry to me, knowing the history.

"When we hired you, we knew that you had some celebrity status and connections, but we never expected that would interfere with your ability to perform your job duties."

Riiiight. That's why you assigned me to that fuckhead.

"I don't think it does. I've done my job to the best of my ability."

"You have done a good job thus far. But the way I see it, there's a clear conflict of interest that impedes you from serving our client, and that's a real problem because the people we represent pay top dollar for our services, and you are not—"

His phone rings. He looks at the screen, and his eyebrows shoot up. He holds a finger up as he swipes to answer.

I blow out a quick breath I didn't realize I was holding.

He nods a few times and shrugs. Then he says, "Got it."

When he looks up at me, his skin reddens, and his facial features tighten. His hard glare sets off alarm bells, even though I already know the worst is coming.

"I need you to figure out your priorities, Luna. Your personal life cannot interfere with the work we do. It's not professional, and it's not fair to our clients. I'm not telling you what to do, but if you want to continue growing with Elevate and reaching your full potential, I suggest you take control of your personal relationships so they don't bleed into this. In the meantime, I have approved the communications to go out. Take care of it. We're done here."

If I want to continue? I'm not fired?

My heart is pounding in my ears, and I'm stunned but not stupid enough to question it. "I will. I do have a request."

He raises a brow and scoffs. "*You* have a request?"

I'm pushing my luck, but I'm going for broke. "Can you communicate to Thierry, through the official agency channels, that it is not appropriate for him to make comments of a personal or sexual nature about me? I honestly thought that would be part of this conversation."

He seems taken aback. A couple of seconds tick by, then he nods. "Draft the talking points and send them to me. I will have an in-person conversation with him and follow up in writing. In the meantime, you will continue to represent him."

I stand and leave. When I get to my office, I close the door and collapse into my chair.

I shoot a text to Maeven.

ME

I don't know how you did it, but I know you saved my job. Thank you.

Her reply is quick.

MAEVEN

Don't do that again. We'll talk more later.

My hands do not stop shaking as I start sending out replies to the different media outlets. I jump on a couple of phone interviews. As I grab my bag to go, my phone rings.

It's Bethany Belmont.

I should've blocked her number long ago. Everything in me tells me to let it go to voicemail, but I answer anyway.

"Everyone gets a freebie, Luna. That one was yours. I don't know how you managed to stay employed today, but the next time you bring up that concert business, I'm going to destroy you and your mom. I hope she remembers the NDA she signed."

All that says to me is that she did her best, but I'm still here. So I lean on that and vent my frustration on her.

"I'm not afraid of you, Bethany," I say, using her name for the first time. She doesn't deserve my respect. "I think we both know you have a lot more to lose than we do. An NDA won't save you once all the dirty shit you do is out and accessible to the world. My mom knows better than anyone but I don't need her to talk. I can talk about how I was mysteriously drugged after Adina ordered me a drink. I suspect she knows more than she lets on about that. I wonder if Thierry will keep quiet to save her. Also, don't call me. Thierry is my client. You and your daughter don't need to communicate with me."

I hang up and walk out. As I'm in the elevator, I scroll through my text messages. There are several from Mami, Sel, Thierry, and Rio.

Seeing his name makes my stomach burn.

I answer Mami and Sel and then hop in an Uber home. I need to think before I say anything to him. I haven't had a chance to analyze what happened today. I keep turning it over in my head and blaming him.

But I'm the one who made the choice and needs to get my priorities in order, as Victor said.

When I get home, his SUV is parked outside.

Rio

The Uber pulls up outside the building, and Luna steps out. I reach for the door handle of the SUV and get out. I don't have to call out her name. She's waiting for me as the car pulls away. Her face is blank, not panicked like when they brought me in handcuffs, or worried as it was when she walked in the room to negotiate with my team. There's no trace of the annoyance in her eyes when she left the station.

There's nothing there.

Cold settles in my chest as I cross the street. It makes me want to turn back, but I'm walking to her anyway. I reach her, lean to kiss her, and her lips pucker against mine. When I pull back, the sadness in her eyes hits me like Thierry's sucker punch.

"Let's go inside," she says.

I nod and follow her in, but my feet want to root to the ground. I want to tell her it's okay, that we don't have to do this. Because what's coming is pressing on my spine. I've been dumped before. I know what the end looks like when it looms—tired eyes that have had enough.

Enough of me? Of my shit?

It triggers memories of Perla except this is not dulled by grief. I'm fully feeling this moment. We go up the stairs. The echoing of our feet against the walls and empty hallway is intense. I've never noticed before. The first time was probably because I was coming up to pick her up for the baseball game, and the idea of seeing her had my heartbeat pounding in my ears. The night before the concert, I could only hear the gnawing pain. But Luna's hand was there, guiding me. Today, the sound of every step bounces, rebounds, and unnerves.

Because this is the end.

At the top of the stairs, a few feet from her front door, she pauses.

"Luna." Her name falls from my lips with the need to tell her we don't have to do this. I can just go.

She turns around, and with one look at her face, teary-eyed, I can't say the words. There's no way in heaven, or the fucking hell I know so deeply, that I can walk away from her by my own doing.

She opens her mouth, but words won't come out. She takes my face in her hands and kisses me.

The door to her apartment swings open, and we break apart. Her mom steps out into the hallway with a huge smile on her face. "I couldn't wait until you came in," she gushes and extends her hand toward Luna.

A diamond ring, a huge sparkler, shines on her hand.

"Mami," Luna gasps, staring at it. Then she smiles just as big as her mom and throws her arms around her.

From inside the apartment, a tall, dark man in a blue suit steps out. Luna goes to hug him as Raquel watches. Her smile is full and bright, like someone who has everything. It's a dagger straight to my heart because I'm losing everything. But I step up to hug her because she deserves to be happy.

"Rio." She smiles at me and hugs me. Then she introduces me to her fiancé.

"Congratulations," I say.

"Thank you." His smile matches hers. He has every reason to. "We'll get to know each other better soon."

"We're headed to one of Darren's business dinners, but we will need to celebrate sometime this week," Raquel says then frowns while looking between Luna and me. "Is everything okay?"

No, and please don't leave so it doesn't have worse. But her mom has always been kind to me, and this is a huge moment for her. I can't ruin it for her.

I put my arm around Luna and smile like I'm not bleeding inside. "Yeah."

"We have to celebrate this weekend. Sel is going to lose her mind, and we have a wedding to plan." Her voice is light, but her hand tightens on my lower back as if she's trying to hold on.

"Love you, *Mariposita*." Her mom kisses her and walks out with Darren hand in hand. I remove my arm from Luna's shoulder, and we go inside.

She dumps her purse on the table and moves to the living area. Her back is turned away from me with rigid shoulders. It intensifies the sinking feeling in the pit of my stomach. I cross the room and stand behind her, placing my hands around her waist. She leans back against me, and we're silent for a bit.

I breathe the dark fruit scent of her hair and close my eyes. "You can say it. I know where this is going."

She spins around, and we are face to face, almost as close as we were in the stairs when we kissed. "How can you know where this is going when I fully don't?"

"You do, Luna. We know each other well enough. I put your job on the line and made the world talk about you again. You didn't sign up for this, and Elevate is going to be on your ass. I don't blame you. I would dump me too."

She flinches. "This is not your doing alone. I made a choice today that changed everything."

"Because of me."

"Yeah. But you didn't ask me to. I volunteered."

"To save me, Luna. And you don't need to do that. I have money and people to do that. I don't ever want you to lose your career for me, even if I think you are better than that place."

"I know what you think about the agency and my job, but I told you this is important to me. And obviously, you are more, because I thought nothing about almost throwing all of it away. And I would do it again." Her eyes are clear and focused on me.

"What can I do?"

"Can you stop being insecure about Thierry?" she asks. "Can you be okay knowing I will continue to work with him? Can you ignore a bunch of childish messy men when they question you for supporting me?"

I shake my head. "No. Because it's not about that. I worry about you and what they'll try to do to you."

"Do you trust me?"

"With my life, but you're not the problem. He won't stop coming after you. He won't be able to help himself. He's destructive."

"But I'm telling you none of that matters," she insists. "I took measures today to make sure it doesn't."

"You don't need this job, Luna. You have all the other work you do. You have every cent I own at your fingertips."

"I didn't go to school all those years and bust my ass to get straight A's to depend on a man, not when my dream job has been laid before me, not when I've spent years getting the necessary experience to be able to land it." She shoves a hand through her hair and walks up to me.

She places a hand over mine. "You're not okay with this, and I get it. But I can't sacrifice this for you because I'm going to resent you. This is my dream. You're already living yours. You got built back up to number one, touring sold-out venues all over the world. Now it's my turn, and I'm not willing to give that up."

"I would never ask you to do that, so say it," I beg her. I can't take any more of this.

"I love you too much. I see myself putting you first, and I don't want to be that woman whose ambitions get lost in a man's. I also don't want to be your downfall. You were doing so amazing, and you did this because they used me to bait you."

"Say it."

She shakes her head.

"We don't need the words, do we?"

I kiss her because I can't help myself. "I'm always going to love you, Luna Zaira."

And I walk past her and out of the apartment.

26

Luna

I think I've forgotten what color looks like. The thought almost makes me laugh. It's ludicrous but true. For the past three weeks, I've only been going from my apartment to the office and back. Lots of gray and beige, along with New York City white subway tile, and brick backgrounds that blend into each other. When I'm home, I oscillate between zombie and obsessed, moving around my place like a horse with blinders on.

The vibrant shades of orange, yellow, and red from the trees that line the highway are so bright it makes my eyes feel like they're in a fish tank.

"Where are you taking me?" I ask Maeven as she speeds her way up the Cross County Parkway. "There are parks and trails closer to both of us."

"There are, but I wanted a more private venue. I know you hate the attention you're still getting, and I want you to be comfortable and honest."

"That's not anxiety-inducing at all." My voice is dry, more than I intend.

She chuckles, taking the exit at full speed. Her nifty Lexus 350 handles the curve with smooth ease. "Not my intent. I want to know how you are. We're heading to a safe and well-guarded area to walk and talk outside. You may see one or two celebs, but it won't get out. It's a safe space where people are not photographed or harassed."

We go through a gate where we sign in and park. There are a few luxury cars in the lot.

I look at the entrance to the trail and exhale, my gaze fixed on the colorful forest with vibrant leaves on the trees and ground before me. "It's beautiful."

"It is. So...talk to me. How are you?"

I think of the last three weeks when I have been stuck in my office or my room, online looking for an apartment ahead of *Mami's* wedding. When I'm not doing any of that, it's even worse. I watch the concert feeds that Sel sends me, obsessing over every detail, every expression on Rio's face, trying to decipher how he really is handling stuff. I try to sleep to avoid thinking, only to wake up early and pack or work on Morena & Miel stuff.

"Fine, I guess," I finally say.

She says nothing, but I can feel her gaze burning the side of my head until I sigh.

"Thierry's been busy, so I thank God for that. It keeps my mind occupied."

She shakes her head. "He triggers so many memories of me in the trenches with Mateo; it's wild. But I'm glad it helps you not think about it...unless he's just a mask and you're still thinking?"

"I think about..." I measure my words and shake my head. I can't tell her.

"I'm not just Rio's. I'm yours too." She rips the Band-Aid off by saying his name.

I keep walking like the pain is not about to double me.

"What I'm trying to say," she starts again, "is that I would never betray your trust. You've been cooped up for three weeks, and since Sel is away, I can sub. I'm a good girl's girl." She smiles.

"I do know that about you, but you're no one's sub."

"You said it." She shrugs, and we laugh.

"I'm trying, Maeven. I'm waiting for the day when I don't have to fill every second of my life with something to do so I don't miss him." *Or no longer fill my nights with his performances.*

She waves me on, and I continue.

"I don't get it. We weren't together all the time, but I miss him like a limb. It's like the time I had my finger in a cast and couldn't use it. It was there, and it hurt, but I couldn't move it." I blow out a breath. "When I have a minute to breathe, I wonder what he's doing or if he's okay."

"Well…" she says, "you know what he's doing. You got your enforcer infiltrating the camp."

She means Sel, and it makes me smile.

"She's there for Tito. She's so in love." And even my heart smiles for her because I love to see her happy. Though Sel tries to sound matter-of-fact about it, the truth is she's giddy when she talks about Tito.

"Main objective, yes. But we both know she plans to keep an eye on Rio. I think part of him knows it too, but Tito is happy, and he loves him like you love Sel." She smiles too. "And that keeps an open line to you. And vice versa, right?"

"Yes," I admit, because Sel reports everything she sees. "I worry about how he's handling it inside. I wonder if he feels alone too, because…" I stop because my throat clogs, and I shake my head until it clears. "I don't want to be someone else who abandons him."

"You're not. It didn't work out then. It doesn't mean it won't later on when you are both ready. Normally, I'm so used to seeing breakups that I don't blink, but you two hurt my heart. My comfort is that I know you'll find your way back to each other as long as you both keep an open mind and heal."

And there's that feeling in the pit of my stomach—the same one I got when she called and invited me out last night.

"Why do I feel like you're setting me up for something, Maeven?"

Her lips flatten. "Well, I—"

We hit a windy curve, and two men walk toward us. One is very tall with an athletic body, wearing a matching tracksuit. His skin is a rich, beautiful brown, and his eyes are like piercing honey. He must be at least 6'4". The other man is shorter, but at least 6 feet tall, and has a slender build and a buzz cut.

"Maeven Tatis, imagine finding you here," says the shorter man.

"Hi, Dane. It's good to see you." She intends to keep walking, like she doesn't notice the way he's staring at her.

He isn't deterred. "Let me introduce you to my client, Giovanni Ortiz."

"Gio," the taller man says as he shakes her hand, but his gaze is on me.

Maeven extends her hand. "This is—"

"Luna Santos," Gio says and offers me his hand. It's big and warm, like his smile, but his handshake is firm.

"Nice to meet you." I look at Maeven, ready to get going.

"We will leave you to your walk," Dane says.

"See you around." Gio's eyes are sparkling with unmistakable interest.

We keep walking, and Maeven looks back and chuckles. I follow her gaze, and both men are staring at us. I turn back and look at her, shrugging.

"I'm getting a call by the end of the day."

I frown. "A call?"

"Yup. About you. Giovanni is going to ask for your number. Dane will be calling to try to secure it for him."

"That's weird AF," I say, thinking about Rio asking for my number the first night we met.

"Welcome to the celeb world. Weird ain't the word."

"Dane is going to call about you. He was *bobito* staring at you," I tease.

"*Bobito* is how he's going to stay. I don't shit where I eat, plus I already had one of his friends, and one thing about this girl is that I clean messes, I don't make them. But back to you. What am I telling him?"

I shake my head. "I don't know. I'm not ready for stuff like that."

"Think about it."

"I will, but I think you need to tell me what you wanted to talk about."

She stops walking and faces me. "I'm only sharing this with you because I trust you and you are my friend. I don't want it to blindside you. I'm putting Rio in another contractual situation."

My stomach dips, and I squelch the urge to press my hand to it. I shake my head but clear my throat. "He's dating someone."

"No, Luna. He's on tour right now and is doing a collaboration with another artist from *Fichal Mundial.* They want to push her more, and Rio is hot right now. He's also on tour, and they want to keep the buzz on him. So, it's a good opportunity for them to capitalize. It won't be at the level the two of you had. It will just be pushing the song and doing promo."

I see us at the Knicks game when we were both so unsure but almost kissed. "Are you going to coach them too?"

I can't help the pain in my voice. Her face goes a little red. "Luna, no. It's not like that."

Are they going to kiss like we did in the stadium and the world faded around us?

"Listen to me," she says, hooking a hand on my arm the way Sel does. "It's not real. It's never going to be like it is with you. It's just a promotion tactic."

We finish our walk with what feels like a storm cloud looming over me. I'm sad, hurt, and though it's irrational...betrayed. It hasn't been a full three weeks.

In the moment, I develop a new plan. I need to move on—and fast —because if I see him with someone else, it's going to eat me up inside. When we pull up outside my house, I turn to her before I exit the car. "If Giovanni calls, give him my number."

Rio

I shouldn't send the text, but I'm so pissed I don't care, and feeling reckless enough to scorch our quiet peace, earth, and everything with it. Luna went on a date with some fucking football player, and I'm in Colombia unable to show up to her house to talk to her. She's smiling up at him with all her teeth, on the fucking red carpet of some ridiculous award show. Meanwhile, I'm here, trying not to punch a wall. So I hit the one thing I can: the send button.

RIO

> So much for 'I'll love you forever.' My kisses are still wet on your skin. But you look beautiful, Mami. I wish the smile reached your eyes.

To deepen the wound, these gossipers on TV keep talking about it. I shouldn't be watching, but the venom is too tempting for me to avoid.

The female anchor is giddy. "Luna is a lucky girl. She attracts heavy hitters. They were introduced by their publicists, and the tea is that Giovanni lost his mind for her and asked her to come to the Stars of Tomorrow banquet. You see the way he looks at her. Lord." She fans herself while her tongue hangs half out.

The designer, a small-framed and light-skinned man with black hair and round glasses, resembling Christian Siriano, is also salivating. "Can you blame him? 'Cause ba-*by*, she came to shine. That body is bo-dy-ing in a double-asymmetric cut midnight-blue dress that clings to her body like butter. This is how you bounce back after your ex is already out there soft-launching a new relationship. We're looking at you, Rio."

My teeth are about to shatter from me grinding them so hard.

The woman presses her lips as if she's trying to suppress a smile. "It's the battle of the exes because Katya is gorgeous and sexy, but Giovanni is good enough to eat, and we don't need crackers. I guess Luna said, *you went there and now we're all going to hell.*"

The three of them cackle, and I'm ready to explode. I'm dialing Maeven, who answers on the third ring.

She doesn't even say hello. "I've been expecting your call."

And I go off. "You fucking set her up with that asshole? What the fuck, Maeven?"

"Okay, let's dial it down. We went for a hike, and he and his manager happened to be there. I know Dane, so we made the introduction. When they called to ask for her number, I couldn't say no—"

Her voice is calm, as if she were explaining breathing to someone who's been trapped in an elevator for hours.

"Why couldn't you say no?" I'm almost yelling.

"Because Luna is my client too, not to mention my friend. It's her decision."

"Are you serious right now?" I ask.

She sighs. "Babe, you're in a budding relationship right now. PR is a lot about optics, especially for someone like Luna, who has achieved a small level of celebrity status. She may not be as famous as you, but people know her, and she needs to keep her money flowing for Morena & Miel."

"You know what my budding relationship is. This is for real. This fucker wants her. He's drooling over her, and she's over there smiling like she's..."

I trail off.

"Rio. All she did was go to an award show with him. You're going to be on a song with Katya, grinding and looking like you're about to tear into each other. You can't expect Luna to sit at home. She's too gorgeous for that."

I hang up on her because there's nothing I can say that will end the conversation well. *Is she fucking kidding me?* She's the same person who was almost in tears when I told her we broke up.

My phone pings with a text from Luna, and I know I shouldn't look at it. I should let it sit because it's only going to piss me off more.

LUNA

Congrats to you, Boo. I know a soft launch when I see one. IYKYK

Yeah, the red-hot anger floods me like a cloud. But I force a breath.

ME

Hmm. All I did was go out to eat. You're over there on a formal outing. You win, I guess?

LUNA

Not a competition. Just having a good time.
You should get out and get some sun.
Colombia is too beautiful to stay in and pout.

The fuck-off lingers on my tongue.

Tito and Sel walk into the living area of the hotel suite, and when our gazes meet, she spins around to go back into their room.

"Don't run."

She faces me. "I figure you need Tito because I'm probably only going to piss you off more. I don't want to be put out in the streets in a foreign country."

"Stop trying to be cute." I point at the screen.

Sel shrugs. "It's a date, Rio—a public one at that. You're acting like they went on a getaway to a Caribbean island and jumped off a cliff together."

The images of the Dominican Republic flash through my head, and I have to close my eyes and stop the images because I don't know what I would do if she were to go away with someone.

I would catch another case.

Her phone rings, and she looks down. "*Tía?* Hi. *Bendición.*" She listens and nods a few times and then hangs up. "That was Tía Raquel. She wanted to know if you were available to take her call."

I nod, wondering why Luna's mom wants to talk to me. She's texted a few times to make sure I'm okay but nothing more than that.

My phone rings a few seconds later.

"Hi, Rio. How are you doing? And I mean, how are you really doing, not some pleasant lie you make up for the cameras."

My face tingles because I was going to tell her how great I'm doing so she can go tell her daughter. Instead, I go to my room to talk to her. "I'm trying to handle things maturely and not lose it but making *un puro tollo.*"

She chuckles. "That's the most honest thing I've heard in a while. Life doesn't come with instructions, so we are bound to make messes."

"How are you doing?" I ask.

"Busy with wedding planning and moving my stuff to Darren's

before the big day. I'm happy because I love him and this has been a long journey for us, but a little sad not having my *Mariposita* live with me anymore."

Luna has to be torn about that, too.

"That's going to be weird for both of you."

But now she'll have someplace where she can be private with that fucking idiot. *Don't think about that, Riomar.*

"Yeah, but I don't want to make this uncomfortable. I was calling to invite you to the wedding. It's going to be a small event, just family. Darren and I would love to have you there."

There's something funny in my chest. It's always present since the night she had me stay over and then gave me the blessing I so needed. She's been supportive since I've known her.

"Thank you. This means so much to me. There's a big place in my heart for you. There's nothing I would love more than to be there, but it's your day, and I don't want to make it awkward for you...or her."

"I get it." But her voice is soft and a little sad. "I wish..."

There's a long pause on the line and a knotting in my belly. She wishes we were still together.

"Me too," I admit.

"Hang in there. Just because it's not the right time doesn't mean it won't ever be."

And that's what I keep telling myself, but every day, I feel like the space between Luna and me grows wider. "Thanks."

"*Bueno*, go and make the girls dance, *muchachito fresco*."

I laugh, remembering that Luna said that's what her mom called me when she first heard my songs.

I make a mental note to do better. I will stomp on my jealousy and not let it get the best of me.

I scroll through my Instagram feed and come across Luna's post. It's a carousel with several photos, 'Get Ready with Me,' where she goes from sitting on her desk at home and giving a quick walk-through of her makeup to her finished look in front of the gold mirror.

Ready to celebrate the #StarsOfTomorrow and today.

I go through all the slides more times than I think is healthy. All the photos are of her alone. *Thank God.*

As pissed as I was earlier, I wasn't wrong. There's something sad in her eyes. Maybe it's because of all the time I spent staring at them that I know them like my own. Or maybe I'm looking for clues to convince myself.

Either way, I'm not going to send another text to her about it... but I hit the heart icon and grab my notepad from the stand.

I think of how beautiful she is in her dress and how I never got the chance to take her to a show or walk the red carpet with her on my arm.

There are stars out tonight
Shining bright against the night sky
They try to outshine each other
But you're the stellar one

Reina de la noche
Queen of the night
Con el Brillo mas intenso
Y presencia fenomenal

I watch you from earth
Light years away
Wishing for one more moment
To touch the hem of your dress.

I'm in darkness
You're the light
Tengo hambre y tu eres mi pan
Without you, I know I'll starve.

27

Luna

I can't get enough of Mami's smile. It's radiant and, when she looks at Darren, full of love. It tickles the corners of my eyes, but I blink away the tears. No tears on her big day. That was our agreement because we cried enough two nights ago.

I'm standing on the side, chatting with Giovanni, but I can't keep my eyes off her. I'm looking forward to living alone for the first time, but I'm a little heartbroken not to have her down the hall. And after the last five weeks of my life—shit, after this last year—I don't know if I can take more change coming my way.

"You okay?" Giovanni asks.

I smile up at him. He's really handsome and warm. He was sweet when we went to the award show. I'm glad I invited him to come. It's kept my relatives from asking about Rio.

And you couldn't spend the whole time thinking about him.

"Yes, just happy for Mami and Darren. They've been together for a while, and watching them finally get married is my favorite thing."

"Well, your family is getting down on the dance floor. You want to dance?"

229

I open my mouth to say yes when the song switches. Rio's voice croons from the speakers.

Se que extrañas mis labios en tu espalda.

And I swear it's a flashback because I think of us in his house in Samaná where he, like the song says, ran his lips up my back. I do miss that, more than I would dare to admit to anyone.

Thankfully, Sel appears by my side with Tito.

"*Tía* wants to throw the bouquet because they're ready to head out."

"I'll be back," I tell Gio.

We join the assembly of women who are waiting as my mom turns around in the sleek, long, white, high-neck halter dress. I don't particularly want to do this, but it's tradition and my mom's day. I'm not going to be sour about it.

"How's it going?" Sel asks.

"Good. It would just be great if I could stop hearing my ex's voice blaring from the speakers."

She winces. "Yeah, that's gotta be awkward. I don't know what the fuck the DJ is doing. That's messy AF. But Gio seems nice."

"He's a doll," I say, watching the way he talks to Tito.

"But he's not Rio."

I turn to face her. "He doesn't have to be. And Rio had the chance to be here. Mami invited him."

"He didn't want to make it weird for you." Her voice is unusually soft.

There's a tug at my chest. As hard as I'm trying to move on, during the ceremony, I wished his face was the one I looked into.

"Here we go," my mom yells and starts the count. "One, two, three."

She sends her bouquet over her head, and it's headed our way. I side-step it, and it ends in Sel's hands.

Everyone cheers as my cousin stands there, her mouth open. Her gaze shifts from me to Tito. He looks like he's about to faint. I laugh.

An hour later, I'm in Gio's Bugatti, cruising on the way to my place.

"This car is cool."

"Thanks," he says, brightening up. "It was the first thing I bought when I signed the new contract. I had it custom-made especially for me, featuring red snake leather. It's my nickname."

"Red snake?"

He nods. "Yeah, because they say I move silently like a snake, and red was the color of the jersey for my first team, The Vipers."

"Oh. I didn't know that."

"The fans gave me that name."

"I'm learning so much about you. So, is it safe to say that cars are your passion?"

"Oh yeah. I love everything cars. I even fall asleep to racing videos or the sounds of tires rolling on asphalt."

He's so animated and excited about it.

And I wonder if Rio still falls asleep to the videos of *El Yunque*.

No, Luna, stop.

"Do you ever go to the races?"

He nods. "When I'm not training or in season. I can take you if you ever want to go."

"I've never been, but it sounds like fun."

No, it fucking doesn't, but I need to try new things.

"Is it going to be a problem that your cousin is traveling with your ex?" he asks, and in a flash, the air inside the car becomes charged and heavy.

"Sel is in a relationship with Tito. That's why she's on the tour."

"I noticed that, and that's why I ask. Her boyfriend was cool, but I could tell he didn't have much use for me. Probably because of his boss."

They didn't seem like they talked much.

"Tito is more like Rio's brother," I correct him. "But to answer your question, no, there won't be any problems. I mentioned that I want to take things slow. I don't want to get into a relationship. I'm not ready for that yet."

"I get it. I just want to know the hurdles I have to jump to get to you." His hand rests on my thigh, and though it's not unpleasant, I want to swat it away.

"We are getting to know each other, and I think that's where your worries should be. Friends first, and then we can see where that takes us."

It needs to be different from what happened with Rio, where we went from hate to the deep end of love, literally and figuratively.

He pulls over in front of my new building.

"Friends who kiss or don't?" he asks, leaning closer.

"I...haven't worked that out in my head yet."

"Let me help you because I've got it pretty clear in mine."

Something I've been dreaming of doing for a long time. That's what Rio said about kissing me. And I'm pissed because I shouldn't be thinking about him.

Gio presses his lips against mine once, twice, and on the third one, he opens his mouth, his tongue slipping into mine. It's not unpleasant, but my mind wanders, and I close my eyes and get caught up in the kiss, but it's no longer him I'm kissing. Those are not his fingers at my neck. Or his lips on my jaw, on my cheek, near my ear.

"This is the type of friendship we should definitely have." His voice jars me, forcing my eyes open.

And it's a shock to my system.

"I should go upstairs."

"Let me come with you. We can just watch a movie."

Why does everything he says remind me of someone else?

"No, I'm tired from the moving and the wedding. I won't be good company."

"I'm sure that's not true," he insists. "But I won't press."

I breathe a sigh of relief and unbuckle my seatbelt. He flips up the car door and comes around. He walks me through my building door. I swipe the key fob to unlock the entrance door and kiss his cheek. "Thank you for coming today."

28

Rio

Tito's been sending photos all afternoon and giving me a play-by-play of everything that's going on.

It's a gift and the biggest fucking curse.

Luna's wearing a fitted turquoise dress that clings to her curves, framing her like a goddess—the *diosa* that she is.

> TITO
>
> Sel said L went to hang out with that guy at her place.

That was the text that sent me into a crazy rage and brought me here, outside her building, like a fucking stalker.

Then another text comes in from my cousin.

> TITO
>
> He's not there. He just dropped her off and left.

I barely read the text when I get out of the car and cross the street.

A couple is coming out of the building, and I ask them to hold the door. The man's about to ignore me, but the woman's mouth drops when she sees me. Then, she smiles, and I recognize one of my *Sirenas* when I see one. We pose for a couple of photos, and they let me inside the building. The woman even uses her key fob to let me up on the elevator.

In front of Luna's apartment, I knock on the door.

The footsteps echo, and the light in the peephole changes, but she says nothing.

"Let me in."

She still says nothing.

"I can hear you breathing. Come on. I just want to talk."

"It's not a good time, Riomar."

I lean my forehead against her door. "*Abreme. Por favor.*"

The deadbolt clicks, and the door swings open. She's still wearing the dress, and God, the photos are nothing compared to the real thing. The color is more vibrant in person, and her perfume is bold with dark fruit and rosy notes. It inundates my senses and I want nothing more than to bury my face on her neck and run my nose over her whole body.

"Wow. *Que bella te ves.*" Even as I say them, the words don't sound quite right. "No, you're breathtaking. *Una diosa.*"

"Rio..." She shakes her head, turns on her heel, and walks into the open-concept apartment. It's different from the place she shared with her mom. This is more modern, like her bedroom, with a lot of space between the pieces and a table decorated in a style that the professionals insisted on for my places here and in the Dominican Republic. Behind the green sofa is a large, framed photo of the view of the coast of Samaná. It's one of the photos she took from the hill. It makes me smile.

"It looks beautiful."

"What are you doing here?" The anger rolls off her in waves.

"How was the wedding?" I ask.

"Great. Mami is super happy." She smiles, and her body relaxes. "She was so nervous."

"How long is she going to be away on her honeymoon?"

"Six weeks. They're doing the trip and then going to DR after."

"You won't be with her for Christmas. That's going to be weird, right?"

She's not asking me to sit. We're standing like two boxers waiting for the bell to ring.

"Yeah, we are not used to being away from each other for long, but we were going to live separately anyway. Well, if she had it her way, I would have already moved into their house, but they need their privacy as a couple."

"So do you." The second the words are out of my mouth, I wish I could swallow them back, because a light switches in her eyes, and they go from soft to sharp to murderous.

"Yes, I need my privacy too." She throws the words at me in the same cutting tone.

It irks me. "Where is he now?"

She shrugs. "He had things to do."

With her looking like this? I scoff.

"What?" she asks.

"What could he be doing that is more important than being with you right now?"

"He came to my mom's wedding. That was the important part of the day." She lands the blow easily, and I wish it didn't hurt so much. I wish I had not spent my whole day lamenting that I wasn't the one there to hold her hand as her mom got married, as her life changed.

"He should be here holding you, whispering in your ear..." I let my gaze slide down her hourglass, stalling on every curve of her body. "Kissing you out of that dress."

Her chest rises with her breath. "There will be time later for all of that."

"Fuck, Luna. My eyes are so full of you right now. I could stare at you all day while running my hands up and down your body. I can't imagine having the right to be here and leaving you. They would have to pry me off and away. He doesn't deserve you."

She rolls her eyes. "Or maybe he's just respectful of my wishes. Have you thought of that?"

And my heart quickens. *She didn't want him here.* I smile and take two steps toward her.

"Why didn't you want him here?" I ask her.

"Who said I didn't?"

I inch closer. "You just did. You said he respected your wishes."

"I'm tired. I had a long day, week, and month. I just want to relax in my space, but I guess that's too much to hope for, because here you come to disrupt it."

It's meant to be a jab, but it doesn't pierce me.

"You said you want peace, but you opened the door."

"Because you asked."

"I ask you for a lot of things: a second chance, a kiss, your forgiveness. Can I tell you what I think?"

"Only if you leave right after."

I cross the distance between us and lean to whisper in her ear. "You don't want him here tonight because *tu sabes que el zángano* ese is not going to get it done."

She scoffs. "Are you serious right now? He's not a *zángano ese.* You're just jealous."

"Yeah. I am," I admit. "Because you went and started seeing someone when we were barely over."

"Rio, what is this? You're in a whole relationship."

Her nonchalance needles me. "You know damned well what *that* is. You know it's not real."

She shrugs. "Isn't that how we started? How long did it take for us to break the boundaries?"

"So it's the same with any woman? You're not special? Any woman can bring me back from the place where I felt nothing, where I couldn't love, and make me crave her every second of every fucking day?"

She holds out a hand. "I didn't mean to imply that. I just meant that you could give yourself a chance with her."

I take her chin in my hand so we are eye to eye. "*Como, Luna?* How am I supposed to do that? I don't want her. I don't want anyone else. I only want one body, one mouth, one pussy. And I know it's the same for you."

She shakes her head, trying to pull away, but it's in her eyes as they well with tears threatening to spill.

"Did he try but couldn't kiss you right?" I kiss the corner of her mouth and run my tongue over it. "Or did you close your eyes and pretend it was me?"

She shoves me away. "Get the fuck out."

I'm stunned, but I hit a nerve. It's written all over her blushing skin. "That's it, isn't it?"

"I said get out."

And my stomach plummets because I know I'm right, but now she doesn't want me here. I turn and begin to walk at a fast pace. She's right on my heels. I reach for the door, but she turns me around and throws her arms around me. Her mouth crashes against mine like *a fiera* I always say she is when we're alone.

I push back, staring at her.

Her chest is rising and falling. "Come on. Let's fuck."

My heart lurches. That's not what I expected her to say. "Everything is on your terms. Always."

"Yeah. And just for tonight. Take it or leave it," she says.

I don't answer her with my mouth. I shove the door closed and pin her against the wall.

"I'll take you every time, Luna. *Donde te pueda cojer te cojo.* But I'm going to mark myself everywhere in this place, in every cell of your body."

"Shut up and fuck me."

I crush my mouth to hers and reach for the hem of her dress, lifting it high over her hips. I cup her ass.

"Come on, I'm ready," she says, bucking her hips.

"Did he get you ready?"

"No."

I slip my fingers into her panties. She's so wet and hot. "Who got you like this?"

"You," she screams.

I turn her around and slide her panties down. I don't even bother to pull down my pants. I just pull out my cock and pound her with her hands braced on the wall until she whimpers. I slide her panties off and unzip her dress. She's like a rag doll as I take her clothes and mine off and leave them on the floor.

Then I grab her hand and lead her back into her living room. And I see all the places where I want to have her. I'm going to write myself into every corner of this place.

I sit on her pretty emerald couch and open my legs, inviting her to climb on me.

"You want it? *Ven cojelo.*" It's a taunt, me pushing my luck because she admitted how much she wants me.

And there's that angry look in her eyes. She doesn't pass, though. No, she climbs on my lap and takes a fistful of my hair, crushing her mouth to mine.

Her hands on my hair pull hard, and my dick springs to life again.

"Hurt me, *Mami*. Break me like you did my heart."

She blinks a few times, and there's a light in her eyes of surprise and almost sadness.

"If you're not going to forgive me, fuck me. Use me. I can't fuck her either, so let me use you."

Her gaze narrows, and she bypasses my lips to bite my neck. I open her legs and use the three fingers she loves to prep her and then guide her to my cock.

She moans, and I let her ride me with her teeth clamped on my neck until she goes limp and takes me along with her.

Luna

"Luna, we should—"

I stop him with a hand in the air. "No. I'm not interested in talking, just fucking."

His eyes are round, and there's something almost resentful in the way he looks at me. But he nods and stands.

"Where are you going?"

"Can I have some water?" His tone is testy.

"Look, if you can't handle this, it's fine."

He laughs, and it's a little ugly. "I can't handle it? You must have me confused with your little boyfriend."

"Fuck you."

"You have been, for hours, but you can't get enough!" he yells and then lowers his voice. "And you never will. But, come, let daddy top you off again."

It's like a heated slap over my face. "Let me rephrase that, fuck off." I hop off the bed and head to the bathroom. I jump in the shower and let the hot water slide over me. I'm so hot I should steam the whole bathroom. This is so bad. *We* are bad right now. I'm mad at him like I hate him, but just the thought that I won't have him tomorrow brings tears to my eyes, and I'm glad the water is running and taking them away. The emotion rocks my chest, and I let the water ruin my blowout and run all over me.

When the door slides open, I try to swallow the emotion, but I can't, and then I find myself pressed against the wall of the shower.

"I'm so fucking pissed at you, Luna. But the truth is that I'm glad to be the one that fucks you and makes you come. I would rather be on my knees on your bathroom floor, eating you, than lying in someone else's silk sheets."

He kisses his way from my neck, down my chest, palming my tits, and sliding his hands down my torso until he lowers himself to his knees and buries his face in my mons. He kisses and sucks his way to my folds and licks me until I'm whimpering.

And then we shower. While he dries off, I go to the kitchen and get some water for both of us. Then I lie on the bed on my side, and he lies across from me. We're staring at each other like boxers on a rest period. No words, no touching, just gaze to gaze.

I wake up in the middle of the night. He's asleep, with his hand over mine. My chest shrinks, the tightness creeping up to my throat, trying to strangle me. I shake my head and climb over him, bracing myself on my knees, not to put any weight on him yet. When I lean closer to his face, he smiles, and I kiss my way from one side of his full lips to the other. I tease him with my tongue to open his mouth, but it stays closed, as do his eyes.

"I know you're awake."

He doesn't move.

"You were just smiling."

He still doesn't move.

I slide my lips down his chin, kissing down his neck to his chest. His stomach muscles contract as I lap my tongue over them. I peek up, and he's still lying down, eyes closed, and still. My tongue glides over one side of his Adonis V, and my fingers trail down the other side until I have him firm in my hand. His intake of breath is sharp, and I chuckle as I work him over in my fingers.

I tip him into my mouth until he hisses, and my walls contract, almost feeling him there. I savor him, moan, and bring him deeper.

His hands shoot to my head and grab chunks of my hair, pressing me as he bucks into my mouth. My hips emulate the motion against the mattress.

He yanks me off him. In my next breath, I'm on my side, and he gets behind me, flipping a leg over him and pushing into me. Then he turns me to face him.

"Your mouth smells like me," he says, reaching between my legs, stroking me in slow circles. I reach back and pull his head, licking around his mouth until he kisses me.

His hand leaves my clit and wraps around my neck, putting pressure. And this is how I want it—raw, without emotions. I need him out of my system.

The orgasm takes me by surprise, rocking my entire body, making me moan loud while arching against him.

He takes my mouth again and lets himself go, kissing me through his release. It's gentle and loving.

Loving.

Fuck.

But I couldn't fight this feeling even if I wanted to. I surrender to it, letting it overwhelm me.

The buzzing wakes me, and I'm still in the same position, contorted against Rio. His hand is on my tit, and my ass is pressed against his dick. I spot my phone by the pillow. Giovanni's name appears across the screen.

My eyes shut. *Shit.*

"Pick it up," Rio says, kneading my tit.

"No. I'll call him back."

His hand stills, but he kisses my ear. "Come on. He could be worried."

His mocking tone ticks me off. "He knows I'm right where he left me."

"But never again how he left you. Do you think he woke up in the middle of the night, alone, realizing the mistake he made?"

I push away from him and get off the bed. "I'm not playing this insecure game with you."

The phone rings again, and I ignore it, going to the bathroom to clean myself up. We've been messy this whole time, and my skin is sticky with all our body fluids—sweat, saliva, cum. I leave the bathroom as Rio comes in.

When I get back, the phone rings again. This time, I pick it up.

"Are you okay? Did I wake you up?" Gio's deep voice comes through.

"No. Yeah. I'm still tired."

From fucking. God, why did I pick up?

Rio crosses the room and heads to the living room, and my heart starts pounding fast. *He's going to leave.* Panic begins to set in. I can't let him.

"Luna?"

"I'll call you later, okay?"

I hang up, drop the phone on my bed, and rush out. Rio's throwing his jeans on. He pauses to look at me. "Short call?"

I throw off my robe. He lets his pants drop and sits on my couch with his legs open.

"One more time and then you go," I say.

I straddle him and ride him until we both come. And my eyes fill with tears because there's no way I can let him go. The last two months without him have been hell. It's not fully living, but this shit is not right either.

"Now, we're both fucked," he says, freezing me on the spot. "You're going to see me no matter where you look. You ruined my sanctuary because I can't go home without seeing you everywhere. And now it's the same with you. You won't be able to fuck anyone here without seeing me."

The cold wave blows through my chest. I climb off him, staring him in the eyes. I'm taken aback. But the anger there fuels my own.

I scooch to the corner of the couch. "Get out. I don't want to see you."

He pushes off the couch and throws his shirt on. He stands there, staring at me.

"Even when you hate me, you'll never stop loving me."

The haze of red behind my eyelids is so strong it threatens to burn me.

"That's where you're wrong, Rio. I'm going to erase you from my heart like you never existed."

"Good luck with that." And with that, he's gone.

Rio

I ride my bravado all the way home. Like a motorcycle, speeding through the road, making me feel invincible. It's me. *I'm still the one she can't get enough of.* She won't be able to forget me. I walk through the door, passing Tito's room, and I hear his laughter and Sel's voice. And time screeches to a halt like a car hydroplaning to a crash that never stops. Reality wrecks the bubble. They're happy while Luna and I couldn't be further apart. In my room, I close the door and face the bed. The empty fucking bed. I spent the night with her, fucked her into oblivion, only to come home alone. To lie in a bed without her, feeling empty and hollow. I spot my notepad on my nightstand and dive for it.

Me quemas con tu cuerpo
Para destruimer con tu indiferencia
Solo soy tu un juguete
Y tu una niña caprichosa.

You pick me up

Then drop me aside
You fill my world
Then leave me to die.

I'm an orphan
Huerfano de tu amor
I'm thirsty
Pero ahogandome en mi calor

Tengo quien me toque
But she's not who I want
My dick wants to say yes
Pero mi mente doesn't react

It's my heart
It refuses when it's not you
Because it plots against me con mi mente
Y no deja que piense
Y le prohibe que sienta
Until someone tu nombre mienta.

Mami, no le deseo este infierno a nadie
Solo a ti
Le pido a Dios que tu cuerpo llame mi nombre
con desesperacion
Porque sabes que el nunca is going to fuck you como yo.

Y para que te sientas mejor, it's the same for me.
I know no peace sin ti.

Still waters run deep
Es Rio
Aunque me consta que nunca se te olvida
Yeah...hahaha...You can't forget me either
Bueno que nos pase.

29

Rio

Every time I sit in Dr. Jacinda's waiting room, I have a brand-new Luna thing I need to talk to her about. Today is weird because I don't have to be here. This isn't part of our schedule. It's either I come here or I go out, and I don't trust myself in the streets. The hurt is too intense, and I see myself trying to cope in the old ways.

That's how I find myself staring at the wall of books. I'm waiting for her in the quiet. Music is my enemy right now because she has become my muse. So, I'm in punishment with my thoughts...like most of today.

The door cracks open, and Dr. Jacinda steps out with a short but attractive woman with jet-black wavy hair, killer curves, and insanely high heels. She's familiar, and when her gaze lands on me, her bold red lips spread into a smile.

"Hi, I'm Mel."

And that's when it hits me. Amelia Solis. She looks young, like a regular pretty girl, and not a *Jefa de Jefas* in New York—except for the designer clothing and the sharp edge in her eyes.

"I'm Rio."

She chuckles. "I know." She looks at the doctor and back at me. "I won't tell if you don't."

"No," I say and then add, "You've gotten me out of a lot of stuff. But you made sure Luna didn't get fired. I'm most grateful for that."

She winks at me and leaves through a side door. People are waiting for her there.

Dr. Jacinda waves me in. Her office is always neat except for the usual tables where there are scattered boxes and figurines. She explained that it's for people to play if they're into it.

We don't ever sit at her desk or any of those tables. Instead, she has rocking chairs by the roaring fire. It's always cold in this room, and I wonder if that's a technique of hers. My Caribbean heart is happy for the fire.

"I'm sorry you had to encounter another client. I try to space out my appointments to honor your privacy. However, at times, I'm unable to plan effectively when we receive last-minute requests from two parties, which is what happened today. This is also a great segue to, what's going on?"

"I spent the night with Luna last night," I blurt out.

"Okay. Good thing?"

There's such a calm demeanor about her, and she's always unassuming, which is annoying today. I need her to fill in the blanks. If it were good, I wouldn't have called her. I know she can tell but forces me to say the words.

"I don't know. Parts were good and the rest is fucked...sorry."

She folds her hands on her lap, delicately. "I'm an optimist, so tell me the good, and we'll get to the fucked after."

Fucked.

The word coming from her jars me, and she smiles because she must know she shocked me. "Is it the word or my age that bugs you?"

"Both," I say. "I feel bad enough that I said it, but I didn't expect you to repeat it...it's hard talking to you like this."

"Rio, I'm a mother of five and a soon-to-be grandmother again. That requires lots of sex and sex conversations. There's nothing you can tell me that I have not heard or experienced. So why don't we bypass the assumptions, and you tell me what happened and why it's affecting you to the point that you called me, of all people...voluntarily."

I don't know what to say, except, "I want to be respectful."

She smiles softly. "You're never disrespectful. On the contrary, you have impeccable manners. Speaking about your feelings and experiences in a raw and very personal way does not change that. Last time, you told me you miss Luna so much it hurts. Last night, you got to spend time with her. How did it happen?"

She remembers everything.

"I went to her new place because I saw the photos of her mom's wedding. She looked beautiful and happy, and that *zángano* went with her as her date. So, I was..."

"Jealous."

"Yeah. I showed up. We argued." I go through the whole story, including the times we went at it like savages, sharing details I could never tell anyone else but her and a priest.

When I finish, she asks, "Do you need some water?"

"Do you?" I shoot back.

"Yes." Her response is so dry, I laugh, and she chuckles.

She grabs us bottles of water.

"Why did you say that to Luna at the end? It sounds like a curse."

My body heats up all over again. "I was pissed. We spent this night together, and she took his call."

"But you told her to answer. Was that just a taunt?"

I shrug. "I don't know."

She hums. "I think you do, Rio. What did you expect her to do?"

"Tell him to fuck off," I almost yell and take a sip of my water.

"Because her *macho* was there?"

I choke on the water and end up coughing, but I admit, "Yes."

"Did you communicate to Luna that you expected to get back together after you spent the night together?"

"No. She didn't want to talk, just fuck. Her words."

Dr. Jacinda nods. "But you agreed."

"Yeah," I say. "I wanted her."

"Then why would you expect her to say that to the person she's seeing? Because it was a transformative dick experience?"

My mouth falls open, then I shake my head. "That's not it."

"Because that's what you agreed to. You love this woman, but agreed to one night of just physical pleasure, knowing it wasn't going to be enough."

I don't like the way she's judging me. "Maybe I wanted to get her out of my system."

"By being more intimate with her? This is the woman you took to the most sacred place in your heart. You trusted her with your mom when we—" she gestures back and forth between us "— had barely been able to touch the subject. Why on earth would you think this would be the way to get her out of your system?"

I hate the reminders, as if the memories of her in my *casita* don't constantly live with me. I stand and walk to the window. There's no air coming through them but just being able to look out into the street lets me breathe better. "I don't know."

"Dig deeper, Rio. You know the answer to this."

"Because I want to know that she still loves me like I love her. That she still wants every part of me and finds it hard to sleep because I haven't texted or called her. I wanted to see for myself that asshole wasn't enough. I want her to forgive me."

"But you told her that you want to haunt her."

Because she haunts me. "I'm not perfect, Dr. Jacinda."

"No one is." It sounds more like deadpanning than reassurance. "What are you going to do, Rio?"

I shrug. "I'm headed to Europe for a few concerts. Maybe give her time to cool off and then come home and try to talk to her."

She nods. "I think that is a good plan."

"Or maybe I should try to move on like she is trying to do."

Her lips purse, and she moves them around like she often does when I give her something to think about. "Rio, I'm weighing how I say this carefully, but I find that full honesty is always best. Neither you nor Luna should be trying to be in relationships with others. You both need to figure out what this is, because you will fall into patterns that are not fair to other people or healthy for you."

Luna

Is this hell?

Because I keep thinking things can't get worse for me, and then they do. Hank sneezes again into his hands. The gurgling sound of something liquid being expelled hits the tissue. My stomach turns, saliva floods my mouth, and I have to turn away. My coworker and I exchange gazes, and I pinch my lips to stop any words from getting out—or to stop from barfing because he follows up by blowing his nose, and the squish of snot has nausea clawing its way up my throat.

We've been sitting here for forty-five minutes in sensitivity training. Meanwhile, I am looking for ways to stop feeling murderous about the fact that fucking Hank knew he was sick and had the nerve to show up to work today, on the day we are stuck in a conference room.

"I'm sorry, guys. I thought I would be better by now."

You should've kept your ass home.

"You should go home, Hank," Vickie, the head of HR, says.

I'm about to agree when the door opens, and Victor pops his head in.

"Luna, we have a situation."

And I see the heavens open. I grab my phone and spring out of my chair, following Victor to his office. He goes in and sits behind his desk. This is a lot like the time I almost got myself fired for Rio.

Fucking Rio. I avoid thinking of him like the plague since our night together.

"What's up?"

He sighs. "Thierry's been caught on camera going into a hotel room in Vegas with two full-service workers."

"Are you fucking kidding me?"

He raises an eyebrow. Probably because I don't swear at work, but it's the norm at Elevate. The F bombs drop on an hourly basis like breaking news.

"I'm sorry. I'm not in a good mood, and Hank is in there sick and spreading God knows what."

He frowns. "He has the Norovirus. Why did he come to work sick?"

"Because it's Hank. And this is ridiculous with Thierry. He and Adina just got back together again. The statements I sent to *People Magazine* and *Big Apple Mag* have barely left my inbox. I know he pays us well, but every week brings something new and worse than the last. It's exhausting."

He bobs his head. "Yeah, no kidding. I have Bethany Belmont up my ass, demanding that we fix this."

I scoff. "Fix what? She needs to find her daughter a new man. He's never going to stop being a fuckboy idiot."

Victor smiles. "You *are* in a bad mood. You know? The first couple of weeks you worked here, I wondered if you would be too nice for this job, but this past month, you've been vicious."

Because I'm still seething at my own stupidity with Rio and that's bleeding into every aspect of my life.

"Let me go call Thierry and get the full story so I can find the right angle to spin it."

I go into my office and close the door. I pull out my work phone and dial.

"Hey, Luna," Thierry starts.

"No pleasantries. What happened now? And please give me the abbreviated version."

"Someone's in a mood," he says, adding, "I was hanging out with these two girls, and someone at the club took photos and videos. Somehow it was taken in the hallway of the hotel."

"Somehow?" I ask, not understanding how he can be so cynical. "You didn't see people walking behind you and recording you in a hotel hallway?"

"I was busy."

Yeah, with each handful of ass.

I pinch the bridge of my nose. "There's no way we can say you and Adina were on a break, is it?"

"Not really. We just got back together." And there is no emotion in his voice.

"Why are you doing this to her?" I blurt out and then course correct. "You know what? Don't answer that. I don't want to know, and I don't care."

"You guys used to be tight." It's as if he doesn't remember why we're no longer friends.

"It doesn't matter. How about something like this: Thierry is focused on his career and personal growth while rebuilding his relationship with Adina. It's a one-step-at-a-time process, and his personal life is not up for discussion at this time."

"I like that," he says.

"I'll run it by Victor and send it out. Route any communications my way. Do not try to answer them on your own. And please try to stay away from messy situations."

I send the email to Victor, who responds with a thumbs-up right away. I answer the emails from media outlets and hop on a couple of interviews. I'm home by three in the afternoon, sorting out our to-do list for *Enlace* so I can email Sel and set out our calendar for the next month. The new shipment for Morena & Miel arrived. Baggy athleisure jumpsuits that are so soft. We have a meeting to discuss them and the other new pieces this week.

I miss Sel so much. We've never been apart this long. This tour will be on for much longer, and I can't wait for her to come back to town.

Something else fucking Rio took from me.

As if summoned, a text comes through from her.

SEL

Girl, this shit is a trip. I think you made him impotent.

ME

What?

I begin to sort through the items.

SEL

K is trying to be all over him. He's ignoring her.

I push my phone away. As much as I love my cousin, I don't want to hear about him. It's enough that I see him on my TV, my feeds, everywhere...including every corner of this house. I need a break from Rio.

"Because FUCK him." My words bounce off the wall as my chest heaves.

Damn, maybe I need a nap. I'm tired and in a funky mood. I lie in my bed. There's a funny feeling in my stomach, and if I get sick, I'm going to murder Hank, that fucking germ-ridden asshole.

I wake up disoriented, with my stomach feeling like an oven, hot and simmering. I grab my phone from the pillow. It's two in the morning, and I have a bunch of messages and missed calls.

> SEL
>
> Did you die? I've been calling you. Call me back.

I hit the call button, and she answers. There's so much noise I can't hear her, but she waves at the screen and then tips the phone to the stage. Rio is in the middle of it, and I can see him singing and moving those hips in a way that is so familiar it conjures many memories. Some from my unfortunate backslide sexathon with him.

She switches to text and sends me the link to watch the concert.

> SEL
>
> Call you when we're out of here. It's too loud.

I shouldn't, but that doesn't stop me from tuning in to the live feed on my phone while I cook some Ramen. At this point, I'm watching so I can hate him some more. I hope his pants tear or fall off, but the girls would enjoy that too much. Shit, if they see how gifted he is in the dick department, it would make them more obsessed than they already are.

And he knows how to use it too.

He's smiling and dancing without a care in the world. I take the noodles to my bed and project the concert on my TV screen. I can barely pass the broth through my throat.

Giovanni sends a message.

GIO

Hey, stranger. I hope you're doing well.

ME

I'm good. You? You guys are on a winning
streak. Great to see.

We are still casual friends. I ghosted him after the night I lost my
damned mind and let Rio plow me all over this apartment.
Stop thinking about that, Luna.
I couldn't face myself after backsliding. I also realized it's not fair to
drag anyone into the mess that is my love life...or lack thereof. But we
can still be friends.

GIO

I'll be in New York in a few weeks. Maybe we
can grab a bite?

ME

I would like that.

I'm about to type a message apologizing for disappearing when the
music stops, and Rio announces a guest, "Let's welcome, la reina,
Katya."
And my stomach flops, with his voice echoing in my ear.
Lo que mi reina quiera.
This fucker just called her what he once called me. I see red, which
intensifies as Katya steps onstage in her sheer jumpsuit and sky-high
stilettos. No, not just stilettos, YSL Opyums. *Those are my dream.* She
rushes to him, and he catches her in his arms. She plants a kiss near his
mouth.
On my fucking spot.
I can't look away. They start singing their new slow song, where he
sounds like he's trying to seduce her, looking at her like wants to eat her
alive. He tells her he had a dream about her.

You were wearing your best outfit, tu desnuda piel.

And my tongue drew maps of pleasure on it
Your moans are the soundtrack
Tu pones lo verbal
Yo pongo lo visual
Cuando tenemos sex, baby es un ritual
It's not just bellaqueo
Esto es espiritual.

When her verse comes on, he sits on the stage steps, and her hips roll in sambas while she stands between his legs, singing to him with that angelic soft voice. His eyes are on her ass, his smile from ear to ear, as he follows her movements like a hypnotized fool.

My face grows hotter, my stomach is boiling, and this fucker stands up, his body rubbing against her, next second he's *perreandola* with his face near her ear. Like we were that night at the club, after our first kiss, when the world could have collapsed around us and we wouldn't have noticed. That's when I lose my mind and almost throw the noodle bowl on the nightstand. I grab my phone and start venting.

ME

Glad to see it's all scripted.

So much for it's not the same as what we had.

I guess a month does change EVERYTHING.

And you had the nerve to come de ridiculo dique jealous to my house.

Mirate la sonrisa, degraciao. If you smiled harder, your face would break. Azaroso.

Even after hitting send, I can't stop watching the undulating of her hips. She's so comfortable singing with her head on his chest. I should tell him to fuck off too.

No, Luna, unsend all that shit. You sound jealous and fucking unhinged.

Yeah, I need to unsend all of that. But I don't want to. I want to text him all the swear words I know because he was here *azarándome la vida,* but look at the fucking smile on his face now.

The nausea rises so fast and furious that I have to clutch my throat. One second, I'm in bed, and the next, I'm running for my life to the bathroom. In my leap from the bed, I knock my noodle bowl onto the floor. I barely make it before I start throwing up. Every thirty minutes, like clockwork, I'm in the bathroom.

Fucking Hank.

Worst of all, a message comes through from Rio.

And then another message.

Fucking Rio.

And a third.

Because I never hit unsend on all of mine.

Fuck me.

Rio

ME

Would it make you feel better if I confirm it?

Would that feed your delusion that you did the right thing by breaking up with me?

Would it make you feel good about being with someone you don't want to be with?

And you want to talk about curses? Tú me azaraste la vida a mí.

I stare at my texts back to Luna and no longer feel the anger I did once the concert was over and I checked my phone. I was livid last night, texting like a fucking *loco* and so pissed I skipped the after-party to come back to the hotel. I called her, and she didn't pick up, just like she hasn't bothered to answer.

Nothing pisses me off more than being ready for the fight, only to be ignored.

I'm embarrassed too. I shouldn't be denying shit. She broke up with me, used me as a sex toy for a night, and told me to get the fuck out.

Easy, Riomar. You're warping the memories.

I blow out a mouthful of air as Tito comes out of his bedroom to sit in the suite's living room. The suite has three bedrooms. He occupies one with Sel. I have the other, and there's an extra one with two beds for my barber and my assistant.

"So?" Tito asks, dropping himself on the couch. "What's up?"

"Where's Sel?" I look in the direction of their room. I don't talk about Luna when she's around.

"Went for a walk to talk to her mom and to see if she can finally get a hold of Luna." He chuckles. "I think she low-key hates you for last night."

I roll my eyes. "She and her *loca*-ass cousin."

His eyebrows shoot up. "What happened?"

"She blew up my phone, blasting me for the performance with Katya."

Tito purses his lips. "You had to know that was coming. It looked pretty intense...she looked ready *para dartelo ahí mismo,* and you looked ready to take it."

And that's what pissed me off the most. *I almost moved on.* "At one point, I was."

"But?" he asks.

I shake my head, not ready to tell him or anyone how I was feeling Katya one second, and the next, she triggered a memory of that video Luna sent me dancing to my music, hips rolling, hair wild. Then Katya smiled back at me, and my fucking dick died.

"Luna got me fucking crazy. Katya has an insane body, and she's so laidback and sweet."

"She looks like she would be down for whatever you want too," Tito says.

I shrug. Because yeah, she is. She's insinuated it many times. But it's not going to happen while I am still so hooked.

Even the fucking song we have together is about Luna. I wrote those lyrics for her.

"But she's not the one you want."

And it galls the fuck out of me. "The one I want—"

The front door beeps and then opens as Sel walks in with several bags in hand. She nods at us but keeps talking on the phone. "Yeah, I bought you the Portuguese rose water, Ma." She looks down at her phone. "I gotta go, Luna's finally calling me back. We have to talk business."

Her name stirs anger in my chest. She can call Sel back but leaves me on read. I don't need her insanity anyway.

"Hey, babe. Oh no," Sel coos. "You're still not feeling good. Fucking Hank gave you the Norovirus. How did you get noodles all over your floor?"

"Heeey, Luna," Tito yells, smiling at me. "We miss you."

I flip him off, which makes him laugh.

"Hold on," Sel says, taking out her AirPods. "Tell him now."

"Love you, Tito." Her voice is soft and a little hoarse.

"Feel better, *Prima*."

I want to punch the smile out of his face.

Sel smiles, and because she's an agent of chaos, says, "Rio's here too. Want me to put him on so you can say something to him?"

Luna doesn't miss a beat. "Yeah, tell him I wish he was here. I would kiss him so I can shove each and every single one of these Norovirus germs down his throat. I want him to feel as good as I do right now. Maybe he can fucking dance it off and barf or shit himself onstage."

"Luna," Sel yells, tapping manically on the phone screen. "Stop, you're on speaker."

"I don't give a fuck. I feel like shit and that fucker—"

Her voice cuts off.

Tito bursts out laughing. "Man, she sounds like my girl."

Sel comes back to the sitting area, a little red and apologetic. "I'm sorry. She's not feeling well. She beasts out when she's sick—always has. And the Norovirus is no joke."

I remember her in the hospital after she got drugged. She was nasty work back then, too.

"It's fine. Tell her all I heard is that she wants to put her tongue back in my mouth."

Sel's eyes widen, and she shakes her head. "Hell no. I don't gaslight my cousin when she's sick. Luna has a temper."

Tell me about it. *I have the texts to prove it.*

"I'm going to send her some soup from our fave Dominican restaurant. Let me call her back."

She heads to the room, and Tito chortles. "Jesus, that was… something."

I shrug like it's no big deal. "I hope she feels better soon or not. I don't care."

But I jump on my phone. Maybe I'm crazier than her, because I'm on the site, ordering her something before I can question it.

"Want me to distract Sel so you can be Luna's hero?"

And it's almost pathetic the way I nod, and he springs to his feet.

Fuck, I'm a simp.

I go to my room and sit in my bed with my notebook in hand.

Soy prisionero
De tu Orgullo
De tu ira
De tu falta de corazon

A restless soul at your mercy
You beat my heart
Stomp on my feelings
Blame me for it
But I don't run
At the first sign of distress
Stockholm kicks in
And I'm back begging
Praying
Wishing for you

Culpable
Te sentencio

You're a killer
A murderer
With a ruthless heart
And a steady hand
Mataste un amor lindo
Es Rio, Mami

Luna

"Should I come home?" *Mami* asks.

I can barely lift my head from the back of the couch, but answer, "No. Of course not. I'm not a kid and you're on your honeymoon."

I'm so sick she's probably the only one who can handle me and make me feel better when I'm like this.

"*Mariposita*, why don't you talk things out with Rio?"

"I don't need another reason to be aggravated." My tone is so harsh, I regret it. "I'm sorry. You know how bad I get when I'm sick. The Rio era is over. He's in Portugal with his new girlfriend."

I get hot all over thinking of them last night. There are still so many ways I can cuss him out.

"Luna, you know what that is. You also haven't mentioned Gio since the wedding."

I take a sip of water, but it makes me gag, so I put the glass down. "I'm not seeing him anymore."

"I know," she says. "That's my point. You can't be with someone else and you're not happy without him, so it's worth a shot to try and work it out."

I remind myself she doesn't know about the night of her wedding or our text tirades, so of course she wants us back together. I can't keep talking about this. I feel shitty enough. The doorbell rings and I see my out. "I miss you, *Mami* but I have to go. Someone's at the door."

It's a delivery from Faye & Fleur and I let them into the building.

Then, drag my feet to the door slowly. I'm so weak, but Sel hinted she was sending me soup, and the excitement of that alone helps me go the distance. When I open the door, I'm facing what can only be described as a white wall. It takes two people to bring it into my living room. They hand me an envelope but won't take a tip from me.

"That's been taken care of," the man tells me.

I see them out. As they leave, a food delivery guy hands me a bag with handles. It's from my favorite Dominican Restaurant. *Sel came through!* I smile and thank him. He won't take my money either.

Then, I close my door and head to the dining room but the packaged white wall package takes up a big part of my living room. I wonder if it's from Gio. He messaged about going to dinner and I get this. My stomach growls but I want to see what it is. I place the envelope on the couch and cross the distance to stand in front of it. It's almost my height.

I tear through a corner of the film and the flowery fragrance invades my senses. There are different colored roses. I need to see the whole thing so I tear the remaining film.

It reveals a framed arrangement of various colored roses, dahlias, and greenery, mixed with succulents, peonies, and berries. It takes my breath away, and without reading the card, I know this is not from Gio. I can only stare at it with my heart pounding in my throat.

I grab the card from the couch and sit. I open the small envelope and pull out the card.

I'll take you whatever way I can get you, cooties and all. Throw out the flowers, if you want, but eat the food so you feel better.

My eyes well up immediately. How can he take me to radical emotional poles in a matter of seconds? We are in this dichotomy of beauty and disaster. And I want him with all my heart but it's not good. Not the way we are now.

I eat my soup and fall asleep staring at the flowers. I wake up to their scent in the morning and I decide. I'm going to talk to him. We can't have another episode like the one we had the other day.

I open my phone but my notifications are wild. Rio and Katya at a soccer game, laughing with beers in their hands.

The haze of red behind my eyelids is back with vengeance and I open my message app to his name and then stop. No, I'm not going to do this again. I'm not going to freak out. I know this is PR. I'm a publicist who knows exactly how it works yet I still react the way I do and that's what's mostly wrong. I need to stop this.

I navigate to his info on my phone and scroll down and block him.

Now I'm not tempted to text him and I'm not going to watch his concert videos either.

30

Rio

"Luna's looking good, man," Niko says.

And fuck me, she is.

We're in Maeven's office discussing my next album when she came on TV, doing an interview. That lace white shirt under her blue jacket has my hands itchy and my throat dry. She's lost weight, and she looks a little tired, but she's a vision for my eyes, as always.

"Let's talk about today's trending topic. That's why we have Luna Santos with us today," the anchor says. "Luna, what is happening with our favorite break-up-to-make-up couple?"

"Thanks for having me, Jake. I think, as always, the gossip rags are making too much out of nothing. People who love each other sometimes go through challenging times. Thierry and Adina have a long journey together. They're young and trying to find their rhythm. Love that serious won't quit."

"Wow, coming from you that is high praise, after everything you've been through in big part through your association with them."

She shrugs. "We put all that behind us a long time ago. They're in a committed relationship, and I represent Thierry now. We know it was a misunderstanding."

"Well, since you're talking about putting the past behind, the one that can't seem to do that is Rio. He was caught fighting online with Noryel DD this weekend. Do you think he'll go back to his old antics?"

My spine stiffens, but I keep my eyes on her.

The smile doesn't slip, and her demeanor remains easy.

"I think we need to start paying attention to messy people who provoke others. Rio is human, just like everyone else, but people sometimes only look at one person in a particular situation. When boundaries are crossed and people put their hands on others, they shouldn't be surprised when they get a response. Just like when you have keyboard warriors who think they can type anything, and it won't bring them consequences."

"That's a staunch defense."

She chuckles. "I think I'm being fair."

He pretends to think. "Wait, is it uncomfortable for you to talk about Rio? I mean, given your history together?"

The smile stretches on her lips, but the light in her eyes is the same one she had when she blacked out and told me to get the fuck out the other day.

Oh shit.

"Not at all." Luna chuckles. "That's also water under the bridge. Rio and I are besties right now. We went through a lot during our time together. That bonds two people. We don't get to talk all that much because he's on tour, and I'm busy with work, but when we said we support each other all the way, we meant it. He's family, like one of my cousins."

My body lurches forward like she kicked me in the balls.

"Ouch," Maeven says.

Niko puts his hand on my shoulder. "That's fucking diabolical."

"I know Sel is somewhere proud as fuck of her," Tito adds.

Maeven turns around and pins me with her sharp, WTF gaze. "What did you do? Why is she so mad at you?"

I say nothing, but she rolls her eyes and grabs her phone.

"Hey, Luna, I have you on speaker. I just watched your segment on the *Jake on 5 Show*. Is there something I should know?"

"No," Luna says, her tone is calm and matter of fact. Meanwhile, the air feels like dragon fire on my skin.

"Why don't you come to the concert in Central Park with us tonight?" Maeven asks.

"Thanks, but no thanks," she says with laughter in her voice.

"Hot plans?"

"Yes, it's my birthday weekend, and I'm going out of town. But even if I didn't have plans, I would just stay home to watch time tick by."

Esme's hands fly to her mouth.

Maeven looks at me pointedly. "I think Rio wants to say something to you."

I open my mouth, but Luna beats me to the punch.

"He can keep it. Love you, M."

And she hangs up.

She fucking hangs up, leaving me there, seething, with three people staring at me.

Rio

"Why can't I know where you are, Sel? Are you two hanging with a bunch of machos or what?" Tito's eyes close after he says it, like a jackknifing 18-wheeler is coming straight at him.

We both know she's going to blast him, but I need to know where Luna is.

"I know you're fucking lying right now. What the hell is this, Tito? I don't want you to know because..." She pauses for three ticking seconds. "Wait a minute, I know what this is. Tell Rio if he wants to know where Luna is, he can text her. Oh, wait, she blocked him. Has to be for a reason, right?"

"Sel—"

"No," she interrupts Tito. "And because you want to be in all solidarity with your boy, let me put you where he is. You're on a time-out now. Don't fucking call me. I'll call you when we get back."

The line goes dead, and Tito gives me that look he gives people who try to come at me when I'm doing a show.

He wants to lay me out.

"I'm sorry, *primo*."

"Are you fucking kidding me, Rio? She's not talking to me now." He puts his hand in his pocket and brings a box out. "I was planning on proposing to her when she got back."

I'm stunned. "Fuck. Tito. I'm sorry."

I feel like shit. My issues always bleed out onto him.

"I deserve this shit. She told me not to get involved, but it's not right that she won't tell me. I wouldn't tell you if she made me swear."

I grimace. "You would, though."

He gives me a death stare, and then we both burst out laughing.

"Yeah, you're my bro. I want you to get your girl."

Luna

South Beach, Florida

The sky is blue like the water, and the temperature is a beautiful eighty degrees in South Beach. We escaped the crisp New York winter to come to Florida, where the sun is kissing all over my skin, but Sel is raging like a category-three hurricane in August.

"The fucking nerve. He's over here letting Rio talk him into shit like a little boy. I cannot fucking believe Tito." She breathes hard, puffing out her cheeks as she releases. "I'm so hot right now."

"They're family. You and I do shit like that for each other. How many times have you told me what Rio is doing during the tour?"

"You're not wrong, but I'm still pissed off. At least we know how to play the game. You don't go *toxica* when I tell you things."

"Apparently, I only go *toxica* when I see shit on my screen. That's why I blocked him, so I'm not tempted to blast him or flip out when all he is doing, is his job." My skin still heats up thinking about the lap dance he gave that chick in Brazil the other day.

"Yeah, but Rio crashes out every time a man is near you. But you want the truth?"

I roll my eyes at her. "When are you ever not fully truthful?"

She looks away to the water. "When I act like I'm okay that the two of you are not together. As much as I give him shit, I love what you guys had. He loves you so hard. He's different with you too. There's so much pain in his eyes when your name gets mentioned. Tito was so afraid that he would go back to his old ways in the first few weeks after..."

My heart sinks. "He didn't, though. As mad as I am, I'm proud of him for that. It's easy to give in to the anger." I shake my head. "It wouldn't work between us. Sometimes I think it's bad for you when a relationship is that intense. When you love..." I trail off.

Sel has tears in her eyes, which she wipes quickly.

My throat clogs, and I try to swallow, but I can't. My eyes well up, but I finally find my breath. "I love him too much...like, it's not normal. When someone consumes your every thought...it's going to be a disaster. I dream about him, and when I'm awake, I'm constantly reliving every moment of our time together. I've been secretly happy he pissed me off. It's pushing me to do other shit. I have to get him out of my head and my heart."

"How are you going to do that, Luna? He's going to keep coming after you. He has to. He loves you too much, too."

"I'm going to give Gio a real chance. If not him, I'm going for the next guy. I'm going to date and have a chilly and cheeky winter."

She sniffles. "Damn it, Luna. You wait until I'm basically cuffed up to Tito to do this? And you coined it too. Ugh." She curls her lip at me. "Do you know how fun that could have been if the two *primas* went on the prowl together?"

I laugh. "Girl, you couldn't even if you tried. Tito got you hooked."

She chuckles. "Yeah, he does. It's really good with him. He takes care of me, and even though I black out constantly, I don't scare him."

My heart goes out because I've never seen her like this—vulnerable and girly for a man. "I love this for you. He's a good guy."

"Thanks, sis. But let me tell you something. I want all the fucking details. I want to live this *chill and cheeky winter* along with you. I want photos on the gram, because you gotta let them worship that body." She stands. "As a matter of fact, let me take a photo for the gram. We can do a countdown to see how long it takes until Rio puts a heart on it."

We both laugh as she snaps a few photos and then posts them in collab mode.

"Your turn," I say. "Take that tank top off. Let's drive Tito crazy."

"No, no, no." She plops back on her towel. "I'm on my period, and I'm bloated as fuck. No way I'm putting this belly on the gram."

I roll my eyes. "You're crazy. Your body is hot, and..." I drift off because one word echoes in my ear.

Period.

I haven't had my period in a while. I grab my phone and go to my tracker, and there, in pink hearts, is the last time I had it...almost six weeks ago. My heart drops.

It was supposed to come right after Mami's wedding.

"What is it?"

Could I be... No, I can't be.

"Oh shit, Sel."

"What?" she asks, frowning.

"My period."

"It's coming?"

I shake my head. "No. I haven't had one. It's been over a month. And I kept forgetting to take my birth control pills, so I stopped them."

Her eyes go impossibly wide, and her mouth drops open. "Oh shit."

"Oh shit," I repeat.

She waves her hand as if trying to slow down. "This doesn't mean anything. You've been upset and under stress, and you just had the flu." Her shoulders droop. "Oh fuck, Luna. You were barfing all over the place for days."

"We need to find out." I spring to my feet and start grabbing all the shit.

"Wait, we can't go to a pharmacy and risk anyone seeing us. It's fucking Miami. People know you, and if they don't know you, they know Rio. All it takes is one photo of you or me in the prego aisle together."

"Let's order it online or from a pharmacy and have it delivered, then."

And she does, while my mind races all over the place.

I marked you.

Now I fucked your home for you like you fucked mine for me. You don't have a sanctuary like I don't have mine because of you.

I hope you hear my voice in your ear and see images of us in every corner.

He cursed me, because now I may carry part of him inside my body.

31

Rio

"Sel is fucking evil," Tito says, flinging his cell phone away. "I know that's her doing."

I reach for my phone and open it. It's a photo slider on my Instagram feed. In the first one, Luna's lying down on a towel, all gorgeous, glowing brown skin in a barely there red bathing suit. The image sends a flash of need straight down to my dick, because Luna naked against me is the ultimate fantasy I now beat off to.

But, it's not meant to be. Luna back with me, laughing, kissing me, lying in my arms.

Not meant to be. She sent me to *la mierda*, and I'm already there, but I don't see my way back.

"You need a minute with your phone?"

"Shut up, Tito," I say, not looking at him. Instead, I put the phone down and return to my computer. I'm reading a book about oceanography, but I'm having trouble concentrating. There's so much in my head. I handled it all wrong, and now I have lost her. I really did. All the signs are there. She blocked me and won't talk to me. Sent me *pa la mierda*, but I can't stop loving her.

And I have to stop bugging her. I can't become one of those creeps who won't take no for an answer or who makes her uncomfortable. And what happens when she gets a macho...

The thought sends a burn down my chest, and I reach for the one thing that calms me these days. I open my notebook and let my pain bleed on the page.

I jumped again
Down the cliff into the deep
Not because I'm reckless
Because I hate being this sober

I need to erase it
The feeling of your hand in mine
The softness of your chest against my cheek
The smell of your hair on my pillow
Your shape in the corner of my eyes
It all needed to go

It backfired
Porque no habia nadie to tell me they loved me in the edge
And instead of the siren sound of silence
I'm drowning in a sea of despair...again
With the siren call of your voice in my head

My heart weighs a ton
It's dragging my chest down
It's not meant to be in that cavity because
I gave it to you, but you turned it down
I don't know how to turn this around
My brain doesn't know how to act
It refuses to feel another great loss
It rages against devastation
It's too weak to carry this cross

A veces quiero que seas Feliz

Te amo de todos modos
Otras veces se me cruzan los apellidos
Y mando la razón al lodo
En esos momentos te envio todo
El rencor, el deseo, la ira, el amor, mi amargura, el odio

Te devuelvo el hechizo
Te deseo que no duermas
Y que te levantes sudada
Writhing en tu cama
Después de gritar mi nombre en tu sueño
Porque tu corazon, and your pussy, extrañan su dueño

Tu sabes que lo soy, Mami
Tu boca puede decir mil cosas
Pero debería ensañarle a tus ojos y a tu cuerpo a mentir
Still waters run...you know
Ni tengo que decirte mi nombre
Tu mente te lo grita a todas horas.

I read my words and blink. *Shit.* I read it again, and the music plays in my head, a soft intro that grows larger, soft, sexy, and *brutal*. And for some reason I can't explain, I page through my journal, reviewing the entries as I do before meeting with Dr. Jacinda.

And I see it, our *story*. I've been bleeding on this page since the night at the Coliseum. It's all here, in my language, the cadence in the words and music playing in my head. It's an album with an intro and definitely an outro.

No, not an album. I couldn't sell this, because I wouldn't want anyone else to touch it. Just me. Only me and a producer. And not just anyone. Someone I trust to do this justice.

I grab my phone and text Niko.

ME

Remember those tracks we worked on way back? I want to do a mixtape.

NIKO

Sick. When? Who's the producer?

ME

Tonight. And you.

NIKO

Bruh. What? 😳

ME

You in?

NIKO

Fuck yeah. Vamo a romper.

Twenty minutes later, Tito and I arrive at Niko's place. My friend takes one look at me and shakes his head.

"*After the Rain* Part II?" he asks, referring to my first mixtape. The first one we worked on when we were coming up. It was in the bedroom of his parents' apartment.

But I shake my head, because this is not that. "I'm about to open a vein to let the poison out."

My meaning dawns in my friend's eyes.

"Fuck, are you sure?" Niko says.

"Rio..." Tito starts.

I stall them both with a hand. "We're doing this, and we're releasing it. If the label wants to sue me, so be it."

"*Hablale*," Niko says to Tito, throwing his hands up.

"You can't do this without your team knowing," Tito insists.

I take my phone and shoot a text to Esme, Kresh, and Maeven. Then I put my phone on airplane mode.

"Let's do this."

It takes us four hours to select the tracks we want from the vast arsenal we've mixed together over the years. While he and Tito eat, I play them and rehearse the songs. The first couple of times are rough, making me question what the fuck I'm doing.

How do I even let this shit out? I know people are going to call me a simp for this one. But the more I think about it, the less I give a fuck.

This my ode to us. A ballad to my *diosa*. Because I've never felt like this before about anyone. *Luna es única*. Our love unlike any other.

The next time I hop on the track, it's natural, like it's made for the words. I can feel it sucking the poison from my wound.

Tito shoves a plate at me while Niko gets the equipment ready. "Eat it."

I do as he says and wolf down the burger and fries. I chase it with a large glass of water, and then I drink another.

"Let's go," Niko says.

I get up from my chair, with the burn in my chest, and walk to the booth. Inside, the silence is thick, and the world disappears. I'm standing alone like I was when I wrote all these words. He signals, and I close my eyes.

I prayed for this, God
Begged you for light
I should've known what you would do
You brighten my way
So I can see the whip coming as you flog me
But it's okay.
I'm ready to bleed
For mi pecado de amarla and the love that haunts me.

Es Rio
Bienvenidos a la Sangria
Pero no la que se bebe.
Hahaha, esta es la que te limpia
It's The Bloodletting.

It takes us overnight, minimal sleep, and a lot of emotion, but I'm purged. My brain is spent, my body exhausted. I lie on the bed, making a list of things that are going to change.

I'm going to move the fuck on. I'm going to give myself a chance to love again now that I freed myself and her.

Goodbye, Luna.

Luna

It's my birthday but I'm not in a club.

The sun finds me on the porch of the hotel, across the street from the beach. I've been here for hours because I couldn't sleep.

Positive.

Seven times.

I stared at all the tests on the floor, not knowing what to do first: throw up, run, or scream. Sel tried her best to get me to come have dinner with friends of hers who moved down here, but I just wanted to be alone. I pretended to sleep when she got back.

I'm pregnant.

The little still voice kept torturing and reminding me. The beautiful room began to feel like a prison, and soon the walls began to close in on me, trapping me. I threw all the tests into a Ziploc bag and put them in my weekender bag. I threw on my shoes, grabbed my phone and keys, and came down here to the beautiful porch, decorated with vines and flowers, of our boutique hotel. The night concierge came to check on me, and I had to reassure him I was okay. I stared into the sea until the sun rose and turned the black velvety waves into a blue mirage.

It reminds me a little of watching the sun rise when we arrived in Samaná but in a different kind of way, because that was soul deep like nothing else. The call of your *tierra* is something that touches every corner of your being. There's nothing like that heat and smell on the island. It feels like yesterday sometimes and others like an eternity. I can't even explain it. *It's all about him.* When I remember, I feel it all— Rio's hands on my skin, his nervousness when we arrived, our time in the casita, his smile at *El Cabito* after we resurfaced from the water.

My eyes well, and the restlessness is back. It's been rolling in like a dark wave and retreating when I feel like I can't breathe anymore. It will roll away again, but I can't sit, or it will set. So I stand and go down into the sand. Maybe a walk will help me clear my thoughts.

I am having his baby when we don't even communicate like normal people. I lashed out. He lashed out. I blocked him. Pregnant.

I laugh out loud. You can't make this shit up.

It's crazy that I can pinpoint the day it happened. The night of my mom's wedding. The night we rutted like angry animals. It wasn't any of the times he loved me but the day he cursed me to miss him and never be at peace. The day I hated him for making me want him as much as I did.

After I was so angry and raging, I lost focus. I threw myself into my work. Even sick with the flu, I was not paying attention to anything. I just didn't want to think about him anymore.

Was that even the flu?

It doesn't matter. Rehashing won't make it better. But I still need to find a way to talk to him, tell him what's happening.

But how do I even begin that conversation?

I start small. I unblock him.

32

Luna

New York

My eyes are fried. I stare at my screen and continue to review my draft of this crisis-response plan. I'm so tired I feel dumb. I've been looking over the same email for way too long.

"Thierry Banks is in hot water again. A woman he was partying with posted photos in his bedroom. Of course, social media is on fire."

I mute the TV because I already know what's happening. It's the call that woke me up way too early after a restless night. I've been sorting through the numerous emails from Adina, her mother, and media outlets seeking a statement. Dumb-ass Thierry is panicking. Bethany Belmont is demanding I do something immediately. This lady really thinks I am her employee.

My phone pings with a text from Maeven.

> **MAEVEN**
> Your response statement looks good.
> Mama's proud of you.

I chuckle.

😊 High praise from the best. Now my life is made. Honestly, I don't know how you do this every day.

My phone rings. She's calling me.

"I sense an SOS," she says before I can say hello. "What do you mean by how I do this?"

I try to laugh it off. "Don't mind me. I'm tired."

"Spit it out, Luna," she orders.

My stomach starts to burn, because she's so perceptive. And I don't want to give up too much or expose all my doubts. Or worse...my condition? I'm already questioning too many of my decisions. At least I can discuss work-related matters with her. She's the only one who truly understands.

"I don't know, Maeven. I ask myself if this is what I want. Is this what I busted my ass for in college? Do I want to spend my days cleaning fuckboy messes?"

She sighs. "It takes a lot out of you, especially because I imagine part of you feels sorry for Adina. That makes it even harder. As you know, I dealt with this before..."

She's talking about her former client, Mateo de la Cruz—New York's darling, home-run God, and patron saint of fuckboys everywhere. He had a scandal every week.

"I couldn't handle something like that day in and day out."

She chuckles. "Of course you could. You're definitely cut out to do this. I think the issue is do you want to?"

"Yeah," I say.

"Mateo was a challenge for me. He was also an exercise in how far I could stretch my limits and my spinning skills...until he got hurt one Christmas Eve. I saw the damage that sticking by him was doing to someone I cared about and the emotional toll it was taking on me. It was Christmas, and I was away from those I love because he was an idiot and needed to be put in a hospital. It gave me perspective, and I knew I had to get out. I wish I could say I was smart and walked away. I stayed longer. Then one day, I drafted a plan for him, gave him my notice, and walked away."

"That's what I want to do," I blurt out before I can think it through.

Without missing a beat, Maeven switches to FaceTime. In two seconds, her face fills my screen. Her skin is radiant and flawless, even without makeup. But she frowns, staring at my face. "I want to say this while looking at your face. Clients like Thierry wear you out but shouldn't make you question your love of PR."

I nod. "I know. It's a combination of things. My time in the public eye was a bit much. I miss dedicating my time solely to small businesses. Every time I have to write a plan to handle fuck-shit, I tell myself I should be creating a new product with Sel for Morena & Miel. The past few days have significantly altered my perspective. If I'm going to put in this kind of time, I want to work for myself. I don't want to clean up for serial cheaters, or deal with Adina's neurosis or Bethany's need to control the narrative. I learned about what matters."

She's quiet for a minute, and I regret my rant. She was a good mentor, and it's like she wasted her time with me.

"Walk away, Luna."

I'm stunned. "What?"

She smiles. "You are 1,000% right. You have other ideas, interests, and talents. Most of all, you have all this knowledge that can be better used in the service of your passions."

"But shouldn't you be telling me to give it more time... Seriously, what if I'm just venting, and now you have me on the verge of quitting?"

She laughs. "You were not just venting. You may not have known it, but you needed this talk. Putting more time into this won't change your mind. Sometimes we can be sure of something in a very short period of time. That is called instinct. I didn't listen to mine, but I'm advising you to follow yours and your heart."

My eyes well up, and I look down, only to stare at my belly. The doctor confirmed the pregnancy yesterday, and I haven't been the same. It's one thing to see it on a pharmacy test and quite another when a professional confirms it.

"I don't know if I trust it anymore."

"Are we still talking about work?" When I don't answer, her brows raise. "I'm here for you as always. I am still your publicist, and like a priest or lawyer, whatever we talk about stays between us—but mostly as your friend."

Something wet drops in my hand, and for a second, I'm confused until I realize it's a tear.

Fuck.

"Listen—" She frowns, looking at something on her screen. "What the fuck? I'm going to kill his ass!" she yells.

"What's wrong?"

Maeven looks at the screen again, and when she does, there's something mixed with the obvious anger in her eyes.

She groans. "Rio dropped a mixtape."

His name alone wakes up the fluttering in my belly. I went to bed thinking about him, about us, about the six-week consequence of our last time together.

It's the size of a grain of rice with eyes, nose, and lips. Lungs and kidneys are developing, as the doctor told me.

"Is he going to be in trouble with the label?" I ask.

She shakes her head. "No. He told us yesterday, and there's a clause in his contract that allows this. But I haven't even listened to it. Let me go handle this. Before I go, your plan is perfect. Send it along with your resignation letter."

For the first time all morning, I feel better. I text *Mami* to tell her.

ME

Quitting this job. Going back to my roots.

Then I prep the package, write a standard resignation letter, and send both.

Victor calls me almost immediately, and the conversation takes over an hour. I'm firm on quitting. He's disappointed and upset about it.

I thank him for the opportunity and hang up.

MAMI

Just landed. Good girl. It's not for you.
Coming over this afternoon.

I check social media, and I'm confused. Thierry's name is no longer on the top trending topics. His name was pushed way down by Rio. He's trending number one, followed by Sangria, bloodletting, *mi diosa*, and then Niko *El Rebelde*.

Mi Diosa? My heart starts pounding, but when I click the topic, all I find is people talking about Katya.

I switch to my notifications, and I see the mixtape alert. I navigate to his YouTube channel. The mixtape is pinned to the top of his page, and the cover image alone makes my stomach drop.

It's the cliff at *El Cabito*. He took the photo while we sat at the restaurant. It was right before we decided to jump—no, before I convinced him to jump.

I take my laptop and go sit on the couch. The second he starts speaking, goosebumps pop out all over my skin, from head to toe.

You brighten my way
So I can see the whip coming as you flog me
Now, I'm ready to bleed.

The pain in his voice brings tears to my eyes. It must be about his mom.

And then the first song kicks off, and he's talking about a woman he doesn't want to be attracted to.

If you don't want me to kiss you, don't open your mouth.

The Knicks game comes to mind. That's when it dawns on me. *Oh shit...that's about us.*

An hour later, I'm an emotional mess. He took me on a journey of what we lived through together, like I don't go through it in my head at least twice every single day of my life.

I cry like I've needed to for months. Our love was real, palpable, beating. The last track tells me it's over for him. It's in all the details and the title: "Bloodletting." He bled me out like I'm venom.

But I can't do the same, because he's in me so deep and alive. All I can do is cry and cry because it's over. It hurts like hell. I bawl until the headache brews, and then I close my eyes. I don't know when I fell asleep, but when I open my eyes again, my mom and Sel are in front of me, staring down at me like something is wrong.

"I've been calling you for hours, Luna. You text me that you're quitting your job then don't answer my calls, and this one"—she points at Sel, who is pale behind her—"is freaking out and won't tell me why."

The nausea rushes up my body, and my brain tells me to start running. I barely make it to the toilet. Everything comes up in waves until I'm coughing and crying at the same time.

I heave until my body calms down. Then, I get up, wash my face, and brush my teeth. I look in the mirror and try not to yelp at my reflection—swollen eyes in a gaunt face as I swish mouthwash.

When I come out, my mom is sitting on my bed. Sel's hovering at the door. Mami is looking at me with those Dominican mom eyes—the ones that miss absolutely nothing.

"How far along are you?"

"Six weeks," I say. "Rio's baby."

She rolls her eyes. "Shocker. Well, what are we going to do, *Mariposita?*"

I know what she's asking, as so many moments cross my mind like they did during my pitiful listening party of one earlier. His smile the first time we met. His relief the night before the concert when I told him I was with him. His haunted eyes in the *casita*. Our kiss underwater.

You had my soul in your hands
All of me was there.

He doesn't know it, but he took my heart with him along with all the love he felt.

But he left me a part of him, and I can't help but place my hand over my belly.

Mami bursts into tears.

"We're having a baby," says Sel and then starts to cry too.

I don't cry. After the last few hours, I don't have any more tears left.

"You're moving in with us." My mom sniffles.

I shake my head. "No. It's time for me to grow in life and business. I'm going to have a kid who needs me."

"When are you going to tell Rio?" she asks.

"I don't know."

"That mixtape happened, and he doesn't even know about the baby. Can you imagine when he finds out?" Sel shakes her head. "He's going to go nuclear."

I can practically hear his angry voice and accusations, and what if he doesn't believe it's his baby? I'll die if he makes me have to prove it.

The nausea is back, and I rush to the bathroom like a bomb detonated in my belly. I sit on the floor later, mouth sour and exhausted, when Sel brings me my phone.

"He's texting you."

My heart takes off, pounding away as I look at my phone. Three texts.

RIO

You won't get this, but I need to say it. This wasn't to hurt you.

I just needed to tell our story. Because it's real.

Now that I did, you're free of me. I won't bug you again. Goodbye, Luna.

Rio

"When we do the song in France, we should kick it up a notch. I'm thinking a Moulin Rouge-style set with a bed. When the intro kicks in, the lights can dim, and I can dance and climb on the bed with you, on top of you," Katya says the minute we sit on the jet en-route to Amsterdam. Her jet-black hair brushes back and forth across her shoulders as she explains. The excitement is clear in her delicate oval features.

It sounds sexy and exciting, and I think the crowd would enjoy it. She's been pitching ideas for the last hour since she got to the private lounge to wait for our flight.

"Yeah, we can talk to the set designers and see what they come up with."

Her hand goes to my face. "You look so tired. Get some sleep."

She doesn't sit next to me but lies down on the seats across from me.

I haven't slept for two nights. I'm exhausted, but the minute I lean back in my seat, words start swirling around my head. But I try to force myself to sleep. Twenty minutes later, I give up and retrieve my notepad from my backpack and give in to the muse.

It only took seconds
Twelve palabras from her lips
To send my world to hell
Y empezar mi calvario – again

Soy Rio

I wasn't alone anymore
The light was shining on me
But I'm now in the dark again. Yeah, again
In a world I no longer know who I am – otra vez

And it's because the moon went away
Leaving me like a winter day
El sol no me calienta
I'm no longer visible
Only exposed for the vultures
I'm a breathing carcass

Perdi la luna
Perdi su mirada
Nada brilla sobre mi
Desde que no tengo su amor

Me siento solo
Necesito de ti
Nada mas llena mi alma as I live

Wishing for la luna to shine on me.

I stare at the notebook, with my face tingling and heart racing.

"What are you writing?" Katya asks, lifting her head from the seat.

I look up at her and am frozen in place but snap the notebook shut.

"Just my thoughts."

She shrugs and goes back to her phone. And I return to my purgatory, because that is where I must be.

I let out my blood for nothing. Luna is still standing there like my personal hellhound, haunting me, ready to tear my flesh from limb to limb and let me burn.

I tried to let Luna go, but my heart laughs at me. Because the words are still coming. *She's never going away.*

Fuck. Me.

To be continued with Lost Between el Rio y el Mar

THE WORLD OF FICHA MUNDIAL

Ficha Mundial Latin Entertainment is a fictional world where Reggaeton Rompe Barreras con Romance. Starting Fall 2025, immerse yourself in a world of interconnected standalones infused with culture, Latin heat, nostalgia, y el sabor de nuestra gente, created by Latinx authors J. L. Lora, K. L. Hernandez, K. Rodriguez, and Shelly Cruz.

In our shared world, Ficha Mundial Latin Entertainment is the higher-arching music label representing the world's most prominent Reggaeton artists.

Works under Ficha Mundial:

Wishing for La Luna *by J. L. Lora*
Staying for La Lluvia by *Shelly Cruz*
Shooting for Las Estrellas by *K. L. Hernandez*
Falling for El Cielo by *K. Rodriguez*

Learn more about Ficha Mundial on our website, FichaMundial.com.

ABOUT THE AUTHOR

J. L. Lora is a Dominican-American author. She currently lives in Maryland, pursuing her dream of writing compelling, sexy, can't-put-down stories about empowered, badass alpha heroines and take-your-breath-away alpha heroes. You can find her and chat with her on social sedia.

Sign up for her newsletter and learn more about new releases, events, news, freebies and much more at **www.JLLora.com**.

Turn the page to discover all my books.

f facebook.com/AuthorJLLora

instagram.com/jllora

BB bookbub.com/profile/j-l-lora

A Love for All Seasons

THE SUMMER I LOVED YOU

THE WINTER OF MY LOVE

THE LONGEST DAY - *Prequel to novella*

THE AUTUMN YOU BECAME MINE

A NOCHE BUENA FOR LONELY HEARTS - *Prequel novella*

THE SPRING IN MY HEART

Ritmo y Deseo

WISHING FOR LA LUNA

Sometimes Love Happens

SOME NIGHTS

SOME MORNINGS

SOME DAYS

WHEN YOU BREAK GIRL CODE

The Trinity

BOSS

MADE

STEEL

Short Stories

ALL I EVER WANTED — *Epilogue to* The Summer I Loved You (online only)

ECHOES OF YESTERDAY

BOUND BY DECEIT — Part of *La Alianza*

En Español

ELLA ES LA JEFA

HECHA Y DERECHA

FORJADA EN EL FUEGO

www.ingramcontent.com/pod-product-compliance
Lightning Source LLC
Chambersburg PA
CBHW051501030726
47592CB00006B/2040